THREE A
BY PAUL CALLOW

THREE AND OUT – THE FILM:

This novel is based on the screenplay, Three And Out
by Steve Owen and Tony Lewis, which was adapted
into a feature film in 2008 by production company
Rovinge Motion Picture Company plc.
Starring Mackenzie Crook, Colm Meaney and Gemma Arterton,
with Imelda Staunton, the film was released in cinemas across the
United Kingdom and Republic of Ireland on 25th April 2008 by
Worldwide Bonus Entertainment plc.

THREE AND OUT
BY PAUL CALLOW

written by

TOM HENRY

Based on the Original Screenplay *Three And Out*
by Steve Lewis and Tony Owen.

Published by
Rovinge Publishing Company Limited
Northway House
1379 High Road
Whetstone
London
N20 9LP

A paperback original 2008

A catalogue record for this book is available from the
British Library.

ISBN 978-0-9558627-0-0

Typeset in Palatino by The Flipside Group, Cranleigh, Surrey
Printed and bound in the UK by CPI Mackays, Chatham, ME5 8TD

In memory of
Tommy Cassidy

TOM HENRY
is a writer and journalist.
He was born and brought up in Lancashire
and now lives near Bristol
with his wife and daughter.

ACKNOWLEDGEMENTS

Thanks very much to Carol and Rob Deacon for providing the necessary peace and quiet - the drinks are on me! Also to my publisher for the questions he raised, the challenges he laid down and his willingness to take a risk. That goes for his editorial team, too. Thanks to Charlie Viney, for his encouragement and advice. Thanks and, as ever, all my love to Melanie Greenwood for her patience and support.
Diamonds are forever...x

CHAPTER 1

"Oi you! Yeah… you. Squirrel-mush. What you lookin' at?"

No older than 18, the biggest and ugliest of the three lads slouching on the Tube platform was as hard as nails. Or so he thought.

The bearded commuter, a copy of *Metro* under his arm and a briefcase by his side, looked away, not daring to catch the eye of the tormentor sneering and snarling at him under his white baseball cap.

His two mates, all paste-diamond earrings and baggy tracksuits, sniggered as the big kid took a step closer to the commuter, giving a hefty tug on the leather and brass leash wrapped around his left hand. On the end of it, a rottweiler with a face like a butcher's mistress bared its teeth and strained to get closer to the man.

"What you lookin' at, tosser?" the kid repeated. "Seen summink you don't like? Or d'you wanner closer look at my sovs?"

He clenched his right fist and held it out like a prize fighter, making sure the terrified commuter saw every jagged, gleaming aspect of the four sovereign rings held out in front of him.

"Leave me alone," muttered the man, looking round for support and sensing the ripples of paralysing fear spreading across the platform, "or I'll call the guard."

"What did you facking say?" shouted the kid. The dog started barking as it squared up for the fight. It knew the routine well.

"'E said, leave 'im alone! Or 'e'll have the lore on ya." The kid swung round to find himself staring into the face of a Cockney woman, no younger than 80.

"D'you want some of it an' all, whitehead?!" snapped the youth. "Or d'you fancy being crapped out on the pavement after Tyson's chewed you up?"

He thrust his jaw arrogantly upwards and deliberately slackened his grip on Tyson's leash. As he did, the dog took a semi-leap forward and barked viciously. The old woman shrank back, terrified of what she'd unleashed. The trio grinned like chimps, and looked round for someone else to intimidate.

But the dog wasn't after her. Instead, it had spotted several mice, dirty and grey, hunting for food between the rails of the Underground line. Entranced, the harnessed animal strained forward for a better look and with it, dragged its young master a foot closer to the platform edge.

The familiar pinging along the rails and the gathering breeze from the mouth of the tunnel signalled an approaching train. The mice scattered and the dog's head jerked from side to side like a tennis fan as it watched them flee. Instinct kicked in and it could contain itself no longer. Suddenly it lunged, and dived off the platform towards the mice, yanking the yob behind it. A gasp of horror went up as the speeding train bore down on the figure in the middle of the track.

Metal shrieked on metal as the wide-eyed driver hauled on the emergency brake. Tyson leapt again, back on to the platform, leaving the kid frozen with fear in the middle of the line. Death, in the shape of a youngish Tube train driver with a mop of unruly blonde hair and a wispy moustache, was staring him in the face. There was barely time to scream, but he managed it, a bellow that bounced off the tiled walls and tore into the ears of the horrified commuters. As the train rammed into him, his final, fateful howl was matched by the same ear-splitting human cry of anguish from inside the driver's cab.

*

"You should eat something, love," smiled the staff canteen woman gently. "Never do death on an empty stomach. That's what I always say."

Paul Callow smiled weakly. News of a death on the Underground travelled fast. He glanced at the lukewarm dollop of bolognaise deposited on his plate, swallowed hard, and shuffled off to sit down, knowing he wouldn't be eating it, or anything else for that matter.

Heaving silently, he pushed the plate out of view and scanned the back cover of the paperback he had brought with him. Dostoevsky. In the past, getting lost in a novel would be his answer to the demands of the real world. But not today. He stared at the words, swimming in front of his eyes, and looked away.

A uniformed arm dropped heavily across his thin shoulders and a big, broad and friendly face leered into his, forcing him to acknowledge it with a weak smile.

"Vic…"

"Hey Paul, how's it going? Er, not too good I hear? They reckon there's a trail of bling all the way to Edgware!"

Seeing another driver heading towards the table, Vic winked. "'Ere, Ash. Look who's here? Suicide Syd!"

Ash, leaner and younger than his companion and with a grin that showed off two perfect rows of pearly-white teeth, put his tray down and settled into the orange plastic chair. "Go on, then," he said, leaning forward eagerly, "let's hear all the gories."

"Oi oi, Ash, hang on a sec," said Vic, sensing a story worth hearing. "Let's just have a bit of background before we get all the juice. First time out, was it, Paul? Always a bit of a choker, first time out."

Paul shook his head, trying to clear out the memory of the kid's face and the penetrating scream. "It really was… just… I can hardly…"

"I know, mate," said Vic, drawing Paul in a little closer. "But it wasn't your fault, was it? One of those things."

Paul sighed. "Maybe, yeah, but even so…"

Ash cut in, wanting more. "Did you see the trauma team?"

The young driver nodded. "Yeah. They asked if I wanted counselling, or someone with me in the cab on the next shift."

"You should go for that," said Ash, looking serious for a second. "Definitely. I've heard one of those counsellors is very hot property indeed. Ask for her."

"I don't need any of it," Paul snapped. "Counselling, guardian angel in the cab, none of it. I just need a break, that's all."

"Course you do, mate, course you do," replied Vic, removing his arm from Paul's shoulders. "You gotta get over it. What did they give you?"

Without speaking, Paul handed a piece of paper to Vic, who read it out loud in his flat, North Eastern tones. "Sick leave – Post Traumatic Stress – Seven Days Only'. Seven days only? The tightwads. You'd get more for murder. What's that you're saying, Ash?"

"Oh, sorry," Ash replied, "I was just thinking out loud, that's all. I remember my first time. I was only a kiddie. It was up at Angel Station. Never forget it. Quite funny, really. I hit a nun."

Paul looked at him quizzically. "And…"

"And what?"

"I dunno? Is it some kind of joke?"

"No," said Ash, slightly offended, "it's a true story."

"See," said Vic, "you never forget your first one. It always stays with you. A rite of passage, I s'pose. The second one… well, depends what it is. Lover's tiff that spills on to the line, then yeah. Old wino with nowhere left to go? Probably not. But the third one? Well now. Now we're talking…"

Paul cut in. "The third one what?"

"Eh?" said Vic, snapping out of the dream he had sunken into. "Er, d'you wanna come for a pint, Paul? Take your mind off it. Nice Bloody Mary down you?"

Paul smiled uncomfortably. Even if they meant well, he wanted his interrogators to go now. He wanted to be alone with his thoughts.

"I don't think so, guys. It wouldn't seem right, really."

"So you're just gonna sit here," said Ash, "and read this?" He picked up Paul's paperback and flipped it quickly from back to front. "Who's this fella, then? Dosto?… Dostov?…"

"Dostoevsky."

"Oh, yeah, of course. Dostoevsky. Yeah, yeah, heard all about him. Paid a fortune for the Hammers, didn't he?"

"He's a novelist," said Paul, stiffening, "he doesn't own a bloody football team."

"I know who he is," said Ash, "I'm just having you on. But d'you know what, Paul?" He nodded to the tatty book. "You wanna get out more, mate. Come on, Vic. Shift starts again in five."

*

He didn't want to – it was the last journey he wanted to make that day – but Paul was forced to go home on the underground. Squeezing in with the rush-hour passengers, crammed cheek-to-cheek and with all sorts of body parts forced to touch all sorts of other body parts, he appreciated the space and the silence that his driver's cab afforded him.

A voice crackled from the intercom. "Could passengers please move down the train? There's room for everyone if you'll all just move up!" Paul obeyed the instruction – after all, it was one he'd given many times himself – and noticed, as usual, that very few others did. Even with a sweaty armpit in the face or something even more unpleasant poking into the back of a skirt, it seemed the majority were determined to grimly hang on to their own personal bit of carriage space.

The train jolted into action and the sudden surge of power caused Paul to lurch into a young female office worker, white headphones in her ears. She glowered at him and turned away again, adjusting her headphones to block out the thrum of the train. He wondered where she'd been, who she was. Maybe in some other circumstance – a bar, or a bookshop – he might have plucked up the courage to ask her. She didn't look a bad person, really. Just frazzled and stressed, like everyone else on the train.

5

But, he thought, you wouldn't ask her anything on the Tube. For a large group of people all shoved together, the silence was overwhelming. To speak to a stranger was to court fear, suspicion, danger. It was the Underground's biggest unwritten rule. Polite Notice – No Communication.

His arm ached from hanging on to the overhead metal bar which dangled from the carriage's ceiling. He could feel the strip lights draining what remained of the colour from his face, blanching it to the most unhealthy, ghastly pale. It had been a horrible day, the most sickening imaginable. Again, he saw the youth's face, twisted with terror, and his own desperate scramble to slam on the emergency brake. The shriek of metal and the thud of steel hitting flesh. Bile rose in his throat and he could feel a cold sweat creeping over him. He had to think above it.

Think above it. It was hard, as the train clanged and shuddered, its passengers swaying to the uncertain rhythm, but he had to do it. In his mind's eye he was in an aircraft, sweeping down from over a mountain to fly just above a Scottish loch. It was spring. Nature was re-awakening after a cold, lonely winter. The water shimmered and sparkled underneath the aircraft and in the middle of the loch, like a pearl in an oyster, was an island. No-one was around. He was alone with the loch, the mountains, the blue sky and the island. It was...

"North Acton! This is North Acton! For security reasons, could all passengers keep their bags with them at all times."

It was a rude awakening from a beautiful dream. Paul snapped into life and with what seemed like half the train, poured out of the carriage and onto the platform, homeward bound. At the station's exit he ignored the free paper distributors as they held out their wares to him, and headed for home, utterly worn out by the day's events.

Towards the end of the row of large, dank-looking Victorian townhouses he squeezed past a brimming wheelie bin on the pavement and up the steps to the front door. Opening it, he stepped

6

into an unlit hallway crowded with bikes and automatically paused at a wicker-topped table, on which lay a pile of post. Rifling through, he found a brown envelope addressed to him and, slamming the front door, he headed to his own flat.

Once inside, he paused to open the letter. It was a bill. By the looks of it, a serious one. Pulling it out, he confirmed what he already half-knew. 'Notice of Disconnection' was stamped in red across the top of it. He sighed, and placed it on a pile of other unpaid demands. He'd have to get it sorted somehow. His driver's salary wasn't bad, but it barely kept pace with the cost of living in London. You ferried all these minted City guys around all day, and came home with nothing.

At least he had his books. The dimly-lit living room was floor to ceiling with them. Books of every size and subject. Surfaces littered with novels; some trash, some classics, some famous, some obscure. Many would have found that cramped, claustrophobic room unbearable to live in, with its junk-shop furniture and old-fashioned lamps. At times, that also included its present occupant. The rest of his life in there he simply tolerated.

There was just one clear space in this cavern of paper and print. On top of a cheap, black-lacquered desk was a laptop computer and a printer beside it. Paul dragged over a chair and sat at the desk. He switched the computer on and with the mouse, clicked open a document. At the top of it, a title: *Love Song For A Lost Generation – A Novel By Paul Callow*. Underneath the title – nothing. A blank screen. An empty canvas. Paul stared at it momentarily, fingers poised on the keyboard. Tonight, like every other night since he'd written the title, nothing would come. Gazing at the shelf above him, he smiled, as if catching sight of an old friend. *Catch 22* by Joseph Heller. He plucked it from the shelf and settled back in his chair to read the classic opening paragraphs.

After ten minutes the laptop gave up waiting for the start of Paul's great novel and a screen saver appeared. It was a large colour photo of a small, remote house, with a grey, slate roof and thick, sturdy walls. It stood on an island surrounded by water as blue as a robin's egg. In the background, the hills glowed with the muted purple of great swathes of heather.

The screen saver caught Paul's eye and, looking up from the book, he clicked on the mouse again, launching his internet browser. Scrolling down his 'favourites' he stopped on an estate agency website. Two more clicks, and he was staring at the same property that appeared as his screen saver. It was still there. Still for sale. 'Loch Tyne House. A real rural retreat for just £240,000'. Get away from it all in Bonnie Scotland." A slow, broad smile smoothed his careworn features as he mentally strapped himself in for another plane ride over the mountains.

*

Monday morning, and a clap of thunder in the skies above East Finchley, plus an angry black cloud, pregnant with rain and its waters about to break, quickened the pace of commuters heading for the station. Among them, a fat, middle-aged man in a suit and a crested tie, running flat-footedly for all he was worth. One eye on the rain, and another on his gold-plated watch, he stumbled through the thickening crowd milling at the station's entrance and shoved through a gap in a determined bid to get to the front.

His hair wet with sweat, the fat man paused at the bottom of the stairs to the platform and yanked at his tie, loosening his collar. His temples throbbed with pulsating purple veins and again he checked his watch. If he could just get through this bloody lot clogging up the stairs, he might make it.

Three-quarters of the way up, he heard the sound of a train approaching and, shoving harder through the crush of bodies, made it to the edge of the platform. But as the train rounded the bend, the man's eyes rolled up in his head and with a great gasp of agony he clutched his hands to his chest. His heart, punished by years of abuse, had simply retaliated at this final outrage.

Inside the driver's cab Paul Callow, only a couple of weeks back at work and still in shock, watched in helpless horror as the fat man struggled to stay upright, crushed downwards by the pain of the imploding heart. Paul hammered on the emergency break but it was too late. The dying man pitched headlong onto the tracks and as the train's wheels locked, Paul screwed up his face to avoid the awful inevitability of the next two seconds.

*

"Pauly," said Vic, his mock-sympathetic expression trying to hide one of glee, "Pauly, Pauly, Pauly, Pauly, Paul. What are we gonna do with you, eh?"

Ash, his partner-in-crime, sidled in, blocking any attempt that Paul might make to escape the locker room and the two ghouls who had now collared him, just two hours after the latest fatality on the line.

"Oh, Paul," said Ash, tilting his head like a sparrow, "two in a month. Tut-tut. *Baaaad* boy. Becoming a bit of a habit, this."

Paul bristled. "It wasn't my fault. The guy was dead before I hit him. I tried to stop."

"Course you did, Paul, course you did." Vic's matey arm snaked around Paul again. "Just a bit of bad luck, that's all."

"But the psychological effect's the same, innit," chipped in Ash. "It all counts… in the Big Game."

"What 'Big Game'?" Paul was puzzled. What were they going on about now?

"Ssshhhh," said Vic, lowering his voice, "keep it down, keep it down. This is the game nobody talks about."

"So why are we talking about it then? I don't wanna talk. I just want to be alone."

"Hark at Garbo here," grinned Ash.

"We're talking about it, my son," Vic continued, "because we care about you. And three… well, it's the magic number."

"What?"

9

"It's the rule, Paul," whispered Ash, holding up three fingers. "Three and Out. You hit three people in a month and they pay you off. Retire you. Reckon you can't deal with it up top... It's Three and Out."

Paul, wide-eyed, could hardly believe what he was hearing.

"You're kidding..."

"Are we?" said Ash. "Would we kid about ten years' salary?"

"How much?!"

Ash sniffed, and wiped his nose with his sleeve. "Of course, no-one's ever done it."

"Though you came close in '99," interjected Vic. "What was it... three days?"

"Yeah," said Ash dreamily, "three days. Three days between me and ten years' wonga. Between me and a Ferrari. So bloody unfair."

On the windowsill by the lockers perched a cage. Inside, a sooty-coloured mouse was enjoying a run on the treadmill. Vic ran his fingers across the bars and looked fondly at the creature. Attached to the cage was a sign: *"Mousewood Scrubs"*.

"How long did he get, then, Vic?" asked Ash.

"Well, what are we looking at... eating biscuits, pissing in the wash-basin. I'd say that was a six-month stretch with two off for good behaviour." Vic smiled and ran his finger along the cage again. Paul stared at the mouse, still unable to believe what he'd just heard.

Sensing his curiosity, Ash spoke again. "You know mate, you wanna get yourself on the Central Line. They're always at it there. When does your month run out... since you hit the first one?"

Paul counted on his fingers. "A week today. Monday."

Vic sucked in his breath with cod-drama. "Seven days, eh? That's pushing it. When you on next?"

"Monday. They gave me the rest of the week off."

"A week off!" Vic shouted, before lowering his voice once again. "The rotten bastards. You know why that is, don't you, Paul? So you haven't got a hope in hell of winning the Big Game." He clicked his tongue sympathetically. "Never mind, my son. Another time, maybe?"

The conspiratorial pair walked away, chuckling to themselves. Paul looked into Mousewood Scrubs and watched the creature on its wheel, round and round and round. Going nowhere fast. *Three and Out*. The very word 'out' summoned up the comfort blanket of his favourite dream; a house on an island on a loch, far from anywhere and anyone, and with all the time – and maybe the money – to read and to write.

CHAPTER 2

Paul barely noticed the crush of bodies shoving past him on the escalator out of the station. On any other evening he would have cursed inwardly at the jabbing elbows and well-aimed stilettos of passengers, sprung like rats out of a trap, from the train.

But not tonight. He was thinking of bodies of a very different kind. Dead ones. The journey from the drivers' depot to North Acton seemed to have flown by in seconds. He was still shocked by the fat man's death – the twisted expression on his purple face looming monstrously as he fell beneath the wheels – and could barely believe that in a matter of a few weeks not one, but two people had met a violent end under the wheels of his train.

They were accidents, both of them. Of course they were. He hadn't killed anyone. Not 'killed' killed, like pointing a gun at someone and pulling the trigger. Not like that. He wasn't a criminal. He'd never even seen a dead body before. He'd heard the horror stories. So he thought he knew. But he didn't know. Until now he had no idea how violent death could visit so suddenly. How it could just leap out at you like a guard dog behind a wire fence, without warning, snarling inches from your face.

That said, he had read enough about death, and murder in particular. He had shelves full of books about the subject. So many of his favourite writers – Eco, Carver, Rankin, Koontz – were obsessed by it. So many ways and means of making someone die. He thought of the cheap Westerns he sometimes devoured when feeling bored by the classics. The cheers that went up from the townsfolk when the lone stranger was quicker on the draw, dropping the corrupt sheriff into a bloody heap in the dust. And then there were the calculated murders. The whodunits, the cover-ups and the crimes of passion. Men and women driven to the very edge of sanity, wreaking destruction with the knife, the gun and the poison bottle.

But his options were limited. He couldn't use any weapons or drag anyone kicking and screaming in front of his train. It had to look like an accident. A fight, where someone pushes someone else off the platform, just in time to meet the train? His mind was racing. Maybe a cop chasing a villain along the line, and the cop dives out of the way at the last second?

The chances of anything like that happening, he reasoned, were a million to one. He could ring Ash, he might help. If he could think of something, give him a hand? He'd split the money with Ash, no problem. But would Ash really help him? What would they do? If, say, Ash knew what shift he was on, and knew when his train was coming into a certain station, could he not... persuade him just to give someone a little shove over the edge of the platform? Someone no-one would miss?

He thought of the three youths and their rottweiler. Kids like that hung around stations all the time, terrifying ordinary passengers. Even the transport police were scared of moving them on. There were rumours of knives and guns. Surely no-one would shed a tear if one of those toerags was to receive a helping hand into oblivion?

He dismissed the idea as soon as it came to him. Ash would never do it. For all his talk, he was a decent guy. And so am I, thought Paul. This was murder he was plotting. Killing. Taking a life from someone who wanted to keep hold of it, however horrible they were. He didn't want to kill anyone. It wasn't right.

Outside the entrance to the station he paused, leaned on a crash barrier and stared vacantly down Victoria Road at the belt of queuing cars. Beside him was a newsagent's stand. An *Evening Standard* sandwich board, advertising the paper's late edition, caught his eye – "U.S. SCHOOL MURDER BOY: 'I WANTED TO DIE'". It was all over the papers and the telly. The kid had taken half his class down with him before turning the gun on himself.

Jesus, thought Paul, if he felt so bad, why didn't he just go somewhere quiet and jump off a –

His thoughts were suddenly interrupted by a giant, half-naked woman leering down at him from a billboard on the other side of the road. Her alluring eyes met his own as she toasted him with a glass of something dark and exotic in her honey-coloured hand. "HAVE YOU GOT THE DEVIL IN YOU?" ran the wording across her heaving chest.

Disturbed, he pushed himself off the barrier and walked towards the pedestrian crossing up by the kebab shop. Of course he didn't have the devil in him. There was no bloody devil. No God, no devil. Period. But there was good and evil, wasn't there? Look at Fred West. Pure evil from his boots up. Good riddance to him. But… just supposing you only knew him as Fred the friendly neighbourhood builder, all types of renovation undertaken, free quotation, no obligation? Supposing he'd done you a nice car port? Would he be 'evil' then? Or, say, you'd lived in Vienna in the 1920s, and the old dear in the flat above recommended that nice Mr Hitler, painter and decorator, because he'd done such a good job on her new en suite. "Ooh, you don't half look like Charlie Chaplin,' I says to him, and we fell about laughing! Well, only I did, to be truthful. He had a bit of a funny look in his eye."

So not everyone could be evil all the time. Even the most evil people had to do the occasional sane thing, like vacuum up dog hair or read the sports section. Likewise, normal people – 'good' people – couldn't go through life without the occasional naughty thought. You'd have to be a saint not to. It didn't make sense. Even Gandhi had an eye for the girls, so they said.

Paul knew he was trying to convince himself. His thoughts pitched and rolled through a sea of troubles, wandering and stumbling and rambling more clumsily than a Polish stag night. Out of the fog in his head came Ash's long, silly face, its toothy grin

14

mocking his confusion – *"Remember the Big Game, Pauly... Three and Out..."* Then the little three-fingered hand gesture, like some bloody game show host, and the house on the island on the loch, its door invitingly ajar. If, by some miracle, someone fell under his wheels next Monday, the dream would be his to make real. But it would be a miracle, the longest odds in history. Euromillions had nothing on it.

If, though, by some chance, someone came forward who really didn't want to live another day, and if they could be somehow persuaded that a sudden death under the wheels of a Tube train – dramatic, yes, but probably painless and certainly quick – was the way to go... well? Would that be so wrong? It wouldn't be murder. No. Doctors turned off people's life support systems when the patient's family said they could, and no-one was ever done for that. In some countries, you could assist with suicide quite legally. He'd read about it: terminally-ill people flying off to clinics in Switzerland, where their life was ended. Cleanly, and with their full consent. It made sense if someone was that desperate to die.

Deep in thought, he reached his front door on Horn Lane, and turned the key. The hall light had been repaired and there was noise – music, high-pitched laughter – coming from the flat upstairs. Paul crept inside, hoping to reach his own flat without being heard. He needed time to think; time to reason all this out. What he really, really didn't want was –

"Oh, hi there, I thought I heard the door go!"

Too late. It was Yvonne, who lived in the flat above. Attractive, sociable and single and with a steady stream of attractive, sociable and single mates constantly trooping up to her flat, Yvonne was every man's ideal girl-upstairs. She had ventured a conversation or two with Paul in the past, but she made him feel nervous. Somewhere, shoved behind his shelf of Chekhovs, was a copy of *Bridget Jones's Diary*. He knew this sort of girl and didn't want to find out too much more.

"Oh, hi."

He looked at her sheepishly, trying to square the dark thoughts in his head with her open, amiable face.

"Landlord was here again today," she ventured. "He was looking for you. Reckons you owe him two months' rent."

It was true, but Paul was in no mood to hear it. Without thinking, he pulled out a crumpled, fat envelope from the inside pocket of his jacket and waved it towards her.

"I've got it, see? Right here in my hand. He wants his money, he's got it! Sorted."

"Whoa, easy tiger!" said Yvonne, affronted. "Don't shoot the messenger. I don't care that much if you pay him or not. Not my problem."

She turned towards her door, towards the fun of the party and the warmth of her friends, then turned back again.

"Hey… hang on a sec. You look all stressed out, honey. Bad day, was it? Do you want to come up?"

Flushed with embarrassment, Paul tensed as he tried to get his key into the door.

"Nah. No thanks. I've got… got some work to do."

"Okay," replied Yvonne, "fair enough. But if you change your mind, you know where I am."

Paul shut the door without replying and immediately felt guilty. Yvonne was a nice girl. He shouldn't be so rude. But even if he wanted to – and he rarely wanted to, never feeling he would fit in, or that anyone would be particularly interested in talking to him – there was no way he could socialise, not with what was going through his mind. If Yvonne, or any of them knew what he was thinking…

It was so, so wrong. How could he even contemplate it? He pushed it away. Suicide was a crime. The joke was that no-one was ever prosecuted for committing it. But assisted suicide?

He couldn't. It was illegal. Very illegal. Okay, if you were the wife of a guy screaming in agony with lung cancer and you put a pillow on his face one night, you might get... what? Three years? Two if the judge wanted to get his name in *The Guardian* for his essential humanity. But if you just wanted to do it for the money? And you got found out? They'd throw the book at you, no question.

But what if you didn't get found out? What if you met someone who really wanted to die, and they were happy about it all, and no-one knew anything about it – other than someone died? What then? Was it bad? Or was it doing someone a favour?

What would you do? A nagging voice echoed around his head. What would he do? He couldn't answer it, because he didn't know. Automatically, he booted up his computer, seeking an escape. He clicked on the document entitled 'BOOK' and opened it: *Love Song for a Lost Generation*. He tried to concentrate, but the music from Yvonne's flat was really thumping now, and feet began to dance heavily above him.

Along Horn Lane, the wail of a fire engine, followed by a couple of police cars, tore through the descending curtain of evening. A car door slammed heavily outside, followed by the screams of an angry young woman giving her boyfriend a highly verbal ditching he wouldn't forget in a hurry. Grimacing, Paul shoved his fingers in his ears but as he did so he felt an irritating, insistent buzz by his thigh. The phone in his pocket was going off, and whoever it was wouldn't give up. When it finally stopped, he checked his missed calls. The landlord was on to him.

His flat seemed to shrink to the dimensions of a cell as each noise fought relentlessly with one another for his attention. He couldn't stand another second. Slamming his fist down by the keyboard he snatched up his keys and his coat, shoving a paperback book into his pocket as he yanked open the door and stomped downstairs.

The wing mirror on the passenger side of his battered Ford Fiesta was hanging off again, knocked by some thoughtless moron driver trying to squeeze down the narrow side street, but he was in no mood to take much notice. Grinding the stick into gear, he pulled out of the side street and headed up Horn Lane. If there was just ten minutes of peace and quiet to be had somewhere in this city, he would find it.

Within two minutes he was stuck behind a line of cars at some traffic lights. He drummed his fingers impatiently on the dashboard, trying to think of anything but the conversation he'd had in the drivers' rest room not three hours previously. *'The Rule... ten years' wages... three's the charm... it's Three and Out.'*

Bloody Ash and Vic. He switched on the old cassette radio, hoping to drown out their snide voices. Traffic was at a standstill. This time of night always turned into a crawl along Horn Lane, but it almost never gridlocked completely, unless something had happened. That ambulance before... was it going to a crash, or some incident? Paul fiddled with the dial, trying to pick up the London traffic news. As he did, a gap opened up in front of him and to the immediate serenade of horns behind he lurched the Fiesta forwards, leaving the stereo stuck on Radio 4 News.

"It's been a North London landmark for more than one hundred years," drawled the reporter, "but Archway Bridge is fast gaining a reputation as a suicide hotspot, and not just among local people wanting to end it all. After a recent rise in fatalities, police are concerned that the bridge might be attracting victims from outside the borough."

He didn't stop to think. He didn't even check the oncoming traffic as he grabbed the steering wheel and hauled it around to the right, flooring the accelerator and causing the car to squeal into a U-turn that wouldn't have disgraced *The Sweeney*. If there was anyone on that bridge now, right this minute, maybe he could... just talk to them. See what was what. Find out why they wanted to jump off that bridge, onto the bonnet of a car or smack into the tarmac. Why there? And who were they, these people who wanted to die?

*

After a battle through the traffic, he'd finally reached the top of Archway Bridge. He parked his car and, buttoning his coat, walked to the first section of the railings. The bridge was ornate, Parisian even, with three wrought-iron lamps on either side. "Too beautiful to want to jump from," he thought. Then he leaned over. The view to the top of the bridge from the road was deceptive. From up here it was a long way down. If you jumped, your chances of survival were small. If you did live – by some miracle – you would be in a hell of a mess.

Paul shuddered and rested his chin on his hands along the top of the rail. What seemed like a million lights glowed in the distance. Aircraft criss-crossed the night sky above him. Below, car after car after car drove past. There was no escape from the relentlessness of it all. If only he had the money. If only…

He heard a scrape and a footstep. Someone was coming. On the far side of the bridge, a man. Paul shrank into the shadows, fearful, but curious to see what might happen next. He looked behind him. It was clear. If he needed to run, he could. There was no telling who might be lurking about, or what state of mind they'd be in.

Paul held his breath as the man approached. Then, right in the middle of the bridge, he stopped. Paul could see he was middle-aged, bearded and scruffy. The right profile? He looked like a mental case, but who could tell? Half of London was mental, but most people did a good job of hiding it. The man leaned over the parapet and, lighting a cigarette, took in the view. Would he jump? Was he just thinking about it, planning for it?

It was now or never. Paul stepped out of the shadows and, clenching his fists nervously in his pockets, walked towards the man. He had to ask him. He had to know. How would he introduce himself? "Scuse me, mate, before you end up as a large Pepperoni with extra salami on the road down there, could I ask you if you'd rather do it under a train a week Monday?"

Ludicrous. He shouldn't be here and yet he couldn't turn back.

The man's face glowed red under the pull of his cigarette. It's like bloody *Gorky Park*, thought Paul, silently cursing himself for reading too many Cold War novels. But he was about to lose his man. With a short, sideways glance at the approaching figure, he flicked his fag end over the bridge and walked back at speed in the direction he'd come from, leaving Paul trailing in his wake. Even if he had caught up with him, there might have been a million reasons the man was on the bridge. And not one of them to do with vaulting off it.

The opportunity, such as it was, was lost. Dejected, Paul sloped back to his car. How the hell did you strike up a conversation with a potential suicide? "Evening sunshine, got something on your mind? Your violent death? Never mind me old china, it might never 'appen, come down and have a nice cup of tea. We got Sky Sports in the nick..."

But only coppers seemed to do it that way, and most times it was enough to make the suicide absolutely sure he was doing the right thing. He could go a bit easier. Something like... what? "You don't wanna do it that way. Might end up in a wheelchair. Life's really not worth living then. London Underground's the way to go. I can show you a nice little high-speed bend..."

Christ. This was terrible. He couldn't hang around every bridge and tunnel in London, waiting for a chatty depressive to come wandering by. There had to be another way.

As he approached the car, his heart sank as he saw a yellow square placed under the windscreen wiper. Another sodding parking ticket to add to the pile of unpaid bills and fines. But he was wrong. It was some kind of flyer. Looking round, to see if the leafleter was still in the area, Paul plucked the flyer from under the wiper and quickly glanced at it. 'Lonely? Desperate?' it read, 'Need help? Don't despair. A sympathetic ear is just a phone call away. Call The Samaritans 08457 90 90 90.'

There was nobody else about. Whoever had left it on his car was long gone. He stared at the number then shoved the leaflet into his pocket, but he couldn't bury it for something bulky was blocking its path. The book. He pulled it out, looked at the cover and almost laughed out loud as he shoved it back inside his coat. It was *Crime And Punishment*, by Fyodor Dostoevsky.

CHAPTER 3

He had what – six days? It was going to be difficult – impossible, some might have said – but he couldn't pass up the chance that had been offered so generously by Fate. If there was someone out there who, for whatever good and valid reason, had decided that their life was no longer worth living and were 100 per cent committed to meeting their Maker, whoever He maybe be, Paul would find them and would ensure that they did not die friendless and alone. Then, after a respectful amount of time had passed, and the cheque from London Underground was safely resting in his account, he would pay back what he owed, load all his books and his computer into his car and head for his new life in Scotland. He saw himself leaving the car parked at the loch's edge and, with the help of a gnarled but friendly ghillie, steering a rowing boat, packed to the gunwales with books, across the loch to the island, and Loch Tyne House.

There he would realise his dream. With no noise, save the call of golden eagles and buds gently bursting into life on spring trees, he would fulfil his creative destiny. In these surroundings *Love Song For A Lost Generation* would surely write itself. No irate passengers, no stations, no rats, no queues, no landlords or utility companies. No noisy neighbours and idiot colleagues. Nobody. Nothing and nobody to block his creativity. They were all to blame, all these people demanding his attention when he should be writing, and he wanted each and every one of them out of his head. Was there a Callow tartan he wondered idly?

He was determined. But where would he begin his search? He could hang out outside a hospital. Sometimes he saw patients in their night gear, smoking fags by the main entrance. But if you were that dogged about having a fag in a dirty grey nightie in the middle of a London street, there had to be something seriously wrong with you, surely? Or did there? They could be in for anything; anything from a bunion to a brain tumour and back. Besides, those who were seriously ill, the most likely candidates for a willing appointment with Death, were probably too sick to even get out of bed.

He did what he always did whenever he was faced with a tough decision. Later that afternoon he went over to one of his favourite bookshops in Camden Town. There among its shelves he would surely find the inspiration he needed. The smell of coffee from the in-store café pricked at his nostrils as he slowly scanned the self-help section from left to right. There was a lot about positive living, it seemed, but very little on the gentle art of doing yourself in.

Next to him was a smart young guy in a tight-fitting, highly styled brown leather jacket, expensive-looking jeans and polished trendy winkle-picker shoes. He had picked up a book and was studying it intently. Paul gave him the once-over and wondered what he was reading. He didn't look the bookish type. Much more outgoing. A hairdresser maybe, or an estate agent. The garrulous type, up for a lot more than staying in with a good book.

Curious, Paul took a step closer and gazed at the book the young man was absorbed in. He couldn't make out the full title, partially covered up as it was by the man's fingers, but he could see a bit of it. Something, something, something 'Suicide… something, something… Guide.'

He'd found it. *The Good Suicide Guide*. Or something like that. And, maybe, he'd found him. The one he was looking for. The collaborator.

Noticing Paul, the young man looked up from his page and smiled the broadest of handsome smiles. As he had done to him, he gave Paul a lingering inspection, which appeared to hover for several seconds around the groin area. They looked into one another's eyes, and as the young man stepped forward he placed the book, cover down, on a display unit. The gesture distracted

Paul, and he glanced down at the book, and its full title: *Coming Out Is Not Social Suicide – A Gay Man's Guide*.

Without skipping a beat, Paul gave the young man a matey nod and a tight, closed smile before turning away and picking up another book in distraction. The young man's expression fell into puzzlement as Paul delved deeply into *The Menopause And Me*.

After a polite interval he left the shop and in the growing dusk, trudged along Chalk Farm Road, head down, hands in pockets and deep in thought. There were only two ways this could happen; out-of-the-box thinking, which required a leap of the imagination he wasn't fully sure he had, or a random encounter with someone prepared to go along with the scheme's essential madness. In the time he had left, he couldn't imagine either happening with ease. Suicides didn't generally announce themselves to the world. It was more often than not a secret, solitary act. He'd heard about those who took tablets and then phoned someone, but these were the classic 'cries-for-help'. And he'd never taken such a call anyway. He didn't know enough people for someone to trust him with a near-death experience.

Just ahead of him, a group of Japanese tourists was chattering excitedly and pointing towards the sky. Their apparent curiosity was infectious, and many more people were stopping and staring upwards. He slowed to see what the fuss was about and, turning his head briefly he looked towards the top of the Roundhouse, an old, circular London-brick building famous for its legendary music events. Right at the apex of the building's roof stood a man.

Paul was as motionless as the figure on the roof. Whoever he was, he appeared to be calm, making no fuss, no noise. He had obviously made up his mind that this roof would be his diving board to oblivion, and took no notice of the chattering crowd below him.

Without waiting to hear the inevitable ambulance and police sirens wailing up Chalk Farm Road to the scene, Paul tore straight through the front door of the building and, ignoring the hip young kid in the box office, marched up to a door marked 'Fire Stairs' and once through, ran like hell, two at a time, up the staircase. On the sixth flight he tripped, grazing his knuckles as he put out his hand to break his fall. Tears of pain pricked at his eyes, but on he went. This pain would be nothing to what he would feel if the man had already jumped, £380,000 of London Underground money floating gently, invisibly behind him.

Finally, he was at the top. He almost barged through the fire door that led to the roof, but milliseconds before he wrenched it open, he halted. If the man was still there, a sudden noise might make him jump. Literally.

Paul opened the door like a burglar, wincing with every squeak of the hinge as it opened to reveal a full view of London's impressive nightscape. He stepped through and looked around. To his relief, the man was still there, just beyond the air-conditioning unit, standing motionless at the parapet.

Should he approach him? Cough, maybe, to announce his presence? He didn't dare sneak up on him. There were no rules for this kind of thing. He paused anxiously. *Go on!* urged a voice in his head, *before it's too late!*

"Erm, 'scuse me?"

Nothing, only the throb of traffic below.

"I really wouldn't do that. Not from there. You might not die, you know?"

There was no response. The figure might have been a statue, standing in silhouette against the night sky.

Paul pressed on. "No. You might end up in a wheelchair. Your life really won't be worth living then. I… I can help you. I know a place… on the Undergr…"

"Could I ask you what you're doing here?" An interrupting voice came out of the gloom.

Startled, Paul whipped round to see who'd spoken. It wasn't the man on the roof, but a broad security guard standing in the doorway of the fire exit. He switched on a torch, straight into

Paul's eyes.

"What's going on here?! What you doin'?"

Paul was shocked. The guard had no idea how dangerous the situation was. Still the man by the parapet didn't move.

"I was just trying to see… if he was all right." Paul pointed the figure.

"Course he's all right," replied the guard nonchalantly. "He's been there all day."

"All day?"

"Well, all week actually. Had a few funny looks at first, but people got used to him. They call it art, but I'm not so sure meself. Prefer a nice Monet… You thought he was real, didn't you?"

"Isn't he?"

"Go up and give him a kick. He won't bite. Though you might get a broken toe. He's made of bronze. A sculpture. You must have read about them? All over the shop, they are."

Paul sighed. He'd heard of them. He even knew who the artist – Anthony Gormley – was. How could he have been so thick? Made to look a dummy by a dummy. Great.

*

Does everyone want to live forever? What the hell is the matter with these people?! He had trouble trying to stop an angry voice stamping on his sleep that night. Why couldn't Death be reasonable, and send him someone soon? It wasn't much to ask. There must be plenty of people in God's waiting room. The British love queuing, but still…

A sudden thought popped into his head, and he was so pleased with it that he immediately sat up and put on the light. God's Waiting Room. He'd heard someone talking about this very place a week or so ago, as he browsed through the bookshelves of a charity shop on Highgate Hill. The old dear behind the counter, worrying out loud that her cruel daughter would stick her in God's Waiting Room when she couldn't go on any more. She meant the big nursing

25

home a mile or so up the hill; a low-slung slab of a place, populated by worn out old bones in pink cardigans and their pinched-faced, mean-minded carers. If he loitered outside there for long enough… scrambling out of bed, he rooted under a pile of old newspapers and fished out the Yellow Pages. He flipped the pages speedily, looking for the letter 'N'.

The following day, a box of chocolates in a carrier bag and a bunch of flowers in the other he made his way to the Golden Pond nursing home. There were very few mid-week visitors, and the whole place had an air of being off-duty, like a sink school when the inspectors had finally gone.

As he approached, he saw a gaunt, elderly man, supported by two sticks, shuffle out of the home's entrance. With a wistful look at the large red 'NO SMOKING' sign nailed to the imposing front door, the old man rooted in the pockets of a moth-eaten cardie for his pipe and a tin box of tobacco.

The elderly gent stooped as he filled his pipe, padding the tobacco down with a crooked, yellowy thumb. It seemed to Paul that he had all the weariness of a world long-past weighing heavily on his shoulders. The old man could barely raise his head to light his paper but trembling, he managed it, and exhaled a long, smoke-filled sigh of relief.

The moment had come. Paul looked round furtively, making sure no-one else could see them. He walked up to the man, smiling. What old people liked most in the world was a happy, polite young person, willing to talk to them, and listen to all their troubles. At this moment, Paul was that person.

"Hello," he said brightly. "How are you?"

"Wossit to you?" replied the gent gruffly. Paul was taken aback. He looked a charmer. Showed you never could tell.

"Oh, nothing," said Paul. "It's just, you know, with all this flu around, and the amount of cars on the roads, and, you know, terrorism and…erm… oh, I dunno… BSE…"

"I can't hear you, son," interrupted the old man, cupping a hand

26

to his ear. "Wot you going on abaht?"

Paul raised his voice. "I'm just trying to say, it's a cruel world today, isn't it? Must be hell for you inside that dump. The way they treat old people. It's terrible."

"It's like being one of the livin' dead in there," said the old man, nodding sideways towards the building.

"Exactly," Paul replied, eager to get to his pitch, "and that's why I'm here. You don't have to live like this, you know. I know a place you can go, where it's nothing like this. It's warm and friendly, no demands on you, all your aches and pains smoothed away…"

"Where is this place?" interrupted the old man again. "Molly's Massage on the Seven Sisters Road? 'Cos I've already been there, my son, and let me tell you, it's bleedin' paradise. Be hard to find somewhere better."

Paul was nonplussed. "No, I wasn't talking about anything… earthly."

"Come again? Where were you talkin' abaht, then?"

"Heaven."

"*Heaven!* What about bloody heaven?!"

"I just thought you'd be better off there, and if you'd like to go I can help. I drive an Underground train, and you know what, it's the perfect way to go, no lingering along, just bang and that's…"

The old man cut him dead. "Get to the point, boy. Wassit you're asking me?

"I was wondering… if you… if you… there's no easy way of saying this… I was wondering if you would like to die under my train. Please."

"You don't know who I am, do you son?" the old man growled.

"No. Should I?"

The old man's blue eyes glittered, but not with the kindness expected from someone his age. They were full of fire. Something about him was starting to make Paul nervous.

"Fifty years ago I was your age," he growled, "but I wasn't standing around like a big poof, with a bunch of flowers under

27

my arm. I was too busy cutting throats. They called me Stiletto Stan. Best enforcer the Twins ever had. Now…what are you doin' coming round here, trying to scare me about death and falling under trains. Because if anyone should be scared, son, it's you."

Before Paul could stammer an apology, he felt a sharp whack to his ear. The blow sent him reeling on the gravel path. Again and again, the blows landed with amazing accuracy, to the ribs, fingers, buttocks. Paul tried to fend them off, but it was hopeless. Then, they stopped as abruptly as they'd started.

The old man towered above him, shaking his stick. "Get aht of it," he screamed, "before I do something I really regret!"

Paul needed no further warning. He picked himself up and, leaving the chocolates and flowers where they'd fallen, he backed off down the drive. The old man picked up the chocolates. Quality Street. Nice one. They'd do for the next time Molly paid him one of her 'home visits'.

*

"Is that the Samaritans?"

After traipsing home he collapsed into his favourite chair and came across the leaflet, plucked from his car's windscreen wiper. Maybe there was a way, after all.

"Yes, it is," said a smooth, calm voice. "How can I help you?"

"Hi. Erm. I was wondering… I've got a bit of time on my hands and I thought maybe I could, you know, volunteer. Talk to people. The odd afternoon, or whatever."

"Well, we're always interested in potential volunteers. You would need to go on a training course, though."

"A training course?" Paul's face fell. "Couldn't I just drop by and start answering calls?"

"I'm sorry, sir," said the measured voice, "but you do need extensive training for this. I could send you an information pack, if you like?"

"Information pack? No. No, that's fine. Well, thanks. Thanks a lot. Bye."

28

It was hopeless and yet it was hope that drove him on. Hope that one day he would walk through the door of Loch Tyne House, envelope himself in the delicious aroma of a peat fire and begin the great novel. He had been putting off this moment, but now was the time. The last refuge of the mad, the bad and the totally crackers. He switched on his computer, clicked on the 'Explorer' icon and scrolled down his favourites to Google. Then, with a deep breath, he typed the words 'suicide chat room' into the search facility.

In 30 minutes he had read almost as much as he ever wanted to know about suicide. The whole thing was beginning to make him feel sick. The pills. The potions. The household cleaning fluids, the neat alcohol and the illegal drugs. That was the pleasant stuff. There were in-depth discussions about noose knots and major arteries, hosepipe strengths and masking tape for car windows. It was awful, and it seemed most people were simply getting off on talking about it.

"Anyone here gonna actually do it?" he typed.

A reply pinged straight back from 'Deathwish'.

"Tried tons o'times, dude. Last time, Jack and coke, plus 150 Tylenol. Slit wrist to be sure. Woke up Boxing Day, parents banging on door. Forgotten I'd invited them for Xmas. Patched up in ER, home in time for turkey. Next time, gonna make sure is last time."

Paul perked up. Could he be a 'jumper'?

"Where U? Wanna meet up?"

"Reno, Nevada. Where U?"

"Shit. London, England. U planning 2 visit soon?"

"No. Planning to die."

"Shame. I need help. Wanna talk suicide. Face 2 Face. Soon!"

"Sorry, dude, no can do. Gotta run... over a canyon :-)"

He tried again. 'NE1 out there wanna talk dying? London calling.'

A message dropped back from 'PoisonGirl'.

'Hey. Dying is well cool. Av tried twice. First time da rope broke.

Was cheap shit from China. Second time got found by sum guy walking dog on da Heath. Him cut me down, sorted me out.'

'Well,' Paul typed back in, keen to get the morbid thoughts pumping around PoisonGirl's mind, 'third time lucky. Three and out, ain't it?'

A pause, then another message. "Nah, don't fink so. Got jiggy wiv da guy wot rescued me, got bun in oven, we'z getting wed next month. So got it all 2 live 4! Gud luck wiv your def, m8. They say drowning is nice x x x."

Paul put his head in his hands and slumped forward towards the screen. Not even these crazies could make this happen. He would have to face facts. The Big Game wasn't one he would be playing.

Suddenly, his screen moved up slightly. He scrolled down, keen to see what had prompted it. Another message. For him.

"Hi. You wanted to talk about suicide. I want to die also, but I need a little help. Someone to help me choose the right fork. Are you this person? Shall we 'go private'?"

Paul read, and re-read it. It looked serious, not some goth kid playing round with a morbid fantasy. It seemed genuine.

"OK. Interested. Let's go private. Am Paul."

"Maurice. Welcome."

CHAPTER 4

It was hard to imagine why anyone from Willesden would want to kill themselves. It seemed a pleasant place, not wealthy, not poor, but somehow solid. It felt more settled than Acton, less frenetic and with a heart somewhat lacking in his own neighbourhood. You could see yourself knowing your neighbours here. Try that in Acton and the door would be literally slammed in your face.

Paul came out of Dollis Hill tube station and headed up the high road which ribboned through the centre. The address he was looking for was on the other side of Willesden New Cemetery. He was still early. A wander in a graveyard, with its silent rows of stones, each with a small story about humanity, was a tempting way to use up the time. Today, though, he didn't feel like it. The dead, after all, were already dead. It was the living he was interested in. Or maybe more accurately, the living dead.

Eventually, Paul found himself along a quiet street of bungalows which backed onto the cemetery. It was London suburbia at its finest. The sound of children's voices coming from a playground in an adjacent primary school seemed to harmonise with the birds singing in the park. Ahead, two well-dressed mothers pushed fashionable urban strollers in tandem, their heads close together in new-mum gossip. It was 11am, morning coffee time. Neither the time, nor the place, to be discussing violent death.

Paul unlatched the gate and walked up the tidy path to Number 74. A small front garden was bordered by carefully-planted shrubs. At the door, a sign: 'Saving The Planet – No Free Newspapers Please'. Several black umbrellas were propped up inside the porch, and a shoe rack held a small collection of neatly-arranged footwear. Paul paused, his finger on the bell. He could not imagine

31

anyone with a powerful death-wish living here.

He pushed hard on the bell, determined to see this through. After a couple of seconds the shadow of a head appeared in the front door's frosted glass panel, accompanied by the sound of several bolts being unlocked.

Paul swallowed nervously, and shifted his feet. The door opened, cautiously at first, then fully. On the step stood a tall, foreign-looking man dressed entirely in black. Black shoes, neat black trousers, and a black artistic-looking roll-neck sweater topped off by a bushy mane of grey-black hair. Even the man's eyes looked black, but his expression wasn't quite as deathly as his attire. In fact, Paul thought, he looked quite laid back, amused even.

The man stretched out his hand in welcome.

" 'Allo. Are you Paul?"

Foreign, definitely foreign. Italian, maybe, or French. The smell of cooking food came from behind the man and wafted into Paul's nostrils.

"Yes, that's me. Paul." He accepted the hand, which shook his limply.

"'Allo, I am Maurice. I am pleased to make your acquaintance. Do step inside."

Paul took a step forward, but was stopped by Maurice with a slight upturn of his hand.

"Oops! I forgot... no shoes in ze 'ouse. So much poop on ze pave-ments, and I only have the carpets just one year."

Paul slipped off his Converse trainers and placed them alongside the expensive leather shoes in the rack. Maurice looked pleased.

"Now, come inside. You are welcome. I am looking forward to meeting you since last night. This way, please."

Paul was ushered through a pastel-pink hallway, decorated with 1950s style black and white photographs. Couples in berets kissing outside pavement cafés. Glamorous older women clutching small, pampered poodles. The house appeared to be as neat as a pin. Fastidiously tidy.

Maurice stood aside and allowed his guest to enter the kitchen first. A skylight and a large picture window allowed in a copious amount of light. Judging by the newness of the kitchen appliances and their upmarket brand, Maurice was a man who spent plenty of time in here. The delicious aroma of gently frying onions, garlic and thyme in a pan on the stove was enough to convince Paul that his host was a very fine cook.

"Do seet down, Paul," Maurice instructed, motioning to a wrought iron chair behind a thick glass dining table. "Café?"

"Yes, thanks." Paul looked around. The kitchen work surfaces were scrupulously clean. Above an expensive-looking toaster was a rack of 12 gleaming chef's knives, magnetically attached and laid out perfectly parallel to one another.

Maurice methodically pushed down the cafetière's plunger and removed two cups and two saucers from a cupboard. After he had placed cafetière, cups, saucers and sugarbowl on to a wicker tray he turned to face Paul and sat directly in front of him.

"*Voila*," he said, with a little flourish. He leaned back in his chair and studied Paul like he might the financial section of a broadsheet newspaper, intently and with full concentration.

"So," he said finally, "what brings you here?"

Paul hesitated. He'd expected Maurice to do all the explaining. The brief exchange they'd had over the internet the previous night indicated Maurice's strong desire to die. Surely it was he who needed to speak first.

"Well… I'm here because of you. Because of what you said last night. About dying. I'm here to help you."

"Yes, of course. To help me. And I think you can do this. I look at you, Paul, and I see a man with… *un apetit*. So this will be a moment to savour. But first, I think you are hungry, yes? I have made for you a little starter." He winked. "Before ze main course."

"Oh, no, that's okay. I'm not that…" Paul didn't want to eat. They had business to talk. It was hardly the stuff of a cosy lunchtime chat.

33

"I insist," said Maurice. "We French believe food drives the wheels of social intercourse."

"Dunno about that," said Paul. He didn't like the last word that fell from Maurice's lips, and started to feel slightly sweaty.

"But of course," replied the Frenchman smiling. Maurice got up from the table and began to dish out the contents of the frying pan on to a white enamel plate.

"Please," he said, pushing a plate of fried onion, garlic and sausage in front of Paul. "*Eat.*"

Politely, Paul cut a small portion of sausage and gathered together a heap of onions to go with it, but for the moment he didn't take a bite.

"I am so pleased to meet you, Paul," continued Maurice. "There are not many people in the world who would do this."

"Well, you know, I'm glad to be of help. It's the least I can do."

"Oh no," said Maurice, his voice raising to a slight squeak. "This is a big, big thing you do. The biggest. But... where will we do this thing? In your apartment?"

"In my apartment? No, no. That wouldn't be too good. I was thinking... on the Tube. The Underground."

"The Underground? But how will this be possible?"

Paul was perplexed. Maurice's English was good. How could he not understand the means of suicide on the Tube? There was only one way, surely? He took a bite of the sausage before he spoke again.

"Well, I'll be driving the train and you can... you know... jump."

Maurice jerked backwards, as though a bucket of ice had landed in his lap.

"Jump! Under a Tube train!? Are you crazy?! I'll be killed!"

"Well that's the general idea... isn't it?"

"But what about the cooking?" The Frenchman stared at his guest, open-mouthed.

"Cooking?"

"Yes. The cooking and the eating."

"Sorry, I'm not with you here. What cooking?"

Maurice sighed. "I wish to watch as you eat. Piece by piece."

Now it was Paul's turn to stare open-mouthed. The remainder of the sausage toyed with the idea of disappearing down his throat, but it stayed where it was.

"Eat...what?"

"Me! Who else?! First, we cut off my penis. We fry it, maybe wiz onions. Then the legs, then the arms and so on, until I am all gone. *Poufff!*"

Paul was dumbstruck. Maurice leaned across the table and patted him reassuringly on the arm.

"I see you are worried by this, no? Don't worry, Paul. Many people have done this before. Don't you read ze news?"

The Frenchman reached over and took a recipe book from the work surface. The centre section was stuffed full of newspaper cuttings, all concerning the same subject: Armin Meiwes, the notorious German cannibal sent to jail for killing and eating a man he met on the internet. The pair had talked it over, then out came the sharp knives...

Maurice looked at Paul intently. "You know... they say it tastes a little like pork... how is your sausage?"

Paul looked at the piece of meat in horror. His forked clanged onto the plate as he gagged, and spat out the remaining sausage.

"Oh dear," said Maurice. "There is a problem. Too spicy?"

Paul jumped up from the table, scraping his chair with force on the wooden floor.

"Look, I'm sorry, I think there's been some kind of mistake here. I gotta go!"

Through the pastel-pink hallway he ran, Maurice behind him. Thank Christ he hadn't locked the door. He almost wrenched it from its hinges as he flung it open and, grabbing his trainers, he ran across the garden and leapt over the low wall. As he fled down the road, he heard Maurice's plaintive voice in the distance.

35

"Paul, please! Don't be afraid of my penis! Come back...you must eat me... please!"

In next door's garden an old lady looked up from the rose bush she was pruning, her face the colour of a fuchsia. With a Gallic shrug and a smile, Maurice politely waved to her, and wandered back inside. Paul, very afraid of Maurice's penis, was long gone.

*

Finally, he had ended up where he started, alone on Archway Bridge after the fall of night. The experience with Maurice had rattled him. Dying was a complicated art and those who wished to do it before their time was up were seriously messed up. There was no such thing as a co-operative suicide, Paul decided, especially not one who would willingly throw themselves under a train in a certain place, at a certain time. And for what? He hadn't even had time to explain to Maurice the real reason for visiting him. He might have understood. But would he have gone along with the plan? Not likely. He would have been better off with a one-way ticket to Germany. They did that sort of thing over there.

Paul shuffled his feet in the rubbish-strewn footwell of his car's passenger seat and for the twenty-ninth time that night checked his view of the bridge through the windscreen.

There was no-one there. In the orange haze of a nearby street lamp he could just about make out the words on the page of his book. The hero, if you could call him that, had now murdered the pawnbroker and her sister, and was agonising over the crime and the punishment that would inevitably follow.

He flipped the page, ready for another weighty paragraph of the young criminal's emotional struggle to justify his crime, but he could not concentrate. The events in his own life were proving too full of moral dilemmas for him to take much notice of what some 19th century Russian was up to. For all the knowledge he'd acquired from his reading, very little of it was helping him now.

Paul dropped the book into the footwell, clasped his palms

36

together and closed his hands over the bridge of his nose. Perhaps this is where it would finish. The hope that had driven him on in the last few days had all but disappeared. Despair enveloped him and whispered cruel truths in his ears. He would drive the train until pension day. The novel would never be finished. Or even started. He would live alone, with his books, until someone took him out one day in a body bag. Or he leapt from the bridge himself.

"OH, FUCK IT!" He rocked backwards and forwards in the seat, overcome by the frustration of it all. He might as well go home now and face the rest of his life. It was all over.

Paul began to heave himself across to the driver's side when something he glimpsed caused him to stop dead, hovering above the handbrake with his arms resting on both seats. A vaguely familiar figure, bearded and shabby, was ambling across the bridge. Yes, it was him. The man he'd encountered before on this bridge, who'd stopped in almost the same place. A night stroller. London had its fair share of them, the kind of people for whom a city in darkness held no terrors. The figure flicked a cigarette end casually to one side and again stopped in the middle of the bridge.

Paul looked away, and slid into the driver's seat. His lonely vigil was at an end. He switched on the engine and pulled away from his parking spot. But as he drove past him, the man made it to the parapet, and in one swift movement put his left foot on the rail and hauled himself up. Christ, he was going to jump!

There wasn't a second to spare. Paul slammed on his brakes, booted open the passenger door of the Fiesta and as he scrambled to get out his foot snagged in his trailing seat belt. Over he went, flat on his face. It didn't matter. He needed to get to that guy double speed. He picked himself up and raced towards the figure, now about to step onto the parapet.

"Wait! For Christ's sake wait! Stop!"

The man seemed oblivious to Paul's shouts and was peering over the edge into the chasm below. He was determined to do it. Paul had no intention of letting it happen. He reached the spot, and without hesitating grabbed the figure by the shoulder. "Don't do it!" he screamed.

Startled by the interruption, the man whipped his head round in alarm but as he did so he lost his footing on the parapet and slipped. Paul had no time to grab onto his jacket and the man disappeared over the side. Screwing up his eyes and twisting his neck away from the parapet, Paul braced himself for the sickening thud and screeching of tyres.

It did not come. Instead, a rasping Irish brogue broke the terrible suspense.

"Don't just stand there, you fucken bollicks. Get me out of this thing!"

Paul opened his eyes and saw the man hanging from the rail, a part of the ornamental balustrade caught in his overcoat. Stunned, he climbed on to the ironwork and leaned over to help, but there was no way he could haul the heavy body back over the side.

"I can't unhook it," he said. "You'll have to climb back up."

"You're a fucking arsehole, you know that? Gimme a hand up!"

Paul grabbed the man's arm, heaving him back up to a standing position. His eyes red with anger, or whiskey, or both, the man snarled into Paul's pale face. Even so, his rescuer wouldn't let go of his jacket sleeve.

"Why don't you come back over this side?" said Paul, ignoring the man's glowering expression. "Just for a while? Then we can talk."

"Talk, is it? Is that what you're after? Well now…"

The man was heavy-set and, from what you could see of it under the beard, had a broad, hard face as flat as a landing strip. He was buttoned into an old grey duffel coat and his nylon trousers were smeared with grease stains.

With a grunt, the man struggled back over the rail, grudgingly accepting Paul's help. At the last second he tripped and landed in a heap on top of Paul. The Irishman now had the advantage and he took it. Grabbing Paul by the throat and pummelling the back of his head on the pavement, he began to scream and howl, inches from his face.

"You interfering little gobshite! How the fuck... why can't you leave a man be... you fucking do-gooder gobshite bollicks?"

Paul's eyes bulged as the man tightened his grip on his shirt collar. With every slam of his head on the pavement he felt his whole being ebb away. For Christ's sake, this was the wrong way round. He didn't want to die!

In the distance, the faint wail of a siren. Paul and the Irishman heard it simultaneously. It was approaching. Grabbing the moment, Paul wrenched his head forward and with a gasp of air spoke just one word: "Police!"

The Irishman loosened his grip and with a curse, stood up, kicked Paul in the ribs and started to run. Winded, but full of adrenalin, Paul jumped up and took off in the same direction, towards his car.

The man ran on ahead as Paul threw open the car door and scrambled in. He gunned the engine hard and pulled away. Behind them, blue flashing lights warned of the approaching cop car. The figure in front had nowhere left to run and, skidding to a halt beside him, Paul flung open the door.

"Get in!"

There was no way out. It was either a night in the cells for a breach of the peace, or a ride out of trouble with a stranger. Swearing, the Irishman climbed in, banged the door shut and they tore off into the night, putting a safe distance between them and the law.

For a few moments neither spoke. The stench of stale breath from panting bodies filled the car. Paul stared ahead, shocked, but attempting to concentrate. The Irishman leaned heavily on the door, the side of his face pressed against the window. Then he broke the silence.

"So what the fuck is this then? The Suicide Snatch Squad?"

Paul didn't reply.

"C'mon now. I'm waiting…"

He had to be careful. The door wasn't locked and any second the guy could simply open it and fling himself out. If he was prepared to go over Archway Bridge…

"How about… I buy you a drink? I reckon we both need one."

"Need one? I'd say you fucking well *owed* me one!"

With a look of disgust, and paying no attention to his own filthy, foul-breathed state, the Irishman kicked at the chip wrappers, burger boxes, plastic coffee cups and empty cans at his feet.

"This car," he said finally, after studied concentration, "absolutely fucking stinks."

Chapter 5

"After you."

Paul held open the door of the pub to his new and dishevelled drinking companion. It was the kind of North London boozer which time and the gastropub companies seemed to have forgotten. A clutch of badly-wrapped sandwiches heaped at one side of the bar was the pub's only concession to the notion of food. In the other corner, illuminated by a mind-numbing sequence of flashing lights from a pair of fruit machines, a small collection of hard-drinking regulars gathered around a squat, shaven-headed and tattooed landlord. It was very much a 'mind-your-own-business' boozer. In short, the perfect place to hatch a fiendish plot.

Paul waited for the Irishman to walk by him, his arm straining against the force of the spring-hinged door. The man hesitated for a second, staring narrow-eyed into Paul's tense, tired features.

"Me first? I don't think so. You first. You're buying these fucking drinks, not me. Besides, if I go before you, who's to say you won't drag me back from the bar at the last minute?"

With a small shake of his head, Paul walked in first. The Irishman was going to demand an explanation and a half, and rightly so. Would he – should he – get straight down to business or soften him with a few drinks before the Big Ask? He needed to know tonight, even if it resulted in a punch in the face. Time was almost running out and this – a dirty derelict with nothing else to live for – might be his last chance.

But by the murderous look of him, he would be in no mood to hear how his slicing up under a Tube train could help a struggling writer make a new and happier life in pleasant, mortgage-free surroundings. Paul knew he couldn't risk losing him straight away.

41

He would have to take it easy, at least for a short while.

"Yeah?" The landlord looked from Paul to the Irishman – now slumped behind a table and still glowering from beneath the peak of his battered blue trapper's hat – and back again. They looked a strange pair, but no odder than the gnarled knot of regulars hunched like trolls at the corner of the bar. He'd serve them, but if there was any trouble…

"Erm, two pints of Guinness please." Paul hadn't asked, he just assumed the man would be partial to a drop of the black stuff. He could barely stomach it himself, but he needed to make some kind of connection with this guy, and quickly. It might only be a drink they had in common, but it was better than nothing.

The bloody Guinness was taking an age to pour. From the corner of his eye, Paul could see the Irishman becoming agitated. He looked uncomfortable, even in this shithole. Maybe he did his drinking elsewhere, in parks and doorways, or wherever tramps and down-and-outs gathered. He looked rough enough to belong on the streets. If he bolted now that would be the end of it. Paul could feel his own tension rising as the landlord let the pints settle before adding the last quarter.

Finally, and with a swirl in the shape of a shamrock poured into the creamy head, the landlord handed over the drinks. Paul swapped them for a tenner, not knowing whether to keep an eye on the Irishman or make sure the landlord didn't rip him off in the change. He settled on the former, figuring that the loss of a couple of quid was nothing to what he would forego if the man made a run for it now.

The landlord dumped the change into Paul's hand and went back to the huddled gang of regulars. Paul placed the drinks carefully down on the table, not wanting to spill a drop.

"Is Guinness okay for you?" he asked.

"They say it is," replied the man, apparently misunderstanding the question but actually not missing a beat. "It's full of iron, you know. But then I'm hardly in a position to talk about a long life now, am I? Still, I didn't think I'd be tasting this again."

He put the glass to his mouth and took a long, deep pull before settling it back down on the table, rounding off the fluid sequence of movements with a satisfied belch.

"Cheers," said Paul, forcing a half-smile and raising a glass.

The Irishman leaned back, the brief pleasure gleaned from the first pull on his pint replaced once again with the snarl.

"Never mind 'Cheers'," he snapped "What's your fucking game? What are you – some kind of religious type? Waiting like a vulture for some poor soul to save?"

Paul shifted uncomfortably. The Irishman wasn't up for any niceties. Better to be straight.

"No, I'm a Tube driver."

"Because you can forget about that with me. I've done all the praying I'm going to do, I tell you!"

The man was ignoring him and, by the sound of it, was about to start on some kind of anti-religious rant.

"I'm not religious!" Paul butted in desperately.

"Bloody creeping Jesuses, trying to save their own miserable skins by interfering in other people's business. What kind of shite is that?!"

Without bothering to answer his own question, the man paused and took another long draught from the pint glass. Paul saw the advantage in the man's silence, and took it.

"No, that's not it at all. I want you to kill yourself!"

In his haste to cut the crap with this man and get to the point, he'd spoken just a little too loudly – and at a moment when the last song on the jukebox had finished and another was about to begin. The trolls at the bar dropped into a curious silence, and turned as one towards the direction of the comment. But the Irishman answered their stares with the kind of drop-dead look not to be messed with.

As they turned back to their own conversation, the man focused his attention on Paul, red-faced with a mixture of nerves and embarrassment.

43

"Keeping yer fucking voice down, you gobshite" he hissed. "And you can shove the whole reverse-psychology up your hole!"

"What...? No, it's true. Honestly." Paul's voice dropped to a whisper. "I want you to kill yourself."

Unsure of what he was hearing, but curious to learn a little more about the person in front of him, the man took another drink, swallowed, and pausing for effect, wiped his mouth of the creamy froth which clung to his matted beard.

"Well," he said, half-amusedly, "you've done a grand job of stopping me up 'til now." He tilted his head at an angle like a bird, trying to work out Paul's next move.

"So what do you want? Is it me organs? Let me guess... you're going blind and you want me eyes? Is that it?"

"No, no, no," said Paul, shocked. It was the one thing he hadn't thought of, trying to find someone who would donate their body to medical science. Isn't that what happened to a lot of tramps? If this didn't work maybe he could try the Sally Army...

"No, it's not your organs I want. I don't want any part of your body... honestly."

The Irishman held his gaze steadily, saying nothing. Nervously, but with the urgency to lay down the deal – whatever the reaction – nagging at him, Paul pressed on.

"It's just... I was wondering if you'd be interested in throwing yourself in front of my train?"

He paused while the Irishman digested this information.

"I'd pay you, of course."

There. It was out. Paul took a swig of his pint in an attempt to hide his flushed face. The Irishman looked at him coolly before replying in a voice thick with sarcasm.

"Oh. So you'd pay me? Is that right? Pay to run me down, yeah?"

He hadn't said 'No'. At least not yet.

"Well, I was thinking... in exchange for this service I could give you, say... fifteen hundred pounds?"

The Irishman raised an eyebrow and smiled contentedly. They were signs Paul took to be definite ones of interest.

"Right so. And then I hurl myself under your train without a care, a big fat smile on my face?"

"Yes, basically."

"And fifteen hundred quid in my cold, dead hand?"

Paul looked away involuntarily. Was he being toyed with? He couldn't work it out. The man seemed to be playing it cool, but they were talking no small amount of money here. Maybe he was simply keeping his cards close to his chest? Again he paused, smiling before speaking.

"Well now, that's a *fantastic* deal! How could I possibly refuse? You'd better get me another pint, son, before I change me mind."

Paul was on his feet almost immediately, reaching out for the Irishman's glass. He had missed the tone of the man's voice, honeyed in dripping sarcasm. As Paul turned and hurried to the bar, the man shook his head, a twin gesture of bemusement and disgust.

When he returned, pint in hand, the Irishman seemed keen to carry on where he'd left off.

"So," he continued, warming to his theme, "bearing in mind your carefully thought out plan... what the fuck am I going to do with fifteen hundred quid when I'm dead? Buy meself a fancy gravestone?"

"No, no, you won't be dead," replied Paul. "I mean... well, yeah, you will be dead, but not until Monday. Monday morning. On the Northern Line at 10:06am. Just out of East Finchley. So you've got a whole weekend to... you know... spend it on whatever you want. On... I dunno... A woman, or loads of women?"

The man took a long swig of his drink while he considered the suggestion.

"And what do you think I was doing last night?"

By the looks of him – a crumb-infested beard and several layers of filthy clothes that would walk themselves to the laundrette given half a chance – whatever he was doing last night, it certainly wasn't that. Paul decided not to press him on the point. There was too much at stake.

"Okay. So… eat, drink and be merry? One last time."

"I'm already fat," snarled the Irishman, "me liver's shot and I don't feel much like laughing. Next big idea."

Paul was stumped. "There must be something you really, really want to do and never had the chance to," he stammered.

"Well now," said the Irishman, suddenly taking on a look of sincerity, "there is."

"Excellent! What is it? Just let me know, and we'll do it. Whatever it takes."

"I want to swim with a great white shark. That's what I want to do. No cage, just me and the beast. Eye to eye. There's this fella does it, out in South Africa. I seen him on the telly. Just gets right in there with the bastards, not a worry on him. And he's never had a lump taken out of him yet. I tell you what, I'd fucking love that."

Paul could hardly believe it. The idea of this guy, stripping off his homeless gear and going all Life On Earth with a bunch of man-eaters. He was a loony, for sure. But if that's what he wanted…

"Look, it's a tough call. We've only got a couple of days. But there's always the London Aquarium. They've got sharks. Not great whites, but, you know… big ones."

The Irishman looked at him, his eyes as flinty-black as the beasts he dreamed of.

"Are you taking the piss?" he said.

A sweat of desperation crept over Paul. "Something else then," he muttered. "I dunno… give it to charity? Isn't there anyone you know who could use some cash? What about your family?"

The Irishman spat back. "My family? Jesus… they probably think I'm dead already."

So he had a family. The man's reaction to the suggestion was immediate; raw, even. Paul softened the anxiety in his voice.

46

"A few quid would be a nice surprise for them, then."

The Irishman took another great gulp from the glass.

"Oh, it would be a surprise all right," he agreed. "A fucken surprise that I had any money to give them. I didn't leave them with…"

He tailed off, and stared into his pint. Paul was scared to break the silence, but he had to get him to agree.

"How about you tell me more? Sounds like the money could help?"

The Irishman took a swig that drained his glass to the bottom. "I dunno," he said finally. "Maybe, maybe not? I just don't know."

He banged his empty glass on the table and gestured towards the door. "C'mon, let's get out of this shitehole," he said. "I need a clear head to think, not a skinful of booze."

*

In the pub car park Paul and the Irishman stood facing one another over the top of the Fiesta. The man's mind was spinning with possibilities. Paul was willing to tell him whatever he wanted to hear to convince him that a weekend blowing a grand and a half before dying under a Tube train was the best idea he'd ever heard.

"I dunno," said the man, now orbiting away from Paul's last suggestion. "I can't say I feel great about this, involving the family."

"Yeah, you're right," said Paul quickly, keen not to let him walk away from the whole thing altogether. "It always gets messy with family. How about a day at the races, then? Just take the money and blow it sky high?"

The Irishman banged the roof. "This is mad! Fuck it. It's been what…seven, eight years? I can't go now. Too late."

"You're probably right," said Paul, "let sleeping dogs lie."

The man walked round the side of the car and directly in front of Paul. Had he upset him? The Irishman stared at him intently, then looked at the ground.

"I wanted to, you know? Visit them. I'm not a totally heartless bastard, just in case you were thinking…"

"I wasn't."

"I thought about saying goodbye. Making my peace. I really did. Just didn't seem right."

"Definitely," replied Paul, glad not to have been belted. "I think that's exactly what…"

"How could I turn up looking like this," butted in the Irishman. "Like a knacker without a penny in me pocket. But with that money you're talking about, well… I'm not a religious man, but this might be God's way of giving me one last chance to make up for some of the shite I've rained down on them."

From his old duffel coat pocket he pulled out a crumpled packet of Lambert and Butler cigarettes and lit one. Between the first deep drag and the subsequent relief of exhalation, he'd made a decision.

"Ah, fuck it."

"Yeah, fuck it," replied Paul, echoing him. "Not the family. Go down the dogs instead."

"No, you eejit," snapped the man. "Not 'fuck it, I give up'. I mean 'fuck it, let's do it'. Carpe diem!"

"What?"

"Carpe diem. Don't they teach you anything at Tube drivers' school? It means 'seize the day'. Take a chance. Fuck it, why not. But I'll tell you something, son. If we're going to do this thing then we've got to get one thing clear."

"What's that?"

"A deal is a deal. No backing out, no fucking around. We shake on it and it's as good as done."

The Irishman was staring hard at Paul, and with the reality of his words came a sickening feeling from the pit of his stomach. Was this actually happening? After the past few days, and the mad scramble around London to find someone, was this the one? This sweating, stinking homeless man with red-rimmed eyes and breath like a badger's? Was this the man who was going to save Paul from

48

a fate worse than… well, worse than death?

"You'll do it?"

The Irishman spat on his palm and stretched out his hand. With only a slight hesitation, Paul accepted it before withdrawing, and wiping his own hand discreetly on his jeans.

"I'll do it," said the Irishman.

"A deal's a deal?"

"A deal's a deal. Now…where's this cash?"

"At home. I live in Acton."

"I'd better get in then," said the man. "I've always wanted a ride in the back of a bin lorry."

*

It was late, and judging by the unusual level of quiet in the house, Paul assumed Yvonne was having a night in alone. At least there would be no awkward questions about his unexpected visitor.

The man followed Paul in and as he put the light on in the living room, the Irishman looked around him in disbelief.

"Christ! Live alone, do you?"

"Yeah, why?"

"Nothing. Just a wild guess. Jesus, I've slept in libraries with fewer books. What did you do, ram-raid Foyles? Any chance of a seat somewhere?"

Paul didn't know whether to be flattered or offended. He'd always been proud of his book collection, but the 'live alone' remark stung. He read. Lots. That was his hobby. If he'd wanted a relationship, he could have gone out and found one. Probably. Besides, from the sheer variety and unrelenting misery of the relationships he'd read about, he was happier alone, indoors, and with a good book. He removed a pile of paperbacks from a high-backed green leather armchair by the electric fire and motioned the man to sit down.

As he settled, the man spotted Paul's laptop on the old table.

"That a computer?"

Paul nodded in the affirmative.

"What d'you do with it? Games and all that rubbish? Playing with yourself, looking at dirty women? What?"

Paul snapped the lid shut protectively.

"No, I'm a writer."

"Oh, a writer is it?" smiled the man. "A writer who drives a Tube train?"

"Yeah, well, not for much longer, hopefully."

The man wasn't listening. He was settling himself into the chair, drawing up his jacket around him. He shut his eyes, as though to settle himself down for the night, then opened them again almost immediately.

"So where's this fifteen hundred quid, eh?"

Paul looked around him. He knew where it was. But was this the right moment? The right man? He said a deal was a deal. But he didn't even know his sodding name. He took a brown envelope – the envelope which contained his unpaid rent money – from under yet another pile of books and hesitated.

"Go on, then," said the Irishman, his eye on the bulging envelope, "hand it over."

"This is my rent money. How do I know you won't just take it and go?"

The Irishman shot a look back at him that made Paul recoil in fear.

"What did I say to you?" he whispered menacingly. "A deal is a fucking deal. That means *you* give me the money and *I* don't run away with it. Understand? Now give me the fecking money."

Paul handed over the envelope. The Irishman ripped it open and began to slowly count it. When he finished, he looked up at Paul with a satisfied smile.

"It seems to be all there."

"Does it?" said Paul, who'd watched the proceedings intently. "I would say it was twenty quid over."

"Call it a bonus, then" mocked the Irishman.

"No way," replied Paul, snatching back the note. "We'll call it fifteen hundred. A deal's a deal, remember?"

The Irishman let it pass, and winked at the affronted Paul before drawing himself deeper into the armchair.

"Don't mind if I crash here, do you?"

Paul knew he had no choice. The bundle of money was tucked safely into the Irishman's jacket and his eyes were closing. At least if he stayed here, where it was warm, he wouldn't be tempted to clear off so quickly.

Paul snapped the light off and opened the door to leave.

"By the way," said the Irishman, "what's your name?"

"God, yeah...of course. It's Paul. Paul Callow."

"I'm Tommy Cassidy. Now open a fucking window, Paul, I'm roasting in here."

Paul did as he commanded, and headed towards his bedroom. He lay on his bed, thinking of the miracle that had happened only a few hours previously. Then his heart began to race as he thought about the slumbering figure next door. A man who wanted to die. Who had nothing to live for, except some family he hadn't seen for years. A man who didn't seem to give a shit about anything. A man who had come back to his house, taken fifteen hundred quid off him and was now positioning his unwashed self between his precious paperbacks. A man who could, at any moment, get up and leave. Or worse still, get up, kill Paul, rape Yvonne, steal money and jewellery and computers and whatever else, and then leave. There would be no witnesses, no caring neighbours on this road to hear their screams. He really should stop reading those Bret Easton Ellis novels.

Paul turned over, dismissing his paranoia, and reached into his back pocket for his wallet. He pulled out a photo, the same one which appeared on his computer. Loch Tyne House. Whatever else he did in life, at this moment – right here, right now – he had to trust in Tommy Cassidy. He held the key to Paul's dream, and without him it would die.

51

But Tommy wasn't sleeping. A neon sign advertising the cheap hotel across the road illuminated his face as he lay in the chair, his thoughts turning this way and that. How would it be? He knew the answer to that straight away. She – they – would be shocked, angry, upset, hateful, and Christ knows what else. Sure, she might have married, changed her name and fucked off abroad. Who could blame her, after what happened? Then again, she might not have married. She might – just might – still hold a bit of a torch for him? Granted, it wouldn't be much, not now after all this time, but maybe he could still work the old Tommy magic. Especially if he looked the part. She always liked him looking the business, even if he was useless at actually doing it. He looked round the cluttered living room. All these fucking books. The young fella must have a Yellow Pages somewhere. He spied it surprisingly quickly, lurking underneath a portable TV. He pulled it out, flipping quickly from back to front. He landed on 'C' and stopped. It would be here somewhere. Yes, found it. 'Car Hire.'

CHAPTER 6

A shaft of sunlight pierced a gap in the faded blue curtains that hung lop-sidedly in Paul's bedroom, finding a spot on his bed-creased, unwashed face. He opened his eyes and involuntarily picked a yellowy substance from the corner of one of them, at the same time savouring the fetid waft coming from under the duvet.

When sleep had eventually arrived last night, it had been a long and deep one. His dreams had at last been peaceful, less crowded with the pressuring voices and the grim faces with their mad expressions that had troubled him over the past few nights. He turned on to his back, still semi-conscious, and allowed his body the luxury of waking up gradually, taking in the morning light and the limb-stretching satisfaction of a night of unbroken, serene slumber.

His bladder felt unusually full and with a shudder and a final stretch of his thin legs he hauled himself over to the side of the bed and raised himself, Lazarus-like, out of it. The house was quiet and the early-morning roar of commuter traffic along Horn Lane had subsided to a pleasant background hum, punctuated by birdsong. It must be after 10am. Paul felt a warm, unusual wave of happiness wash across his T-shirted shoulders, the kind you get when somehow you know it's going to be a good day.

Hands on the top of the cistern cover and enjoying the sensation of hands-free urination, Paul abruptly remembered about last night. *Oh shit.* He had found someone last night. He had met a guy who… who was prepared to die. To fall under the wheels of his train. The wave of happiness washed away, to be replaced by a cold, creeping sensation that started from his toes and ran up his bare legs, along his spine and through his tousled hair. He felt as though a spider had crawled up his body and he gulped and swallowed uncontrollably.

The living room. He'd crashed there, the guy. What was his name? Thomas? No, Tommy. Tommy had taken the money, shoved it in his coat and crashed out in the chair. Or had he? Oh Christ...

With an impending sense of dread that overlaid the little hope which still remained in him, Paul crept to the door of his living room and pushed it open slowly. If Tommy was there, he didn't want to wake him. If he wasn't, Paul couldn't bear to find out.

The heavy green curtains were pulled shut, but Paul knew enough about his own space to see through the gloom. The chair was empty. A sick feeling rose in his throat. By the side of the chair was a torn, discarded envelope. Paul walked over to the envelope and stood over it for a second, allowing the full horror of the situation to drop on to him. After a moment he picked it up, hoping to find a clue. Even a goodbye note would have been something, but there was nothing, not a sign, only a lingering, gaggingly sweet smell of old socks and cigarettes.

He'd been fleeced. Ripped off, taken for a ride, shafted, conned, done up like a big fat smelly kipper. How the fuck could he have been so dim? He'd met some homeless drunk trying to kill himself, invited him home, plied him with cash and asked him to throw himself under a train after a weekend on the razz. A plan straight out of a Mel Brooks film. This Tommy had talked about swimming with sharks. A pointless exercise. Why swim with them when you can fucking be one? He was the biggest predator of the lot, and Paul had trusted the bastard. His hopes had taken a battering many times over the past week, but this was really the final straw. On Monday morning, instead of going home on compassionate leave and waiting for the grand finale of the Big Game – a six-figure cheque with his name on it – he would be pounding the streets at the end of his shift, avoiding his front door in fear of meeting the landlord, his palm outstretched for his cash. In every sense of the word, he was a loser.

Paul slumped into the chair where Tommy had been. Tears of self-pity filled his eyes as he looked around his dingy room. Books upon books upon books. His life measured out in volumes written by other people. Every word he had not composed himself another tick on the clock that counted down the rest of his lonely, unfulfilled being. The dream was just that, a dream. And with its closure, the remnants of a life most ordinary blew away like the leaves in…

Beeeeeeeeeeeeeeeeeeepppppppp!!! Beeeeppppp! Beeeeeppppp! Beeeeeeeeeeeeee eeeeppppppppp!!

Paul jerked bolt upright with the insistent blast of a car horn directly outside his window. Again and again the horn sounded, noisily demanding attention. Even by the Formula 1 standards of this road it was a bloody loud noise. There was something else too, a radio blaring jolly, accordion-driven Irish dancing music. What the hell was it? *Who* the hell was it?

Paul yanked back the curtains, in no mood to put up with yet another frustrated, road-raging lunatic. But what he saw shocked him to the soles of his feet. Instead of a half-asleep young woman in a 4x4 that was just too much for her limited mental powers, standing there on the pavement, while casually leaning in through the car's open window to sound the horn, was a smartly-dressed businessman, beaming the sunny crack of a smile across the length of his face.

Paul hardly recognised the figure standing in front of him. He wore a pin-striped suit, white shirt and postbox-red tie with a haircut and a shave that had stripped away his bird's-nest of a beard to reveal a face as smooth and as ruggedly handsome as one of the statues on Easter Island. The man grinned again and motioned Paul to open the window, hammering the horn of the vintage gold Mercedes 220 SEB coupé for added effect.

"Mornin'" the man shouted with a laugh. "Wake you up, did I? How's yer bollicks for spots?!"

It was Tommy, dressed up to the nines and looking like he'd

just stepped out of a management meeting for a quick spin with an impressionable secretary. That a glamour puss in the passenger seat was the only accessory missing didn't seem to bother him one jot. He looked every inch a new man.

Still in his boxers and grubby T-shirt, Paul ran down the hallway and flung open the front door. Before he could speak, Tommy read the expression on his face.

"Thought I'd had it away with yer money, did ya?" he shouted over the insistent jig of the ceilidh music coming from the car radio.

There was no point lying. That was exactly what he'd thought. But here he was, a dirty, homeless, dishonest Irishman who'd stolen away and come back looking a million dollars – even if he was still wearing an air of dishonesty.

Tommy laughed again, but this time there was a sneer underneath it.

"What did I say to you last night?" The hardness was back, the narrowed eyes and suspicious expression.

"Go on, gobshite, what did I tell you?"

"That a deal's a deal?"

"Ah. Mammy's little schoolboy got it in one. A deal is a fucking deal. How many times do I have to tell you? I'll answer that one meself. None. I don't want to say it again. You got that?"

Paul wasn't really listening. He was staring past Tommy at the car. It was a beauty, a triumph of style and engineering on this street of cars as battered and down-at-heel as Paul's old Fiesta. Forty-odd years old and not a mark on it.

"What's the story with the car?"

"Well now," replied Tommy, leaning back, his arm stretched casually over the bonnet, "I could hardly turn up on the bus, could I? Besides," he added, giving one of the spoked wheels a gentle tap with his brand new black brogue, "I've always wanted to drive one of these. 1962. Gorgeous, eh? And now I can."

He smiled broadly again, and straightened his tie.

"Nice suit, Tommy," Paul commented.

"Ah, you can look like the mutt's nuts for five hundred quid now, Paul," Tommy replied. "You ought to try it some time. Make you feel like a real man, eh? I picked up the suit first, then the car. They could hardly refuse me in this clobber."

"Eh?"

"It's a rental. The car, I mean. I can batter the devil out of it all weekend. Come Monday morning, they can swing for their money. Anyway, can't stand here gassing. I gotta go. Beat the traffic on the motorway."

"You're going? What... now? Where...? Hang on a sec..."

Something inside Paul had switched on. How could he sit in his flat alone for the rest of his weekend while Tommy, in his boss's suit and rented Mercedes floored it up the motorway, destination unknown but with a kind of fierce determination to do the right thing, whatever that was going to be? Something was going to happen this weekend, and for better or for worse, Paul wanted to be part of it. A surge of energy rushed through him as he raced back up the steps and into his flat. He threw on a pair of jeans, trainers, an old grey hooded sweatshirt and his black bomber jacket. What else? His eyes darted around his bedroom and alighted on a sports holdall. Without looking, he pulled open a drawer and stuffed its contents into the bag. There'd be a spare pair of underpants in there somewhere. He ran back into the living room and grabbed three paperbacks from a pile by the fireplace. The situation might be urgent, but there was always time for a read.

In less than two minutes he was outside again and pulling open the passenger door of the Mercedes. Caught off-guard as he fiddled with the radio, Tommy gave him a look of open-mouthed surprise.

"Do tell me what the fuck you think you're doing," he said, as he turned the key in the car's ignition and reached for his seatbelt.

"I'm coming with you." There was not a hint of hesitation in Paul's voice. He'd never been so certain about anything.

"In your bollocks," Tommy said, not even looking at him. "Not a fucking chance. I just came round here to say goodbye. I'll see you Monday morning. Just as we agreed."

"No way." Paul was adamant.

"Look," said Tommy, turning to face him. "I'm not having you around on my last weekend. Your miserable face will kill what little enjoyment I have left."

"I'll just stay in the background," Paul said.

"Yeah, that's right. That's you all over. Hovering in the shadows like the Grim fucking Reaper. I don't want it and I won't have it. Get out of the fucking car!"

"No chance," said Paul. "I know a deal's a deal and all that but I don't know you from Adam. I just… I dunno… I just want to see what happens, maybe. I want to see this through."

Tommy looked into Paul's face and softened. The lad was a loser, sure enough, but he wanted to come. He'd be useless if it got very hairy, though you never knew. And he might be a soft touch for a bit of petrol money.

"Okay, but I'm telling you this," said Tommy. "If you piss on my parade, son, I'll have your bollocks in a pudding bowl. No messing."

"Fine."

"Grand. Get your seatbelt on. I have not the slightest intention of treating this vehicle with the respect due to it."

With that, he pulled away from the kerb and almost immediately into a light controlled pedestrian crossing, which was on red. Tommy drummed his fingers impatiently on the dashboard as an elderly woman progressed at tortoise speed across the road in front of him.

But from an agitated, red-faced look he suddenly turned a ghastly shade of white and slumped towards the wheel, one hand on his head and the other clutching his stomach.

"Shit! You okay there, mate? Do you wanna swap seats or something?"

Tommy looked up, his face a mask of anger.

"Fuck's sake! I'm fine. Only ten yards down the road and you're off whining already!"

"Alright! I was only asking."

"Yeah, well, don't."

Tommy reached into his pocket and pulled out an orange bottle of tablets. Rattling a handful out, he dry-swallowed them. As he did so, the light turned to green and on cue, a car behind him sounded its horn.

Tommy didn't respond. He simply wound down the window and with a deliberately slow movement, gave the impatient driver behind a long, lingering middle finger. He closed the window, gently put the gearstick from neutral into first and for the next twenty yards drove like a centenarian. Then, without warning, his foot hit the accelerator and the car thrust forward like a bull at a gate.

Paul could barely believe he was in this dream of a motor with a man like Tommy. Whatever the guy would do this weekend, he would do it like a man possessed. If you were going to die on Monday, you would live that way too, Paul thought. No time for reflection or contemplation. They only did that in books. Tommy was, ostensibly, a dying man. But he was living. Living harder than Paul had ever done.

Nervously, he asked where they were headed.

"You'll see," said Tommy, his hands gripping the steering wheel.

"Come on, Tommy, give us a clue."

"Ever been to the frozen north? And no, I don't mean High bloody Barnet."

Paul didn't answer, so Tommy answered for him.

"No. You haven't, have you Paul? You haven't been anywhere. Apart from rattling around underground on a train. Or investigating the corners of your own hole. That's as good as it ever gets for you, isn't it?"

"Leave it, Tommy" snapped Paul, his head leaning against the passenger window. But it was true. He barely saw daylight, never mind anywhere out of London. Just like the Tube mouse in the cage in the depot. Round and round, dreaming impossible dreams.

"Okay, a clue." Without warning, Tommy broke into song. *"When you walk, through a storm, hold your head up high…"*

"What?"

"Oh for Christ's sake! It's a song, dumbfuck. I'll cut to the chorus… *and you'll neeeeever waaaaaalk alone…* Come on, mastermind, it's not that fucking hard."

"Football, right? Liverpool? Are we going to Liverpool?"

"Damn right we're going to Liverpool. It's where it all began, Paul, where it all began."

"But Liverpool's miles away."

Paul looked pained. They'd never make it back for Monday.

Tommy spoke. "So for a change, get your head out yer arse, son, and have a look at the rest of the world. Enjoy the view, eh? It's a good one."

CHAPTER 7

For the past hour, since they left London, Paul had watched the English countryside unfold along the M1. He had spent so much time underground, and an equal amount tramping through the cold, grey streets of the capital in search of cheap paperbacks and elusive inspiration, that the ruddy glow of the countryside, even along this stretch, with its swathe of perma-traffic, seemed to be lightening his mood minute by minute. He longed to haul down the window and let the wind tear at his face, even if it was only provided by the backdraft from a passing lorry. Besides, Tommy was driving like a maniac. The G-forces involved in leaning out of the window might have cost him his features.

He turned his head slightly to the right so he could get a better view out of the corner of his eye at the driver. Tommy looked like a man who'd been jump-started out of death. Bolt upright, and still smelling strongly of the generous free sample of aftershave he'd given himself in Boots following the purchase of the suit, Tommy gripped the steering wheel like he was hanging onto a yacht in a Force 10. He'd never moved out of the third lane since they got on the motorway at Staples Corner and seemed to consider it his absolute right to intimidate anyone in front of him to get out of the way. He'd utterly ignored Paul's occasional grunts and squeaks of fear as he hammered the vehicle for all it was worth, every bump and join of the road surface sending shockwaves through its hard suspension.

Then there was the singing. It was hard to believe this was a man set to die in less than 72 hours. He'd stopped at a petrol station before the motorway and after filling the Merc, had spent several minutes browsing the filling station's shelves of cheap, nasty cassettes. Big band swing and Euro-pop had been swiftly rejected in favour of something much closer to home. Now, the tape Tommy had enthusiastically shoved into the cassette radio – '50 Great Irish Drinking Songs for Your Entertainment and Pleasure' – appeared to be on its fourth journey around the spools of the machine and with each play he was belting out the words like he ran the band.

"Ahhhh, yer drunk, yer drunk, yer silly owld fool…"

"Tommy…"

"So drunk yer cannot see…!"

"Tommy, please…"

"That's a lovely sow that me mother…"

"TOMMY!" Almost weeping with frustration, Paul put his head in his hands and banged them on the glove compartment.

Jerked out of his revelry, Tommy gave him a look of shock and disgust.

"What?! What's up? Feelin' a bit Tom Dick, are ya?"

"It's not the driving, Tommy," Paul said wearily. "Though I'm glad I brought spare boxers."

Tommy snorted contemptuously at the remark.

"Well, what is it then? Havin' a nosebleed 'cos you're so far out of London? Is that it?"

"No, no. Look Tommy, I'm sorry. It's the music. I can't stand another second of it. Your Irish eyes might be smiling, Tommy, but I gotta tell you that my sodding ears are bleeding."

Again, Tommy snorted scornfully.

"Oh, wit, is it? The Great Writer comes down from his throne to touch us all with his sparkling sense of humour, eh? Well at least I've got a song in me heart, Paul Callow. Unlike you, I'm not walkin' about with a face like a constipated greyhound. What's yer feckin' problem, eh?"

"I just… I thought it might be nice to have a bit of peace and quiet, now we've left London. Put all the noise of that madhouse behind us."

Tommy looked at him, a smug grin spreading across his broad

features. He reached for the radio's volume control, turned the music down and leaned back into the comfortable leather driver's seat.

"Okay, Paul, fair enough. Let's change the record. How about a chat? A nice bit of blather while we drive? Go on, you first."

"What?"

"Come on, let's hear it. The life story. 'How I Became The World Famous Tube Driving Writer'. I want to hear all the juice, all the mad stuff. The booze, the late nights, the women... God, they must be crawling all over a literary type like you!"

"Look, if you're gonna be sarcastic..."

"Not at all, Paul, not at all. C'mon... out with it."

"There's not a lot to tell..."

Tommy was gleeful. "Well now, that's a feckin' surprise! And here's me thinking you were some kind of eccentric millionaire pop star type with a hundred groupies on the go and a heart of gold for the homeless."

"Piss off." Paul was rattled.

"Ah, don't be like that, Paul," said Tommy, delighted to have provoked him. "C'mon... tell me. You're a writer. What d'you write about, eh? Drugs, whoors, bent coppers, terrorists, fast cars – all that kind of thriller stuff, eh? All based on your own experiences, no doubt..."

"Just leave it, will you?!" Tommy's words jabbed at Paul like hot needles in his eyes. "I don't do anything, okay! I just work... driving...and write... when I can."

"Jesus, I'm almost fainting with excitement," Tommy hooted. "You're gonna have to take over the wheel, son. This rock n'roll life of yours has fair knackered me out!"

"To be honest, I wish you'd fucking jumped."

"What? What did you say?" Tommy took his eyes off the road and looked at him murderously. "Cheeky bollicks. .Will I open this door now and leave you like a skinned rabbit on the hard shoulder, hmm?"

Paul sensed the red mist coming down on Tommy, but he

wouldn't back down. He hadn't come this far to take all the crap Tommy seemed to delight in shovelling on him.

"You're having a go, Tommy, but you don't know anything about me. All I know about you is that last night you were ready to kill yourself. I saw you climbing over the bridge, but I didn't hear you singing then. Funny, that."

It worked. Tommy slumped into a tight-mouthed sulk. For a minute he sat in studied silence. Then he spoke up.

"I've had the two days," he said finally.

Paul was puzzled. "What d'you mean?"

"The two days. Bad days, yeah. Plenty of those. But Christ, I've had the good days, too. Some of the best times a man could have. Believe you me, I haven't sat on me arse moaning about life. I just got on and enjoyed it. Most of it."

Tommy's features softened into a smile of nostalgia.

"I had the best craic when I was a young fella like you, you know."

Paul, still smarting from Tommy's remarks, sat in silence. The Irishman was oblivious to him, as he began to reminisce.

"Me and the lads – we were the wild bunch. You know that song… *'the boys are back in town, boys are back in town…da da DA!'*? That was us, down to a tee. We all grew up in the Northside of Dublin. Big gang of us went to school up there, all thrown out for this, that and the other. Our mammies all cryin' and wailin' that we were bound for hell, but we didn't give a shite. We were the roaring boys.

"Dublin couldn't hold us. We'd have all been in the nick if we hadn't left. When was it now… '71? '72? So friggin' long ago I've almost forgotten. There was work over in Liverpool, we heard, so we goes down the North Wall and buys ourselves ferry tickets. One way.

"Six of us turned up for the crossing. Me, Dancer Doherty, little Barry Ryan, John Flaherty, Danny Fitzpatrick. And Mickey Callaghan. Shame that bastard didn't go over the side of the boat. Still…"

Sensing a story about to develop, Paul sat up and turned slightly towards Tommy. Noticing the gesture of interest, Tommy continued.

"We'd no money for a cabin, so we sat out on deck. It was a clear night. We threw the barman a tenner and he brought out four great crates full of bottled Guinness. We sat there all night, drinking our heads off, cracking jokes, chucking the empties into the sea, watching the gas platforms going by. I can see it now..."

"Anyway," he continued, "we got to Liverpool, found some squatty old digs, you know, and went out to work. Did anything. Digging roads, building flats, repairing bomb sites, railway piling. We worked hard but we fuckin' played hard. Jesus... come Friday and Saturday night, we'd be tearing that city apart. Liverpool and Dublin are like twins separated at birth. Different, you know, but they belong to each other. They loved us, and we loved them. Especially the girls. Mickey Callaghan gave half the good Catholic females of Liverpool a dose before he almost scratched his balls off with the pain!"

Tommy laughed, shaking his head at the memory of it. "He was a devil for them. He was running three, four, five of them at a time. Loved nothing better than them finding out about each other and then scrapping over him in some pub. Tables flying, all screaming, hair pulling, biting. He'd just stand there and laugh. Jeez, him and me were the best o'pals."

"Did... you have loads of girlfriends yourself?" asked Paul tentatively.

"Why? You after picking up a few tips then?"

Paul blushed and didn't reply. An uncomfortable subject. Tommy carried on, regardless of the silence from his passenger.

"Nah, not really. I mean, I had my share of the women, but I wasn't driven by my dick, like Callaghan. For me it was the drink. And the gee-gees. Couldn't pass a pub or a bookies without going in. Habits like that leave a fella short o' money, I can tell you.

"I was living upstairs in the house of a family in Old Swan. They

65

were the tightest bastards going. The rent was twenty quid a week – a lot back then – no furniture, no food, electricity meter, and the room the size of a coffin.

"I remember it was Christmas Eve, '74. I couldn't afford the boat home to Dub, so I had to stay with these people. I got in, Christ knows what time, drunk as a skunk. They were long in bed. A note was pinned on the bottom of the banister rail. For me. I pulled it off and read it. 'Dear Mr Cassidy. Tomorrow is Christmas Day and we have family coming round. We would prefer it if you weren't here.'"

"Thanks a bunch, I thought. Kick a man out at Christmas, why dontcha? I wandered into the kitchen and I could smell this wonderful smell. They were obviously cooking the turkey slowly overnight, for the big day, you know? I open the oven door and sticks me head in to get a good waft."

"Well, I'd had more to drink than I thought and suddenly, up came the old heave-ho. All over the fecking turkey! Jesus, never did a man sober up so quickly. I look round to see if anyone's coming, but they're all flat out upstairs. So I grabs a spoon and I stirs the puke into the juices and the gravy. Round and round the tin the bird's sitting in, 'til you couldn't tell anything was different. Just the gravy was a bit thicker, that's all. With extra carrots."

"I hoofed it upstairs and chucked my things in my bag and I banged the door on the way out, laughin' like a fecking drain. I took off round to Callaghan's and we sat up all night, just howlin' about these miserable bastards and their special turkey! Oh dear God!"

Tommy wiped his eyes with laughter at the memory. Even Paul was chuckling.

"Yeah, they were rare ol' times," said Tommy. "All the scrapes we got into. Great days, they were. Pity they didn't last."

"No?"

"No. Sadly not."

Tommy stared into the distance, sighing heavily before he spoke again.

"Some people aren't who you think they are," he said finally. "Me and Mickey Callaghan... well, it was natural to start something up together. A little building firm. It made sense, get our lives on a firm footing, you know? And we were good pals. Trusted each other. He would do the paperwork and I'd organise the labour."

"We were starting to do well. I met Rose and so I was thinking about settling down, kind of. I was still a big man for the horses and the booze, don't get me wrong, but I thought there was money to pay for it, so it was okay. Me and Rose, we got married eventually, big wedding and all that. Then it all went..."

He paused, biting his bottom lip.

"Went what?"

"I took me eye off the ball, son," Tommy said. "Left too much of the important stuff to Callaghan. The fucker was a crook. Taking bribes, sending the heavies round to sort out the competition, that type of thing. I never suspected him at all. Before I knew it, he'd stitched me up for the half the company. I had debts... with other people. Hard cases around Liverpool who would stuff my head up my hole to get their money back. I go to Callaghan and I says, 'I need to take some money out of my half of the firm.' He replies, 'What half?' He'd done a number on me."

"Oh, he was cute alright. Got me on some bullshit legal technicality. I hadn't read the small print. Too busy studying the form, I suppose. I was deep in the shite, you know? And I thought he was a mate. You can never tell, eh?"

"What happened?"

"I begged him to give me what I was owed. No chance. Then I asked him for a loan. 'Okay' he says, 'but you have to win it, fair and square.' Cards. He wanted a game with me, double or quits. If I win, I get the loan and I get the gangsters off my back. If I lose..."

"But you won, right?"

"No. I lost. The cards were rigged, for sure. I lost everything. And more besides."

67

Tommy fell into silence, turning away to gaze at the grey-green fields going by. The spell was broken. Tommy wasn't about to offer any more information and Paul considered it too dangerous to ask.

"Go on, Tommy," Paul said softly, "put the music back on. I'll try and sleep through it."

*

A sharp shove in the shoulder woke Paul up. His neck ached from leaning against the passenger window and he wondered where he was. There was something else, too.

"Hey, lazy bollicks!" It was Tommy. "Good job you weren't driving, eh? We're near Liverpool. And can you answer that sodding thing?" he added, gesturing towards the sports bag at Paul's feet. "It hasn't stopped ringing since Sheffield."

Wearily, Paul rooted in the bag for the blaring mobile and, just in time, pressed the green 'answer' button.

"Uh. Hello?"

"Paul, mon petit chou," said a foreign voice, vaguely familiar. "You are very naughty to run away. Do I not look tasty? I'm sure I am most flavoursome, perhaps with a soupcon of raspberry jus. I make a very tasty jus…"

With an embarrassed flush, Paul quickly pressed the red 'end call' button and threw the phone back into the bag. Why the hell had he given that French madman his number?

Tommy looked at him, but didn't speak. Enough had been said on this journey already.

In 15 minutes the Mercedes had reached the city's inner suburbs. Expensive looking detached houses gave way to tough little redbrick terrace houses, which in turn gave way to block upon block of council flats. The streets were narrow and mean, with metal grilles across many shop fronts and a fair few houses boarded up completely. The city was on the up, so he'd heard, but if there was money floating about, little or none of it had descended here. Paul

68

wondered about the car's chances of survival, a feeling reinforced when they stopped at traffic lights. A car pulled up alongside them and three hard-looking kids sitting in the back scrambled to the rear passenger window to get a better look at the Mercedes' wheels.

"They're not bad people, you know, the Scousers," said Tommy, reading his thoughts. "Not all of 'em, anyway. Salt of the earth. Though you'd have to chain your mother to a fence if you left her outside the shops for a minute."

The car cruised down a main road, past a row of houses which broke for a large, Victorian Gothic church. Almost as soon as he'd passed it, Tommy braked sharply and immediately threw the vehicle into reverse. He reached the church and went forwards again, this time swinging in through its ornate iron gates.

Tommy stepped out of the car and gazed admiringly at the high brick archway which framed solid-looking, wooden, double doors. Paul, glad to be out of the car and into the fresh air, walked back to the gates and looked at the sign. 'Welcome to St Jude's Roman Catholic Church.'

"What's this, then?" he gestured to Tommy. "I thought you said you weren't religious."

"I'm not," snapped back the reply, "I'm a Catholic. Anyway, there's no harm in a bit of nostalgia while I'm here. I was married in this church, you know?"

"Yeah?"

"Yeah. What a do! I was drunk for a week before and for another two after. The ceremony was a bit of a blur, to be honest. Half of Dublin was here. Wonder if it's changed any?"

Tommy grasped one of the large, circular, iron door handles and turned it. The door was unlocked and with a creak he pushed it open. The familiar, lingering smell of incense hit him almost immediately and he recoiled at the rush of memories it suddenly provoked.

"God, it's been a long time," he whispered, to no-one in particular, dipping his hand into the holy water receptacle by the inner doors to the nave of the church and crossing himself. Automatically, Paul moved to do the same but Tommy slapped his hand away with unexpected force.

"That's sacrilege," he whispered loudly, "for a Protestant!"

Paul looked hurt.

"How did you know I was a Protestant?" he asked.

Tommy laughed, the same sneering laugh Paul had heard too many times already.

"You've all the spirit of a wet weekend in Wigan. What else could you be but a Protestant? Answer me that!"

He was getting personal again. Paul responded in kind.

"Isn't it a sin to commit suicide, Tommy? I mean, if you're a Catholic?"

"Isn't it a sin to deliberately run down someone in a train, Paul? I mean... if you're a human being?"

Tommy strolled off down the aisle, his head slightly bowed. Paul watched as the Irishman gazed at the statues and pictures around the walls of the church. Everyone seemed to be suffering in one form or another. Above the altar hung a giant crucifix, with the equally large and imposing figure of Christ hanging upon it. Imagine coming to church every day, he thought, and looking up at that. No wonder they all seemed to drink.

His eyes were drawn down to an inscription on the base of the crucifix. He read the words and felt the same fear experienced by the generations of worshippers who had come here, but for very different reasons. 'He Died,' it read, 'That We Might Live.'

Paul stared at Tommy. He was no less than a human sacrifice and, for whatever reason, willing to be one. He seemed to be looking for something down one of the side aisles. Above a doorway, a dim green light glowed. For a second, Tommy stood outside the door then went in. It was a confessional box.

*

Tommy was on his knees, his head facing a thin metal grille

70

behind which was a curtain. The box had a cloying, musty smell, and Tommy could sense the presence of the priest, his face just inches from his, but invisible behind the cloth.

"Bless me, Father," he began, "for I have sinned. A lot. It has been... a long time since my last confession."

The priest began to mumble some words which sounded like ones of absolution. Tommy couldn't remember the order of things and butted in.

"'Scuse me there, Father, but don't you want to know my sin? I mean, whatever I tell you could be the difference between three Hail Marys and a full-on pilgrimage of repentance to the Vatican."

"Whatever it is, my son," said the priest, "I'm sure that God will listen to your intervention and absolve you from your sins. There is nothing that He cannot forgive."

The priest was about to continue reciting the rite of absolution when Tommy interrupted again.

"Look, Father, there's a problem. It's not what I've done in the past. It's what I'm going to do on Monday."

"Then may God forgive you for what you're about to do," said the priest. "And if you'd care to talk about it further, I'm here, same time, same place, next week."

"But..."

"Go in peace," said the priest, "to love and serve the Lord. Thanks be to God."

He could expand, but Tommy felt a sudden weariness come over him. He stood up, opened the confessional door and strode out towards the centre aisle. Just before the altar was a tiered stand half-full of prayer candles. Paul was by the side of it, absent-mindedly lighting one after another and placing them on the stand.

"They're 20p each," said Tommy, gesturing towards a hole-in-the-wall collection box.

"Isn't that just for Catholics?" Paul retorted. Seeing the look on Tommy's face, however, he quickly changed his mind and fished a pound from his pocket.

"C'mon," said Tommy, "hurry up and stick it in. We're out of here, right now."

*

The car pulled into a parking area on the side of a hill, overlooking a low-rise housing block. Tommy was silent for a long time as he stared at the rows of run-down old maisonettes, the walkways in front of them filled with grubby washing, discarded furniture and broken dreams. There had obviously been demolition and regeneration work at one end of the estate, as a section of the flats was scaffolded and wrapped in thick plastic sheeting. Across it was strung a large white banner, with the words 'CALLAGHAN CONTRACTORS' plastered across it.

"Well now," muttered Tommy, shocked, "just look at that. Callaghan. Done better for himself than I thought. The bent bastard. He must have bought off the whole feckin' council to get this contract. Hard to believe we started off digging ditches."

His face hardened like concrete. "That bastard owes me..." he whispered.

Tommy stared again towards the run-down section of the flats, his expression a mask of guilt and regret.

"This is where you lived?" Paul took in the scene. Tommy nodded in confirmation. This was the Edenbridge estate. Once upon a time, places like this must have seemed like a brand new start for everyone. No back-to-backs or outside bogs. Everything shiny and new. Until crime, drugs and more drugs moved in. Areas like this never recovered and neither did the people. The harsh, pinched expressions as they passed by the car and glowered at what they thought were the rich guys inside told the whole story. Paul, feeling very uneasy, had seen enough.

"Come on, Tommy, I think it's time we went. The car'll be on four bricks if we sit here for much longer."

Tommy chewed the side of his cheek and examined his fingernails. "I dunno about you, Paul," he replied, "but I always think it's rude to visit someone and appear empty-handed. Especially after all these years. I've a bit of shopping to do."

72

"I don't understand," moaned Paul as he followed Tommy out of the late-opening DIY store, the latter striding with determination towards the parked Mercedes, a plastic bag in his left hand. "It's not what I'd call a present."

Tommy ignored him. Reaching the car, he rammed the key into the door lock and yanked the handle open, throwing the object on to the back seat. He unlocked Paul's door and with a pained look on his face the passenger grumpily got in.

"Tommy, what are we doing? Just please tell me what we're doing?"

"I told you," he said with exasperation, pushing the key into the ignition, "I didn't want to turn up empty handed. Not after all this time."

"But... a crowbar? I thought you wanted a present... what's she going to use a crowbar for?"

"If you don't shut the feck up," Tommy snapped, "you'll be using it to get my foot from out your arse!"

Angrily, Paul grabbed his seat belt and clicked it into place. Tommy gunned the engine of the Mercedes and steered it with a squeal of tyres out of the empty car park and onto a main road.

There was little traffic. The city's commuters had long since left for home and the darkness that shrouded the deserted streets kept residents indoors, fearful of the night and those who stalked through it. The main road broadened into a dual carriageway, split in two by a central avenue of mature trees. As they drove, Paul noticed the houses on either side of the road gradually becoming smarter. Pebble-dashed semis gave way to older, detached houses complete with gates, high hedges, security cameras and 'Beware of the Dog' signs. The area was in sharp contrast to the Edenbridge estate, with its grim flats and grimmer residents.

Tommy clicked on the indicator and turned left into a tree-lined avenue, eventually pulling up opposite a very large detached house. It looked about 20 years old and had been designed with all the tasteless flamboyance of the era. A pair of roaring, concrete lions stood guard on top of the pillars supporting two large, ornamental, wrought iron gates. In their paws, the lions clutched medieval-style shields, each embossed with the letter 'C'. A white Jaguar car was parked in the driveway. The house was silent, no lights and no evidence of anyone inside it.

"He's still here, then," muttered Tommy, looking at the car.

Paul stood where he was for a moment.

"Tommy, where are we? What the hell are we doing here?"

He turned to Paul, aggressively thrusting his face close to his.

"It's none of your damn business! I didn't ask you to come along."

Tommy gently opened the gate and instead of using the path, stepped on the grass and headed for the side of the house. Helplessly, Paul followed him, desperate not to be heard.

Half-way along the rear wall of the house, Tommy stopped, and gazed through a window. He touched it gently a couple of times then, from under his suit jacket, pulled out the crowbar and slotted it into a gap between the window and the frame. From creeping worry, Paul was now in full panic mode.

"Tommy!" he hissed, beginning to feel hysterical. "Bloody hell, Tommy! Breaking and entering? Are you mad?"

The Irishman ignored him and, realising the crowbar wouldn't fit, took off his jacket and wrapped it around the length of iron. Before Paul could stop him, Tommy gave the window a short, sharp blow, resulting in a muffled crack and the tinkle of falling glass.

Time seemed to be holding its breath, but from the still night air there was nothing. No footsteps coming around the corner, no dog barking. Tommy shrugged, and stuck his hand through the hole to reach the handle on the inside. Once located, he opened the window fully and put his hands on the frame, getting ready to haul himself up. His eyes shone with excitement and anticipation. He actually looked pleased to be breaking and entering.

In contrast, Paul was dancing on the spot with fear and twitchily glancing behind him every other second. Tommy hauled himself up, wedging his frame inside the window. It was obvious he was having trouble getting through, but Paul was rooted to the spot, staring in horror at the ample, pinstriped backside in front of him.

"Stop gawping," wheezed Tommy from inside the building, "and help, can't you?"

There was nothing else for it but to push him. There was no way Tommy could reverse, even if he wanted to. Paul shoved, and heard Tommy land with a heavy thud, followed by a loud crash and something shattering. Then, a steady stream of curses followed by silence.

What the hell was he doing now? A moment later the back door opened and Tommy leaned out, beckoning Paul to follow. But he was frozen with fear, and after a couple more urgent waves Tommy went back inside.

He could just hang out here and wait for Tommy to do whatever he had to do in there. He didn't want to know. He just wanted this to be over with, but he didn't want to be caught hanging around outside. Suddenly, a small twitch within a nearby bush caused Paul to jump in fear. He shrunk away from the source of the noise. A mouse? A cat? Or a guard dog, teeth bared and jaws slavering, waiting to spring into action?

Paul needed no more persuasion. Tommy was insane, it was clear, but he was safer with him inside than he was outside. Swiftly, he walked to the open door and was met by a torch shining in his face.

"Oh, you made it," whispered Tommy. He shone the torch around the walls of the large rear living room they'd found themselves in.

The walls were covered in swirls of pink, green and electric blue wallpaper, fixtured and fitted heavily with fake gold.

"Look at this," said Tommy in a low voice that suppressed a laugh. "Like a tart's boudoir."

"This is crazy," said Paul, eyes bulging with trepidation. "What are we doing here?"

"Keep your mouth shut," hissed Tommy, "and do as I tell you."

The Irishman pointed the torch towards the stairs and with it, motioned Paul to follow him. In response, Paul grabbed the flap of Tommy's jacket and hung on.

"Tommy, stop! Please, I'm asking you... this is mad. Come on. Let's go! This is mental. What happens if we get caught?"

In response, Tommy snatched the corner of the jacket out of Paul's hand.

"There's no-one here. They won't be back from the club for hours."

"Who won't? Whose house is this, for Christ's sake?"

Tommy looked at Paul as though he were stupid.

"It's the Callaghans'."

"What? Oh no. No, Tommy, this is wrong. This could screw up everything. Come on!"

Tommy had had enough. He wasn't breaking in for fun. The kid was in the way, big style.

"Listen, you little fecker," he snarled, holding Paul by the neck of his sweatshirt and pressing him against an ornate stained glass window, "you've got a choice. Either we do it my way or we don't do it at all."

Paul was terrified. But it wasn't too late. Not quite yet.

"I can always get someone else, you know."

"Go on then," challenged Tommy. "But you're not getting your money back. I'm doing this whether you want to or not, so if you want to fuck off now, be my guest."

Tommy paused, waiting for the reply he knew would never come.

"I thought so. Are you done?"

Huffily, Paul nodded.

"Right. Then shut your whining please and follow me."

Tommy turned back up the stairs, tiptoeing up on the thick, pink shagpile carpet. Two steps behind him, Paul followed with his heart in his mouth. But behind them both, high up on a wall and out of sight, a small red light began to blink...

*

To Paul, every step up the stairs, however well-cushioned they were by the carpet, was one nearer the gallows. He felt bound to Tommy by a kind of invisible chain. He didn't want to follow him to whatever fate awaited them, but he had no choice.

Tommy reached the landing and headed for the nearest door, which was slightly ajar. Without hesitation he pushed it open and walked in. The slight creak as it opened felt like a punch to the pit of Paul's stomach. Anything could happen, absolutely anything. If this man really was the double-crossing hardnut Tommy had described and he was lurking behind that door, it could kick off any second. He had to get Tommy back to London in one piece. The way they were going, it would take weeks to scrape every shred of him off the walls. Suddenly, the plan looked about as feasible as a Bin Laden marrying a Bush.

"Jesus!"

Tommy stopped dead in his tracks. Paul, sick with fear, peered over his shoulder. There, in the middle of the large bedroom was an imposing, sleigh-style double bed and on it, two hillocks of gently rising and falling duvet, a crumpled valley of fabric between them. The movement was accompanied by a tunelessly rhythmic duet of snores and grunts from the bed's occupants.

Paul's bladder was about to involuntarily empty itself on to the pink carpet.

"We've got to go, Tommy!" he hissed. "We've really got to go right now!"

Tommy turned to him. There was not one sign of fear in his eyes, which made Paul all the more terrified. This man wasn't going anywhere.

"They didn't hear me put the window through," he whispered gloatingly, "so they won't hear us now."

He shielded the light from the torch by cupping it with his hands and scanned the room. Within seconds, he'd located a dressing table, full of boxes, bottles, lotions and a magazine or two. In the middle, a large jewellery box stood open, proudly displaying the treasures which spilled over its sides.

Standing just inside the door, Paul watched in horrified fascination as Tommy rooted as quietly as he could through the jewellery box, picking up objects and almost immediately discarding them.

"Fuck," he whispered in Paul's direction, "she must be wearing it."

"What? Wearing what?"

No sooner had Tommy said it than he padded noiselessly to one side of the bed and took in the sight of a fat, fifty-something woman snoring flabbily in her sleep, earplugs pushed firmly in.

Gently, stealthily, Tommy lifted the corner of the duvet to expose the top half of the woman's body. When he had drawn it back far enough he laid it down and followed his gaze from the top of her beefy arms down to her fat, sausage-like fingers. They were covered in gold rings. One ring stood out among all the others for its elegant beauty. Tommy smiled as he took in the sight of the sapphire, set on an ornate gold band. With crafty determination he took hold of the ring and attempted to pull it, millimetre by agonising millimetre, from her middle finger.

It wouldn't budge. It had obviously been placed on her finger in leaner times. Tommy tugged harder, but the woman moaned in her sleep and pulled her hand from his grasp. She turned over heavily, pulling the duvet back round her and flopping her hand over her crumpled face.

Tommy took a couple of delicate paces back to where Paul was standing. He leaned on Paul's bony shoulder and put his mouth to his ear.

"It's no good," he whispered, "we'll have to use soap."

With a flick of his head, he gestured to what looked like an en suite bathroom in the far corner of the room. The door was open.

"Go on now," Tommy whispered to Paul, "there'll be some in there."

Paul hesitated, then took a step towards the bathroom, glad to be out of the immediate vicinity of the sleeping couple. He entered and shut the door gingerly behind him.

Tommy waited, looking at the slumbering couple and following the progress of the woman's be-ringed hand as she nuzzled her pillow contentedly.

Thirty seconds went by. A minute. Twenty more seconds. What the fuck was he doing in there? Frowning, Tommy sneaked over to the door and tried the handle. It was locked. Then, the awful gurgling sound of a toilet being flushed percolated from under the door.

Simmering with anger, Tommy tapped his foot urgently on the bedroom carpet until Paul unlocked the door and came out, a sheepish expression on his face.

"Sorry," he whispered, "I couldn't help myself."

"Jesus," replied Tommy, his jaw clenched. "Did you get the soap?"

Paul passed over the plastic, pump-top bottle containing a full load of thick, white liquid soap. Tommy snatched it off him and handed him the crowbar, pointing to the second lump in the bed.

"If he moves," he ordered, "hit him."

Swallowing hard, Paul took up his position at the other side of the bed and peered in to get a closer look at his would-be victim. It was a man, red-faced and balding with white hair at the temples. He wore a white 'wife beater' vest and was also ear-plugged, his mouth gaping like a goldfish.

Tommy had crept round to the woman's side of the bed and armed with the bottle of soap, was gauging the precise location of the assault. He watched her rhythmic rise and fall. Lining up the nozzle carefully against her ring finger, he squeezed hard.

Just at the moment the nozzle released a spurt of the glutinous liquid, the woman made a sudden movement forward. The soap hit her hand, but also splattered a thick stream onto her face and into her open mouth. Instantly, she started coughing, loud enough to drag her out of her sleep.

Tommy and Paul hit the floor on either side of the bed as the woman spluttered and choked. There was an unbearable, agonising silence as the bedsprings creaked heavily with the force of her beginning to sit up.

Coughing, confused and dazed, her eyes opened, blearily at first. Then, they began to grow wide with horror as she stared down at her hands. Dripping from them in thick, slow globules was a sticky white gloop, the same substance which had matted itself in her hair and was about to slide gently off the end of her nose.

With a scream of shock and disgust, she turned savagely to the man lying next to her and, without hesitation, belted him hard with the flat of her hand in the middle of his back.

"Michael Callaghan!" she shrieked in a voice that would have raised the dead, "you dirty old bastard!"

Shocked out of his sleep, Callaghan scrabbled desperately to fend off the blows from his wife with one hand, reaching for the bedside light with the other and yanking it on.

"What the hell's got into you, woman?!" he roared, looking around him wildly. "What's goin' on?!"

His answer lay on the floor by his bed. In the light of the lamp, Paul was clearly visible. Gripped with terror, he could only smile dumbly at Callaghan and his wife as they stared back at him in shock.

After a second that seemed like an hour, Callaghan spoke. His voice was calm as he weighed up the situation, mentally calculating the odds of the skinny, terrified young man lying on the floor getting the better of him.

"What do you think you're doing there, son?" he asked, as though talking to a little boy.

Suddenly, Tommy leapt up from the other side of the bed. The woman let rip with a shattering scream and flung herself under the duvet.

"Hit him!"

Tommy howled the command to Paul, but it was too late. In panic, Paul lost his grip on the crowbar and it fell uselessly at his feet. Grabbing the advantage, Callaghan jumped out of bed, dropped to his knees and snatched something from under the base.

Everything seemed to freeze. Paul was now staring into the barrel of a sawn-off shotgun and, eyes screwed up tight, he backed away, feeling himself literally up against the wall.

But Callaghan wasn't looking at him. He and Tommy were staring at each other like two fighting dogs, snarling, snapping and baring teeth in mutual hatred. Callaghan spoke first.

"You..."

In the corner, Paul muttered a mantra of expletives, hoping that he might somehow wake out of this living nightmare.

"That's enough now, Paul," said Tommy softly. The silence that returned to the room, its four occupants locked in a horrible, waxwork-like tableau, was unbearable.

"Turned to burglary, have you, Cassidy?" sneered Callaghan. "That all you got left?"

"I only want what's mine, Callaghan."

"There's nothing here belonging to you, Cassidy."

Again, their eyes locked in blazing contempt. In the bathroom, a tap dripped slowly, counting off the agonising seconds as the two men squared up for the inevitable fight.

But from under the duvet came a piercing scream. The woman threw off the bedding and bellowed in the direction of the combatants.

81

"Tommy Cassidy? Jesus Christ! What the bloody hell d'you think yer playin' at?!"

Tommy nodded a little gesture of recognition and tried a gentle smile.

"All right there, Maureen?"

The fat Liverpudlian woman resembled nothing less than an enraged sow. She turned to her husband, her piggy eyes wild with fury.

"Ask him what he's doin' here, Mickey? Go on! Ask him. Him and soft lad there."

It was an apt description. Paul looked like a piece of butter about to melt under the glare of a hot light.

"I'm sorry, Maureen," Tommy piped up, "but I've come for me ring."

Callaghan shifted uncomfortably and raised the barrel of the shotgun a degree higher. He was about to speak, but with a wave of her hand the domineering Maureen silenced him.

"What ring? What bloody ring?"

"The sapphire," Tommy replied. "The one on your finger there."

Maureen puffed into a ball of disgusted outrage.

"What are you on about? Your ring? You're joking, aren't you? It were an anniversary present, that. I've had it donkey's years."

"I know," said Tommy. "You've had it coming up eight years. Haven't you?"

Flustered, Callaghan jabbed the gun in Tommy's direction.

"I've heard enough, Maureen," he snapped. "I'm calling the police."

But Maureen wasn't listening. She stared at Tommy intently.

"How do you know how long I've had it?"

"Because he won it from me in a game of cards," replied Tommy coolly. "It was all I had left. I'd just had it repaired for Rosemary."

Callaghan butted in again.

"Don't listen to him, Maureen, he's talking out of his arse.

Always did. You've seen the shop where I bought it."

Again, Maureen ignored her panicking husband.

"Go on, Cassidy," she said, "tell me more."

"That's it, really. It was a card game. Double or quits. If I could've given him the cash instead I would've. But I couldn't. He took a shine to the ring. Said he needed something for your anniversary. How could I face Rose after that?"

"That's bollocks, Cassidy," interjected Callaghan, "and you know it. You're a fucking liar and I've heard enough."

But now it was Callaghan's turn to taste Maureen's venom.

"Cards? Gambling? Lying? Passing me off with your sordid little winnings? You…" As she spoke, she rubbed her hand in the soap that coated her cheek and began to work at the ring.

Callaghan was starting to crack.

"He's lying, Maureen, honestly. I swear to God… I bought it in that shop, you saw it yourself…"

Working the ring furiously, Maureen finally prised it off and immediately flung it over the bed. It landed on the floor, between Tommy and Paul. Quickly, the pair exchanged glances.

"Grab it Paul," Tommy snapped, not relishing the thought of being pebble-dashed against the bedroom wall by a couple of shotgun cartridges.

Paul stepped away from the wall and bent down to retrieve it. As he did so, Callaghan pointed the gun at him and ordered him to back off.

"Oh put it away, you sad old fool," Maureen barked. "It's not even loaded."

Callaghan lowered the weapon sheepishly and Paul grabbed the ring. With nothing left to say, the pair headed for the door as Maureen laid into her husband, shouting the odds with a gob as wide as the famous Mersey Tunnel.

"Oh," said Tommy brightly, remembering something and poking his head back round the door, "you wouldn't happen to have a box

83

for the ring, would you, Maureen? No? Okay, no problem then. It'll be fine as it is!"

Tommy and Paul pelted downstairs and made for the rear door. But the red flashing light they hadn't noticed as they'd crept up the stairs only minutes previously had done its work. The silent burglar alarm had alerted the police.

As they bolted through the door, they ran straight into a carnival of blue flashing lights. Two police cars screamed to a halt. Instinctively, Tommy decided to run for it, leaping over a low wall. Paul dived into a rhododendron bush, pulling the thick leaves around him as camouflage and hoping that his shaking body wouldn't give the game away.

Shivering, he watched as Tommy came back round the corner with two burly officers grabbing each of his arms. He was protesting, cursing, spitting and kicking, but it was to no avail. One of the cops wrenched open the rear door of the squad car and with a hefty shove forced his captive inside.

The occupants of the other police car were still around, searching the gardens and the perimeter of the wall. Paul clutched the ring so hard it was digging into the flesh on the palm of his hand. If he was caught now, he would be in possession of the stolen goods. Could he trust Tommy to stand up for him if he was pulled? Or would he be bang to rights?

Taking no chances, Paul put the ring in his mouth. Booted footsteps came nearer and Paul cowered low as a penetrating flashlight swept the bushes. He felt the light stop just above his head and with a nervous reflex, he gulped. The ring caught the back of his throat, causing him to gag, but the very act of stifling it forced the jewel even further down. As the flashlight swept away, the ring went down his throat. Now, he was in sole possession of it.

Minutes passed. The heavy footsteps and occasional glimpses of sweeping torchlight through the bushes seemed to have gone. Then, Paul heard the clunk of a car door and a vehicle driving away. Tentatively he raised his head through the rhododendron bush and quickly glanced around. The coast appeared to be clear. A cold sweat broke over him as he realised he'd escaped. But there was still Callaghan and his gun. Somewhere in the house there might be a box of cartridges and a very angry man, who had been made to look stupid and was bent on brutal revenge.

Paul hesitated no longer. He crawled out of the bush and backed down the path until he reached the front gate. The sound of shouting was still coming from inside the house. Paul turned and with all the casualness he could muster, half-walked, half-ran to the parked Mercedes. He grabbed the door handle and pulled. It opened, but even as he went to crouch in the driver's seat he realised, with a thud in the pit of his stomach, that Tommy had the keys. He didn't know how to hotwire it, or whatever the hell it was that you did to steal cars. He had no choice but to abandon it.

Dejected, Paul walked back up the avenue, his hands in his pockets, his head down and his neck pulled into the collar of his sweatshirt. He was lost in a strange city. Tommy was...? God knows where Tommy was.

Paul reached the end of the avenue and found himself back on the wide dual-carriageway. He looked left and right, wondering which way to go. He and Tommy had come from the right, from the estate close to the city centre. He might find a café open there, or a cheap B and B. Or even a train station out of the place. He turned right and as he walked he felt his hopes disappearing as quickly as the ring had down his throat.

85

Chapter 9

An unfamiliar place brings out unfamiliar fears – fears that never seem to apply when you're on home territory. In the past, Paul had vigilantly avoided the potential for getting into trouble in London. He always took certain routes home and rarely ventured out after dark, preferring to sit, night after night, alone and in the isolation of his living room-cum-library, poring over books old and new, marking eloquent passages from them with pencilled comments, storing up words, phrases and expressions that he would use when he was ready to write his novel.

Now, though, he really was alone – miles from home and in a city with a fearsome reputation, deserved or otherwise, for random and explosive violence. Hadn't some kid been axed to death in a park somewhere in Liverpool just for being the wrong colour? What would they do to a skinny southerner, wandering about like a lost lamb around the tough estates and districts which ringed the city centre like a locked handcuff?

He tried not to think about it, even as the suburban roads he was walking turned into urban streets – narrower, dirtier and more threatening. The occasional drunk stumbled by, singing or cursing to himself. Paul didn't dare look up, terrified of the possibility of catching the wrong person's eye. Head down, and pulling himself into the shadows close to the boarded-up shops for fear of attracting unwanted attention, Paul walked doggedly along the grey, greasy pavements, hoping to find a place of safety and shelter. Or failing that, an all-night McDonald's complete with a security guard with the dimensions of a garden shed.

There was also the question of Tommy. He might still be in the back of the police car or, more likely, in a cell somewhere, waiting for a visit from the CID the following day. He would be charged, no doubt, and then bailed. And even if Paul did find the police station he was being held in, he too would be arrested as an accomplice. Callaghan would see to that.

As he walked, he focused hard on his options. The temptation was to simply go home and give up. He'd lost £1,500 on a kind of macabre bet with himself. Maybe meeting Tommy, becoming involved in something completely beyond his control and losing the money was nature's way of telling him that it was all over. The dream house on the island would remain just that, a dream. He would go home, carry on where he left off and pretend none of this ever happened. He had the job, the flat and the books. It was by no means the existence he really wanted, but it would do. It was better – quieter, safer, more predictable – than being pulled into situations like the ordeal he'd just gone through. He owed Tommy nothing, quite the reverse, in fact, though he knew he would never see a penny of that again. Tommy could be looking at ten years for aggravated burglary and who knows what he'd done in his past to make that sentence an even longer one. Even if, by some miracle, he got off or the charges were dropped, Tommy was highly unlikely to come looking for him to give him his money back. He'd said as much before the break-in. Unless, of course, he was desperate for that ring…

*

Less than five miles from where Paul was walking, Tommy, minus his tie and shoelaces, sat in a cell in the city's central police station, held on suspicion of burglary. He had been interviewed under caution by the arresting sergeant and some young female copper, but said nothing. There was nothing to say. When CID arrived in the morning, a statement from Callaghan tucked under their arm, his fate was sealed as tightly as the sterile plastic bag containing the fingerprint-speckled crowbar they would also bring in. He'd employed it to smash the window into the Callaghans', but he'd also told Paul to use it as a weapon. Callaghan had heard him and would make a meal out of that, conveniently forgetting about the sawn-off shotgun now nestling at the bottom of the nearest pond. "What gun was that then, officer? Never had one in me life..." Never mind that Maureen had given him the bloody ring in the end. Callaghan would soon shut her up with a new Beamer or a fortnight in Florida. The bastard.

He wondered if Paul had been nicked. The little whelp probably came out with his hands up, blurting out the whole tale in a dribble of tears and snot. The broken window, the crowbar, the soap, the ring. The ring! He almost certainly would have handed it straight over to the law, like a hot piece of tar. Skinny little bollicks. He was completely out for himself. Him and his bloody weird obsession with suicide. Let his next shite be a hedgehog.

Tommy sighed and let his head fall heavily into his hands. He couldn't sleep. It wasn't that the bed in the cell, with its grey walls and single, unshaded light bulb, was concrete, or that the blanket covering it was thinner than a gnat's pube. It wasn't the noise of the Friday-night drunks in the cells along the corridor, banging on about their rights as loudly as they hammered on their doors, who bothered him so much. God knows, he'd been there a time or two himself in the past.

It wasn't even the thought of going to jail for a long time. He'd been in and out of hostels for years, mingling with the lowest of the low – psychopaths, drug addicts, dossers, drunks, paedoes – the full complement of the deranged and the dysfunctional. Prison, with its routines and regular meals, might actually be something of a relief. Anyway, a long stretch inside would hardly matter now. With a reflex action, Tommy reached into his jacket pocket and from a carefully-folded piece of tissue pulled out a handful of orange pills and swallowed them down. The cops had taken the rest of the bottle from him, for obvious reasons, but had allowed him to keep what he needed for the night. He wouldn't ask for a glass of water. He didn't want to see their pig faces again until the morning.

As the tablets crawled, painfully slowly, down his dry gullet he allowed himself to dwell on the subject closest to his heart. It was the one that tore at him on sleepless nights like this and ate into his very being like a cancer. He'd been so near – so fucking near – to doing what he had come to do. Jesus, eight years without a word to Rose would've taken some explaining but plenty had had it worse and they'd got over it. She would be the same, he was sure, if only he could just get a grip of her – try to explain and tell her he was truly sorry. Whatever she wanted to hear he would say it.

She'd tell him he was full of shite. Fair play, that was true. It had never been any different. "This time next year, Rose my love, we'll be out of here," he would say, sweeping his hand in an extravagant gesture of dismissal around the cramped flat they'd lived in since they were married. "This time next year you'll be in furs – no sweat."

It was all bollocks – just a small part of the guff he gave her on a daily basis. Tight-mouthed, she'd ask him why he never seemed to be making any money when Mickey Callaghan was. "Saving for a rainy day, love, that's what I'm doing. Don't worry now. It's all tied up nice and safe." It was – in the safe at Ladbroke's and in the tills of any number of pubs along the Dock Road. And, eventually, in the scraps of IOUs and other false promises he made to the contingent of Liverpool low-lifes and hard-nuts who lent him money, and eventually demanded its return with a slice of interest fatter that a slapper's backside.

The ring was the final straw. With a few more loans and a bunch of favours owed around the city, he might just have been able to smooth over the fact that he'd lied and lied to Rose over the years. Even the times he'd disappeared for a day or two – out on the lash with the boys, too hammered to come home, or guiltily holing up somewhere, licking his wounds after taking a hit on a horse – he had been forgiven. Oh there'd been the rows, all right; plates hurled, suitcases dumped over the balcony of the flat, but in the end there was always the delicious moment of reconciliation.

Losing the ring was different. She had loved that ring. In a rare spell of playing the devoted husband, Tommy had escorted her down to Boodle and Dunthorne's, the famous Liverpool jewellers, and, with a flourish, produced a thick wad of notes from the jacket of his best suit. She shouldn't have been flattered. She should have known better and should have questioned Tommy harder about the source of the cash, but there he was, the sparkle in his eyes twinkling brighter than any precious stone, and more fool she for believing him. It was their wedding anniversary and Tommy had sworn that the year ahead would be the turning of a corner for the Cassidys. Three months later the ring was gone and right behind it was Tommy. She would never have understood, so he simply didn't bother to explain.

He was a coward and he knew it. The minute he'd gone, a bag thrown together when she was at work and a cheap bus ticket to London, the whole shebang would come collapsing down around Rose's ears like a falling tree. The lies, the money gambled and lost, the debts, the half of the business that never was and the ring – all landing on her like a delivery of rancid horseshite from a thousand feet up. And him leaving her with it all to sort out, along with everything else she had to face. It was the worst thing a man could do, abandon his wife without a word, and he could hardly call himself a man whenever he thought about it, but he had done it.

He knew people loved and respected Rose. He knew she'd be looked after. By and large, they were a good bunch, the Liverpool Irish. They wouldn't see her go under. At the start, he promised himself that he would be back in a few months. He'd lie low in the capital for a while, not tell anyone – even Rose – where he was. Then, he would sneak back up there, pick her up and take her somewhere else. A place they could make a new start. Glasgow, maybe, or Newcastle. Or, God love its dear, dirty self, Dublin. Ireland was booming, and there was work. For the first time in centuries, more people were coming to live in Ireland than were leaving it. Emigrants were returning home. Maybe it was their moment to do the same.

But a few months turned into a year and Tommy still couldn't find a way of facing her. To ring her or write to her might have landed her in trouble. After all, he was still on the books of some seriously heavy people who had long memories. He didn't want to leave her exposed. He also didn't want to be found. The longer it went on, the harder he found it to visualise their reunion. Two years passed, then three. He had a job organising gangs of Polish labourers on building projects around London. It wasn't particularly well-paid, but it was OK. There was money for basics, and for booze and the horses. His memories of Liverpool and those he had left behind didn't exactly disappear but, with 14-hour working days and most nights spent in a drunken stupor, the domestic circumstances of his life before that fateful card game began to fade. More accurately, perhaps, he simply blocked them out.

Then, with no small amount of irony, he was suddenly sacked, replaced by a Romanian gangmaster who didn't drink, didn't gamble, went to Mass religiously and was ruthlessly, coldly efficient in his collection of large amounts of bribe money from poor, would-be workers to secure employment. It was the 21st century, new and harsh, and men like Tommy, who lived like there was no tomorrow but had a streak of decency running somewhere beneath the roguish exterior, were over. He was middle-aged, broke and living in hostel accommodation. If there was ever a glimmer of hope that he might find his way back to Rose, it was now finally snuffed out. Except for this – the one, solitary opportunity thrown to him. The chance in a million of someone literally grabbing him from the brink of death and offering him a grand or more to spend in a weekend. Jesus… he'd been so damn close. Just to have seen her for a minute, drop the ring in her hand, maybe even kiss her goodbye. To tell her that he still loved her and always would. Now wouldn't that have been something?

The pain started up in his chest again and he reached into his pocket to see if there were any tablets left in the tissue. If not, he'd have to call the custody sergeant. He pulled out the tissue and shook it. No tablet. He checked his breast pocket. There was something in there. Tommy pulled it out and looked at it. A till receipt from Waterstone's. When the feck had he been in there? He hadn't read a book for years, never mind pay for one. Puzzled he turned it over. On the back was an inner London number and a name next to it: 'PAUL'.

Of course. Gobshite's number. He'd scrawled it down at the guy's flat from the piece of card shoved under the telephone's keypad. He'd decided to get the haircut, the suit and the car, then simply clear off to Liverpool alone, giving Paul a ring before he set off up north to tell him he'd be back on Monday. He'd changed his mind that morning, but he hardly knew why. Maybe he wanted to show the lad that his money was being well spent.

Tommy stared at the number and carefully folded it back into his breast pocket. Tomorrow, he would have the legal right to make one phone call.

*

Paul had been heading for the one landmark in Liverpool he was sure would lead him to the centre and, after two hours walking, he was about to reach it. The huge cathedral towered above him, its distinctive red bricks a monument to the years of sweat and backbreaking toil that went into its construction. It was the biggest Anglican cathedral in Europe. The sheer bulk of it stopped Paul in his tracks. Tired and footsore, he leaned on a railing and gazed upwards, almost overwhelmed by its silent vastness. He thought of all the effort that had gone into its creation, the patience and determination of the architects, the skill and toughness of its builders. They hadn't given up and this was the result.

Rested, he decided to press on. Maybe, he reasoned, if he could find the river he could find the railway line. This was a port and surely there would be a track leading from it to a main station? The cathedral stood on the corner of a road, and as he crossed over he noticed the name of it on a sign fixed to the wall of the building opposite: Hope Street.

In 15 minutes Paul was walking slowly along the River Mersey. There was a strong tide and the swirling, inky blackness of the river, illuminated by the grand buildings that stood along its bank, captivated and mesmerised him. Many times he had walked the city stretches of the Thames, seeking inspiration for his writing or solutions to the problems of his life, but his desire for solitude was always interrupted by the ebb and flow of traffic up the river, along its banks and over its bridges. There was no peace, no rest.

This was different. He was still alone but now he revelled in the isolation. The salty wind stabbed at his nostrils and forced its way into the back of his throat. Buffeted by the strong breeze, the shriek of gulls overhead, searching for early morning pickings, Paul felt he was somehow being shaken out of a stupor. He thought again about the events of the past 24 hours. Finding Tommy. Persuading him to take part in the plan. Coming up here. The break-in. It had flown by at breakneck speed. It had been... what had it been? Exciting? Was that the right word to describe the feeling of hooking up with a lunatic like Tommy and, within a few hours, taking part in a major-league crime? Well, yes. It was the right word. Thrilling, even. Paul suddenly felt more alive than he had done for years.

Again he paused, standing back to take in the view of the city. The water, and the way the buildings seemed to line up along the riverfront like great liners at berth, gave him a sense of perspective he hadn't had for a long time. Maybe Tommy was gone, but that didn't mean the dream was dead. There were still two days. If he couldn't find Tommy, could he find someone else to help him? It would be hard, impossible maybe, but if he didn't try he would be letting himself down. He reached into his jacket for his wallet but pulled out the picture of Loch Tyne House. Hours ago, skulking like a frightened rabbit in the bushes as Tommy was hauled away, he would have considered tearing it up. Now, it seemed more of a talisman for good fortune still to come. If he caught the first train from Liverpool, he might be back in London in three hours. There was still time to find someone else. He could do this.

*

His wander along the river in search of a railway line had proved fruitless. If a line had been there, it was long gone. A sleepy night porter at a waterfront hotel had pointed the way to the station and after a short walk through the deserted centre he had come upon Lime Street Station, on an incline just above the city's museum and art gallery. When he got there he discovered the quickest train to London departed at 7.30am, no stops, arriving at Euston just after 10am. A small knot of clubbers stood around, some still buzzing from the drugs they'd taken, others already crashed out wherever they could find room after giving in to the demands of their evening. Reckoning that he was in reasonably safe territory, Paul had found a spare bench, rolled his jacket into a makeshift pillow and had laid down. Exhausted by the walk and the events that had taken place, he had fallen asleep quickly and easily.

When he awoke at 6.45am, stiff, cold but not entirely uncomfortable, the station was slowly coming to life. The clubbers had gone and the shutters were opening on the concourse coffee shop as a guy in a red-trimmed uniform swept crumbs off the floor and shooed the pigeons away. Paul stretched, rubbed his eyes and tasted the foulness of his breath. Last night had been unbelievable. Somehow, everything looked different. Despite the crick in his neck caused by the jacket, which made him look like a quizzical whippet, his head tilted to one side in pain, he actually felt changed. He was no longer an observer, but a participant. He looked at the clock. 6.50am. Time for a piss and a coffee before joining the shuffling queue which had already formed outside the undermanned ticket booth.

The coffee helped to warm his hands as he stood in line.

94

Sleeping rough was a colder experience than he'd imagined. He would be glad to get back on the train and sleep in the warmth of the carriage for a few hours before resuming his search. A couple of places in front of him, an elderly couple were having difficulty in understanding that they would have to wait in Birmingham for an hour to make the connection to Norwich. Impatiently, Paul shifted from foot to foot. Now, he just wanted to get on.

A noise came from the depths of the inner pocket of his jacket. His phone going off. Surprised that anyone would call at all, especially at this time in the morning, he fumbled for it. A number he didn't recognise.

"Hello?"

"Paul... mon cher. It is I... Maurice."

Oh for Christ's sake. Paul's heart sank as he pictured the Frenchman on the other end of the line, picking slowly at a stuffed olive and imagining it was an eyeball.

"Leave me alone," Paul muttered into the phone.

"Paul," replied the familiar, wheedling voice, "you must not resist. It is your destiny to eat me. Why not start with my ear? It is so delicate, so shell-like...."

Paul had had enough of the bearded, black-clad freak.

"Listen, you crazy cannibal," he shouted, scattering the ever-present pigeons that had gathered around a nearby bin, "I don't want to eat your ear, your penis, or any part of you! DO YOU UNDERSTAND!?"

With that, he hung up, thrusting the phone back into his jacket pocket. He felt the astonished, horrified stares of the passengers in the queue with him, but was too irate to explain. Extraordinarily, the phone rang again, a split second after the ticket booth clerk tapped on the window to summon him forward.

Paul tore the phone from his pocket, astonished and angry that Maurice had the nerve to bother him again.

"Listen," he said savagely, "just fuck off and leave me alone, alright?"

There was a pause while the caller caught his breath. Then, the laconic tones of a Dubliner, momentarily caught off-guard, but ready with a smart retort.

"Now then," said the voice, "is that any way to speak to your father?"

"Tommy...?"

"Spot on, son. Wanna know where I am?"

CHAPTER 10

Paul hesitated at the foot of the steps that led up to the imposing double doors of Liverpool's central police station. If he walked up there and introduced himself, the chances were strong that he wouldn't see freedom again for another five years, maybe more. He'd picked up that ring and his dabs were all over the crowbar. It would hardly take a Perry Mason to make the charges stick to a jury like glue.

But Tommy was in there, with no visible means of escape, and he needed his help. In truth, they needed each other. All sorts of scenarios ran through Paul's mind as he paused, trying not to catch the eyes of uniformed constables coming in and out of the building. What if he somehow got Tommy out on bail and they made a run for it? By the time the police caught up with them – if they did catch them – Tommy would be dead. Convenient for him, but not necessarily for Paul – the only surviving suspect, now implicated in a suspicious death.

His mind was a tangle of fear and excitement. He could still run away alone, but something inside him was urging him not to. He had to see this through, whatever the conclusion. Paul wasn't good at trusting his instincts. He knew what he knew and that was as far as it ever went. But now, standing at the mouth of a beast which could swallow him whole and not spit him out for a long time, he felt an insatiable urge to go up and give it a poke in the balls just to see what would happen.

He took one last deep breath of fresh air before opening the heavy door and stepping inside. The station smelled like all official buildings – a mixture of disinfectant, cheap carpet tiles and sweat. The desk sergeant barely looked up as Paul stood in front of him, coughing gently to get his attention.

"Yes, sir," he said finally, "what can we do for you?"

"Erm, I've come to see... my dad." The words formed unnaturally on Paul's lips. He felt like he'd spoken in a foreign language.

"Oh yeah," said the sergeant, with disinterest. "And who's he, then?"

"His name's Cassidy. Tommy Cassidy."

"A bobby is he? Can't say I've heard of him. I know everyone in this station."

"No, he's... he's in the cells."

"Oh." The sergeant's expression changed from indifference to one of loathing, albeit in an aloof, professional way. He followed his finger down a long custody list in front of him. "Right then, let's see... da-da-da-da-da-da-daah... here it is. Cassidy. Aggravated burglary. Yeah, he's still here. And your name?"

Shit. Paul hadn't prepared for this eventuality. He could give him a false one. Whose book had he read recently? Ian Rankin. No. No way. He'd heard all coppers read crime fiction. Especially detectives. Christ knows why. Maybe for inspiration?

"Paul." He couldn't lie.

"Paul. Okay, Paul, I'll buzz you through that door on the left, then if you wait around for a mo' I'll get someone to give you a little rub down. It's procedure. Make sure you haven't got a birthday cake with a saw in it."

Paul smiled weakly and when the door buzzed he did as he was told. Thank God he'd swallowed the ring. After a thorough search by a young PC with a thick Scouse accent he was led down a corridor to a room marked 'Interview' and told to sit down.

"D'yer wanna brew?" the young copper asked. "There's a coffee machine down the corridor. It takes 20s. I'll get it for yer if yer want?"

No, he didn't want. It would be his second coffee of the day. This was the last place on earth he wanted to crap in.

After a nervous five minutes spent staring around the bleak, bare interview room, Paul jumped at the turn of the door handle. The young PC opened it and waved his charge through it.

Dishevelled and sleep-deprived, Tommy shuffled in and sat down at the table opposite Paul. He greeted him with a tired smile and a cheery "Hello, son."

"Right fellas," said the cop, "you've got five minutes. I'll leave you to it."

The second the door slammed shut and they were alone, Tommy leaned over the table. His expression changed to one of nervous anticipation.

"Where the fuck did you get to?" he hissed.

"I hid," replied Paul, also tense, his eyes flicking around the room for tape recorders or cameras. "Once they'd caught you they didn't seem bothered about me. Good job too."

"Never mind about that now," said Tommy. "Did you keep the ring?"

"Yeah, I did."

Tommy's shoulders slumped with relief. "Well, at least that's something. Is it safe?"

Paul didn't know what to say. He nodded uncertainly.

"So... what does that mean?" asked Tommy, confused.

Paul opened his mouth and pointed down his throat.

"I thought I'd get caught," said Paul, catching Tommy's startled expression. "It would be evidence. I put it in...it was kind of an accident, I guess."

"You didn't? Don't fecking tell me that you..."

"It hasn't come out yet," Paul interjected, "but I'm sure it won't be long. I'm pretty regular."

"Jesus, thanks for sharing that. I mean, it's going to be lovely now, isn't it?"

Paul shrugged. What could he say? He did what he did, and saved the ring.

"Well," said Tommy, somewhat ungratefully, "don't strain yourself on my account. The magistrate doesn't sit until Monday."

It was the scenario Paul had run through his mind and the very one he really didn't want to hear. The one which would complicate everything, make the whole plan almost redundant.

"No, no," he said, audibly panicking, "that's too late. We've got to be back by Monday morning. Shit. *Shit!*"

"Looks like you'll just have to run some other poor fucker down," replied Tommy laconically.

"For Christ's sake," said Paul, "there must be something we can do to get you out. Think, Tommy, think!"

Tommy shrugged. "I don't know, Paul, you tell me. I thought you were the brains of the outfit. I've been awake all night in this stinkin' hole, and I'm so hungry I could eat a scabby donkey. It's hardly the starting point for the Great Escape, is it?"

At that moment, the door handle turned and the young PC stepped through it with another officer. Time was up so Tommy slowly rose to his feet, his chair scraping on the lino floor.

"Well, son," he said, waving his hand, "it's been grand to see you. Love to your mother, now."

"Hang on," said Paul, looking at the two officers, "just wait a sec. Is there anyway I can get him out of here before Monday?"

"Sure," said the older of the officers, grinning sarcastically, "you're welcome to take him… if they drop the charges."

Bastard. But as they turned to head back to the custody suite, a thought flashed through Paul's mind…"drop the charges". Supposing he could find someone, anyone, who could help? It was a long shot, but worth a try.

"Hey," he called out to the backs of the departing trio. The older cop turned round. "If I can't have him, can I have his car keys back? Please? It's a rental and I don't want to have to fork out for it."

The cops looked at each other. "Wait by the front desk," the older one said. "When we've locked Paddy back up we'll bring them through."

*

Paul had to act fast. No time to mess around. No more long walks.

Glad to be out of the claustrophobic confines of the police station, he ran along a nearby shopping street until he found a cashpoint. He withdrew £50 then looked round for a taxi. But where the hell was he going? Luckily, Paul remembered the route and that, plus the cabbie's knowledge of his home city, took him back to the turn-off for Callaghan's house.

Head down and with the minimum of fuss, he walked up the suburban avenue until he reached the house. With a quick glance to his left, he noticed the upstairs curtains were shut. Maybe they were sleeping in? He'd didn't really care. Quickly, he walked over the road and with a single movement unlocked the door of the abandoned Mercedes, opened it and got in. Another glance at the house. Nothing. He turned the engine over, put the car into gear and moved off without looking back. At the end of the street he took a mental note of the road name – just in case.

He had a plan. A vague one – but a plan nonetheless. He needed to get back to the housing estate they'd arrived at the previous day. It was Saturday, but there was every chance that the builders redeveloping part of the site might be putting in a half-day. They would certainly know Callaghan. Maybe, just maybe, someone would know Tommy.

After stopping a couple of times for directions, he found the estate and the parking space they'd occupied the day before. At first glance the building site looked deserted, but after he locked the car and walked closer to it, he noticed a portable building full of workmen. It was lunchtime, and the men were eating pies and sandwiches, drinking tea and looking through the papers.

He could see they were mainly young, of similar age to himself. Would they know Tommy? There was no harm in asking.

"'Scuse me," he said, conscious of his accent and his interruption of their lunch break, "sorry to bother you. I just wondered if any of you knew a guy called Tommy Cassidy? He's, um, a friend of Mr Callaghan."

There was a chorus of "sorry mate", "never 'eard of 'im'"

and "dunno, la", accompanied by a round of head shaking and shrugging. One guy at the back, his safety helmet propped on the back of his head to reveal non-regulation earrings, seemed to be more interested than the others.

"'Ow old are we talkin', mate?"

"Er, I dunno, really," replied Paul. "Fifties? Fifty-five? Fifty-six? Something like that?"

"Nah," said the man, "not here. I mean, he might have worked here once, but not in the last five years I've been with this lot."

He pointed out of the cabin door to an older man walking slowly out of the estate, his paper in one hand.

"See 'im there? That's Danny Fitzpatrick. He was on the sites with Callaghan for years. If anyone'll know your fella, he will. Go on, catch him up and ask him. Don't forget to buy him a pint. That'll open his gob."

The other builders laughed knowingly. Paul thanked him and ran over to where the man was strolling.

"Are you Danny?" asked Paul, slightly out of breath.

"I am," replied the man, who looked to be roughly the same age as Tommy and Callaghan. "I'm also off for a pint, it being dinner time and all, so if you've got something to say, could you make it quick?"

"Sure," replied Paul. "Do you know Tommy Cassidy?"

The man paused, looking into the distance. "Well now," he said finally, "there's a name I've not heard for a few years. A good few years, too. Tommy Cassidy. And what d'you want to know about him?"

"I'm… a kind of friend of his," replied Paul.

"So he's alive," mused the man. "That'll be a surprise. More for Tommy than for anyone else, I would say."

The man stuck out his hand. "Danny. Danny Fitzpatrick. And you are?"

"Paul Callow."

"Well, Paul Callow, are you not thirsty? I think it's time we had a drink. Mine's a Guinness."

In the pub, Fitzpatrick told Paul how he, Callaghan and Tommy had arrived from Dublin together. How they'd drunk, fought and fucked all over Liverpool. How Callaghan had made it big. How Tommy had lost the lot down the bookies.

"So, that eejit Cassidy's in trouble again, eh," he said. "No surprises. Him and Callaghan – nothing but trouble, the pair of them."

"Oh yeah?"

"Yeah. Big time. Tommy – it was usually the gambling. Callaghan always had an eye for the ladies. Still does, the dirty fecker."

"Is that so," said Paul, warming to Danny. "You know...maybe I'll stay for another one. D'you fancy it?"

Within 30 minutes, Paul was making his excuses to Danny, a slip of paper with an address scribbled on it in his hand.

"Mind how you go now, son," shouted the Irishman as Paul pulled open the pub door. "That Callaghan one's like a bag of cats if you stir him up."

"Don't worry," replied Paul grimly, "I think I've got all I need to shut him up."

*

Unbelievably, Paul found himself once again walking through the concrete lion-defended gates of Callaghan's house. His heart was in his mouth, and he barely knew what was driving him on to such madness. Cautiously, he reached out for the bell, but before he could press it the door was wrenched violently open. There, in a garish yellow golf jumper, a thick gold chain poking over the top of it, stood Mickey Callaghan, his face a wild shade of vermillion.

"You..." he snarled at Paul. "You've a fucking nerve coming here, boy."

Callaghan took a step forward, clenching his fist. If Paul didn't say his piece quickly, he would be turned into black pudding there on the gravel drive.

"Mr Callaghan," said Paul, with as much polite authority as

103

he could muster, "I'm here to ask you nicely. Will you drop the charges against Tommy?"

Callaghan stared at him. There was a better way of settling this. A more permanent solution to the problem. He pulled a mobile phone out from the pocket of his pale blue slacks and started to dial.

"If I were you son," he grimaced, "I'd save your breath for the law. I don't want to hear it."

"Okay, well you had the chance," replied Paul. It was time to play the trump card, the one Danny had given him. He beckoned towards the car. The door opened, and, with as much dignity as she could muster in skin-tight, pastel-pink leggings, out stepped a young woman, done up like a dog's dinner and with a sneer on her thickly made-up face that would have parted the Mersey.

"Oh aye," she screeched, as she tottered up the drive, her high-heels kicking up the stone chippings as she flounced along, "and we all know what you save your breath for, don't we Mickey Callaghan."

"Mary Loughlin!" Callaghan started backwards, his anger melting into a mask of horror, as the vision from his murky doings on the side strode right up to him.

"Hiya Mickey," she said as she reached him, her voice as loud and raucous as a nest of squabbling magpies, "and how's your bollocks? That rash cleared up yet, has it?"

With that, she reached out her manicured hand for the front of his trousers and squeezed, gently at first and then with increased pressure as Callaghan began to double over in pain.

"Mary..." coughed Callaghan, tears of agony tearing at his eyes, "what... are you... doing here?"

"You know," she said, releasing her grip and watching him stagger backwards in shock and pain, "it's a funny thing. I just got talking to Paul here and it turns out he knows you."

"Knows me," Callaghan spluttered, "he fucking robbed me..."

"Yeah," said Mary breezily, ignoring his last remark, "he knows

104

you. And your wife! How about that, eh? Funny, you never mentioned her last bonfire night…"

Panic-stricken, Callaghan looked wildly back into the house. Mary…the little tart… on his own doorstep… shite and onions… what would Maureen…?

Further down the path, Paul watched in amusement as Mary did her worst.

"Remember that night, do you? When you said you wanted to put your big rocket into me flower pot…went off with a right bang, didn't it?! Remember..? No? Well, let's see if your wife can help, shall we?"

The brassy, brazen young woman attempted to side-step Callaghan into the house, but he blocked her path, grabbing her arm.

"Alright, Mary, alright," he muttered, cringing with embarrassment. "I'm gettin' the message. Tell that long streak of piss standing on my drive that him and his mate won't hear any more from me."

Mary turned and gave Paul an extravagant thumbs-up gesture. Delighted, he gave her one back.

"Don't worry," she hissed at Callaghan as he released her arm, "your dirty little secret's safe with me. Married men like you shouldn't go round with bangers in their pockets. Can be dangerous if they go off, know what I mean?"

She turned on her stiletto heels and marched back down the drive. With a flourish, Paul opened the passenger door for her and mock-bowed as she slid in.

*

With Mary safely deposited home, Paul returned to the police station. Callaghan, fearful of anyone else being dragged up from his sordid near-past, had already made the phone call to the police. After five minutes waiting, Paul looked up to see Tommy being buzzed out of the side door, a free man. Paul stood up immediately, keen to get on with the day. Tommy, though, stood at the top of the steps and turned his face towards the early afternoon sun, savouring his unexpected liberty.

He looked at Paul's anxious, pale face and spontaneously grabbed him in a playful headlock, rubbing his hair vigorously.

"Jesus," he shouted, "give the lad a medal! Charges all dropped, eh? Who'da thought you were so feckin' smart?"

Angrily, Paul wrenched himself free.

"It's not funny, Tommy," he growled. "What were you thinking? I could have been nicked too. Anything could've happened. You're gonna screw everything up the way you're going."

"Sure, this was part of the deal," said Tommy. "Remember? A chance for me to sort things out."

"With your family, Tommy," replied Paul, "not with some psycho you used to play cards with."

"Achh, lighten up son," said Tommy dismissively. "Callaghan's been an itch I couldn't scratch for too bloody long. Now I've done it and I feel better for it. So shut the fuck up, and let's get on with the main feature."

They reached the car, Tommy smiling to see his treasured, if temporary possession once again. Still moaning, Paul threw him the keys. Tommy climbed in, shut the door and started the engine. Paul pulled at the door handle, but it wouldn't budge. Locked.

"Tommy, open the door for Christ's sake."

Tommy wound down the window just enough to lean up and put his mouth through.

"I'll pick you up on the way home. See you later."

Paul begged, but it was useless. Laughing, the Irishman wound the window up and pulled away at speed, the car kicking up a cloud of dust as it disappeared. In a fit of temper Paul picked up a stone and threw it, but already the car was around the corner and gone.

Paul looked around. Stuck in this sodding city again. What was

Tommy playing at now? Would he get back on time? Where would he know to pick him up? Suppose he didn't come back?

He sat on a low wall, a sudden wave of depression washing over him. Suddenly, he stopped the mental acrobatics and listened. The sound of a familiar car engine, and getting closer. He looked up to see the Mercedes coming at him from the opposite direction, as though it had done one big U-turn.

The car screeched to a halt next to him, and Tommy once again wound down the window, this time to a more sociably low level. He grinned as he leaned over the passenger's seat.

"Isn't it time you had a shite?"

A broad smile broke across Paul's face. He sidled up to the car and pulled the handle. It was open.

"Get in," said Tommy, "we've got a big job to do. Well, *you* have."

CHAPTER 11

Paul slammed the door of the Mercedes shut, holding a paper bag with a green medicine bottle printed on it. They were parked outside a chemist's, one of a number of shops along an unprepossessing parade a mile or so west of the city centre. While Tommy waited outside, still smiling as he thought about the revenge taken on Callaghan, Paul was inside the shop, asking for a certain product with embarrassment as a gaggle of old ladies waiting for prescriptions leaned in to hear more.

Tommy indicated to the bag. "Did you get it okay?"

"I did," said Paul, "but not without half of Liverpool's grannies watching me. Bloody embarrassing, it was."

"Ach away," Tommy laughed, "it's only your arse. Go on then, pop one."

"How long will it take?"

"God, I dunno. If you got the full strength jobs like I told you, you should be laying a brick within the hour."

Paul pulled the packet from the bag, opened it, and hesitantly prised three tablets from the blister packet.

"Just the two," said Tommy, nodding. "Always better to under-estimate with the old laxatives. Mark my words."

Reluctantly, and with no great pleasure, Paul dry-swallowed the two tablets, grimacing as they went down.

"Good man," said Tommy, starting the car. "Okay, eyes peeled for the nearest burger joint. There'll be a bog in one of those, for sure. To be honest, I might sit in and wait for ya. There's probably time for a decent feed while you're, er, panning for gold in there."

As it turned out, the laxatives took effect far more quickly than Tommy predicted. After just ten minutes on the road, in the hope of finding a burger bar, Paul shouted for Tommy to stop, and the pair headed for a battered-looking greasy spoon café they'd driven past a minute or so previously.

Paul made his excuses hastily while Tommy revelled in the luxury of a bacon butty and a cup of tea. He idled through a copy of the Sun, trying as hard as he could not to linger on the racing page and the tips for the day.

After a few minutes, the toilet door opened and out came Paul. His face was a ghastly white, and his expression haggard. He looked like a man who had been far too close to nature for comfort.

Tommy watched him, half amused, half in admiration, as Paul shuffled to the table, turning his head away from the smell of frying eggs and frothy coffee. Tommy held out his hand expectantly, like a shopkeeper demanding the return of a lollipop from a thieving child.

With a grim expression that spoke volumes about the terrible doings behind the bog door, Paul dropped the shining sapphire ring into Tommy's palm He pulled out a chair and sat down heavily, immediately raising himself up again in gruesome pain. Ignoring him, Tommy turned the ring round and round in his fingers, looking at it with suspicion.

"Don't worry," said Paul, slightly affronted, "I did clean it."

Tommy couldn't help himself. With a reflex action inherited from long lost generations of animal ancestors, he sniffed the ring and, seemingly satisfied, took a clean handkerchief from his pocket and wrapped it up.

"Okay, shall we go? Tommy?"

Paul was already half on his feet, and seemed keen to make a move. The tick of the clock inside his head was growing louder by the minute and he felt a constant, nagging agitation. They had a day and a half. Who knew what else Tommy would do in that time?

But the Irishman stayed where he sat, head cupped in hands and lost in thought.

109

"I don't know," he said finally, looking up. "I'm not sure this is such a good idea."

Exasperated, Paul sat back down again. The tomato sauce that Tommy had wiped across his plate with the remnants of his bread was already starting to congeal. They had no time to linger, no time at all. And yet, the Irishman suddenly looked cowed, frightened even.

"Look Tommy," said Paul quietly, not wanting to push him too far, "what's the deal here? I mean, with your family?"

Tommy sunk his head in his hands once more, contemplating the cold, half-drunk cup of brickie's tea in front of him.

"I walked out on them eight years ago. Not a word to them. Never seen them since."

Tommy shifted uncomfortably on the orange plastic chair, but he still didn't look up.

"Why?"

"Because if I hadn't... if I hadn't, my Rose would've kicked me out anyway. You know I lost the ring in that bloody card game. But that wasn't it, really. I'd already gambled everything else away over the years, and what I hadn't gambled I'd pissed down the pub toilet. I owed people money all over the place. The ring was just...the last straw, I suppose."

He half glanced up at Paul, and suddenly seemed to look much older. All the guilt, the worry, the debt, the boozing and the late nights had etched a road map of suffering into his lined face. He shook his head and turned to face the wall, hardly able to look Paul straight in the eye.

"Maybe I should just leave them some money and have done with it," he sighed. "It's more use to them than any apologies I could possibly make."

It had only been a couple of days, but Paul had never seen Tommy look so down. Even on the bridge – even as he was about to launch himself off – Tommy possessed a fighting spirit. Until now. He seemed to be as crushed as Callaghan's knackers in Mary's clenched fist.

110

"Come on, Tommy," said Paul, trying to shake him out of his despair. "Everyone deserves a second chance."

"A hundred and second chance, more like. I'd left her before, you know, but only for a couple of days. Once the shite had been cleaned off the fan, I went home. But eight years gone... Jesus."

"Okay," said Paul, trying to find a positive, "but what's the worst that could happen? She slams the door in your face. That's it. It can't be any worse than that, surely?"

Tommy snorted in reaction. "You've obviously never met my Rose," he muttered.

Paul looked at him. Tommy was talking like he was already beaten. Like he couldn't possibly take another chance, just to see what might happen. It sounded creakingly familiar, the whole 'I can't, because' routine. Then, it dawned on Paul or rather, it hit like a ton of bricks. Tommy was beginning to sound like him. The excuses and the self-pity, the avoidance strategies and defensiveness. It couldn't be happening. Not to Tommy.

Paul's response was so unexpected it seemed to have come from nowhere. In fact, it was years of insularity and lack of confidence finally seeping out of this uptight young man.

"Well, so what!" he snapped, taking Tommy by surprise. "I didn't come all this way to watch you back out at the last minute. Jesus, Tommy... what happened to 'seize the day'? If you're gonna sit there not knowing which way to jump, then fine, but I'm telling you this. We're going, and you're going to say whatever it is that you've come to say. Okay?"

Paul was bristling with anger. He couldn't believe he'd stood up to Tommy like that. But in the past 24 hours he'd felt a change come over him. He didn't want to sit back morosely, and watch the world pass him by. This was it, the here and now. He didn't want to read about it. He wanted to be it.

Tommy perked up from his slump, sat back in his chair and stared at Paul with new eyes. Well, now. There were few people who spoke to Tommy Cassidy like that and didn't end up chewing tarmac. Somewhere, under all that past-it student clobber and the anti-social, literary genius stuff, lurked a fine pair of bollocks. You couldn't describe them as being made of steel, not quite that hard, but they were tough enough. Walnuts, maybe.

Sensing that he'd struck a chord, Paul followed up his outburst with a much gentler gesture. Lightly, he laid his hand on Tommy's arm and squeezed it.

"Come on," he said, with something approaching tender reassurance. "I'm sure it'll be worth it."

Tommy paused. The boy was right. This was it. Jesus, she'd... never mind what she'd do. If he got to see her face one last time, it would be worth it. Even if it was screaming blue bloody murder.

He smiled at Paul. Not a piss-taking, sarcastic smile he'd thrown him the past couple of days, but one filled with warmth and respect. Paul noticed it. Without a word, but with a mutually flustered feeling, the pair rose as one from the table and headed out of the café door.

*

"Christ alive!" Tommy cursed, as he walked up the third flight of concrete steps to the landing he was looking for. He stopped momentarily, out of breath, and took in the scene. They were back on the estate they'd first visited yesterday.

The walls of the stairwell which snaked around Scafell House were covered in graffiti, illegible efforts by illiterate idiots. Rubbish flowed down the steps like a terraced waterfall, and the acrid stink of piss that seemed to permanently coat every corner forced Paul to hold his nose as he walked.

"It wasn't like this when I was living round here, you know," said Tommy, by way of explanation. "Nah, no. There were decent people here once. Glad to get out of the slums. Now look at it. Worse than any fecking slum. And whose fault is that?"

"I dunno," replied Paul, a few paces behind, "the trash that live round here?"

112

"Drugs," said Tommy with conviction. "That's what happened here. When drugs move in, all sense moves out. It wouldn't surprise me if that fecker Callaghan had something to do with it. You don't get a house like his by pointing a few chimneys."

Tommy lit a cigarette and, careful to avoid lumps of hardened chewing gum, grabbed hold of the rail which ran along the wall and hauled himself up.

"Two flights left," he yelled. "Nearly there!"

At the fifth floor Tommy stopped again, moving off the stairwell and on to the balconied walkway. He tugged the sleeves of his shirt down just below the arms of his jacket and, with a lick of spit, smoothed his naturally tousled hair into a semi-neat parting. He brushed the lapels of his jacket down, exorcising the remains of the bacon butty, and wiped the corners of his mouth for stray remnants of ketchup. He was bracing himself for a potentially bruising encounter.

Paul, lost in thought, was gazing over the side of the balcony. The wasteland below, with its cavernous underpasses, patches of scrubby, needle-strewn grass, vandalised play area and threatening, piss-stained stairwells reminded him of the estate from *A Clockwork Orange*. He would hate to even walk through here at night, never mind live here.

Tommy threw the butt of his cigarette on the floor and thoughtfully stamped on it with the heel of his shoe. He braced himself and walked past Paul to the second door along.

Paul joined him and, at Tommy's urgent command, straightened his tie for him. The Irishman gave his hair a final lick over, then wiped his shoes vigorously on the hem of his trousers. Rose could never stand a pair of filthy shoes over her threshold. In his mind's eye he saw himself 25 years ago, standing on the doorstep of the house in Aigburth she shared with a couple of other nurses from the hospital. He was calling for her to take her on their first date. He was in his best suit then, a shiny Italian designer rip-off he'd picked up for a song in a pub. With black shirt, skinny white leather tie, matching white espadrilles, sunglasses perched on his permed head and bathed in Kouros, he thought he looked the epitome of 1980s cool sophistication. He rang the bell, expecting to see her, but he was met by Sinead, a sarky little cow of a housemate who could barely stifle the laughter at the vision in front of her. "Rose!" she shouted up the stairs, "you'd better come down quick. There's a fella here from Spandau Ballet to see you!"

Rose took it in her stride. He looked a dog's dinner, but she appreciated the effort. They went to the pictures, then the pub, and had fish and chips on the way home. It wasn't what Don Johnson would've called a night out, but then again, Don Johnson wasn't out laying asphalt 12 hours a day and wondering when the recession would get him. And it was the start of a great romance, while the romance lasted.

So here he was again, still hopeful in his best suit. He stared at the door bell. What would she look like? He knew the answer to that. The butterflies in his stomach had turned to eagles and there was an uncomfortable, lavatorial feeling further down. He raised his hand to the bell, but let it drop again. He'd come this far, but at the last second his courage was failing him.

Impatiently, Paul made up Tommy's mind for him and rang the bell himself. This was it. Tommy straightened himself up as though on parade, his heart thumping loudly in his throat.

Silence.

"She must have gone to work," Tommy announced, leaning heavily on the bell. "Ah well. She's not in. There we are."

He made a slight turn to go. Suddenly, and with the kind of exasperation that usually comes with the knowledge that Bible salesmen are on the step, the door flung open to reveal a large, sweating and, above all, very heavily built man, all muscle up top but sagging hard in the middle, clad only in a towel wrapped around his waist. He looked daggers at the pair of them. Tommy, for his part, seemed to be not the slightest bit intimidated by this glowering man mountain wobbling angrily in the doorway. If anything, he was utterly confused.

He took a step forward, and eyeballed the giant.

"Are you fucking my wife?" he demanded.

Now it was the muscleman's turn to stare in confusion.

"I don't know," he said, before half-turning away towards the inside of the flat. "SANDRA!! You married to an old Irish bloke?"

A muffled reply in the negative came from somewhere inside the flat. Tommy stepped back, still confused but also embarrassed at his mistake.

"Sandra? No. That's not the name. Sorry about that. It's alright pal. I must have the wrong place."

"Who were you looking for?" the muscleman asked. "Anyone I'd know?"

"Rosemary," Tommy replied. "And Frances. Rosemary and Frances Cassidy. Well... it might be Sheridan now."

The man shook his head. "Dunno. They used to live here, did they?"

Tommy looked round at the front door. Number 119. Same place all right.

"Yeah," he said. "Would you happen to know where they've gone?"

The muscleman was beginning to shiver in the cold wind which blew along the walkway. He shrugged apologetically and began to shut the door. As it was closing, Tommy caught sight of someone else, coming downstairs. It was another man, completely stark naked, and as cool as a cucumber. With a wink that said 'c'est la vie', the muscleman stepped back inside and shut the door.

"Well," said Tommy, as the door closed, "thanks for that. I'll leave you to your... whatever."

Dejected, and not a little shocked by the interesting threesome that appeared to be taking place in his old home, Tommy trudged back along the walkway and turned down the stairwell. Paul, anxious that all Tommy's hopes and dreams had been dashed in this godforsaken dump, trotted a few paces behind him, keen not to tread on his thoughts.

At the bottom of the stairwell, Tommy stopped and lit a fag. Paul tried to get a handle on his mood, and considered that the only tone he could take was a conciliatory one.

"Look, Tommy," he said, "I'm really sorry. I really, truly am. It was always gonna be a long shot. Loads can happen in eight years. It's been a long time. Let's go back to London, eh?"

But as Paul was discovering, it was never easy to read Tommy Cassidy. He just didn't fall into the 'right' categories. He couldn't be catalogued and filed neatly on a shelf. When the chips were down, there was always a spark of something. Even if it was only his cigarette lighter.

Tommy took a long pull on the end of his fag and stared back at the flats. He shook his head and made for the car.

"Come on, son," he said, "have a little faith. Don't be so fecking defeatist. Something will turn up, you'll see."

As they walked over the lumpy, glass-strew and turd-covered pavement back to the car park, a shout came from above.

Tommy and Paul turned simultaneously. There, five storeys above them, was a figure, waving its arms. The muscleman.

"I found this," he shouted, his voice echoing off the walls of the surrounding flats. "I think it was them."

Out of his hand flew a screwed up piece of paper. It landed a few yards away. Tommy strode over to pick it up and, unfolding it, gazed at it in triumph. On it was an address: '18 Thirlbeck Road, Coniston, Cumbria'.

"There you are," he said to Paul. "The darkest hour is always before the dawn."

"No," replied Paul firmly. "No way."

"Ever been to the Lakes, Paul?"

"No, Tommy. We're going back to London. Now."

"Not now. Eventually."

Without another word, the Irishman set off back towards the car park. It was insane. Another one hundred-odd miles away from London, and the end of the Big Game. But with the car keys in one hand and the piece of paper in the other, Paul knew Tommy held all the aces. At a pace, he followed him like a lost sheep. He didn't want to be left behind again.

116

CHAPTER 12

"It's strange," said Tommy, running his finger down the Cs in the index at the back of the UK road atlas he'd just purchased. They'd stopped at a service station on the M6 to fill up. Relieved to be away from Liverpool, but anxious to get to their destination in as little time as possible, Paul was fidgety, twisting the plastic straps of his sports bag as Tommy, tongue shoved into one corner of his mouth, scanned the map.

"What's strange?"

"This," he said, jabbing his finger at the map. "Coniston. The Lake District. What the hell would she be doin' up there? She's a city girl, through and through. From Cork. The only time she ever comes into contact with the countryside is when it falls on to her dinner plate."

"People change, Tommy," replied Paul.

"True enough. And some of us just get worse. Still… the Lake District? Surely there'd be nothing up there for her?"

"Escape? Peace and quiet? Inspiration?"

"Nah," said Tommy dismissively, "that's not her. Sounds more your thing, to be honest. You know… a touch boring. Sorry, don't mean to be rude there."

"No offence taken," said Paul, the image of Loch Tyne House seeping into his imagination like a drop of honey on hot buttered toast. "Some of us like solitude."

"Not my Rose," replied Tommy. "She wouldn't be up for any of that golden-daffodils-bloody-Wordsworth malarkey. She loves the bright lights. The razzle dazzle. The glitz and the glam."

"Or is that just you, Tommy?"

"Well, maybe," said Tommy thoughtfully. "There used to be the occasional mention of a country cottage. I thought it was just one of her dreams. Never quite saw the attraction meself, starin' at sheep all day." He looked at his watch. "We'd better get going," he said. "There's only a few hours before it gets dark and they turn all the lights off after Kendal."

"Do they?" said Paul, incredulously.

"Do they bollicks! God, you really did come down with the last shower, didn't you? But I'll tell you what, there's not much up there. We're gonna need this bloody map."

Throwing the atlas on Paul's lap, Tommy turned the key in the ignition and pulled out of the service station. After a minute or two, he switched on the radio and twiddled with the dial, looking for something that suited him. He eventually settled on Classic FM.

Tommy leaned back in his seat and turned up the volume. The station was playing Schubert's Symphony Number 3 in D Major.

"How about this, eh? This is the life." He turned to Paul with a broad grin. "D'you know what? I feel like Inspector fecking Morse."

"Inspector Clouseau, more like," grinned Paul.

Tommy laughed. "Yeah well, you might have a point there, son. It's the wrong motor, too. Maybe we should have nicked Callaghan's Jag while we were at it. But, you know, I've got us this far. We're doing what we said we'd do, are we not?"

"Less of the 'I', Tommy," Paul replied. "Don't forget who got you out of the nick."

"True," said Tommy reflectively. He looked at Paul again. "Hey, we're a good team, aren't we, me and you?"

"I think that's a compliment. I'll take it as one."

"Do so," said Tommy, winking, "do so."

Paul reflected on Tommy's words. The Irishman had abused, taunted and frustrated him to the point where he could have screamed in his face and pushed him off Archway Bridge himself, but somehow, and Paul didn't really know how because he hadn't experienced anything like it before, Tommy had pulled him close and shared the madness of his life with him. What was a purely selfish arrangement on either side had turned into something else. Mutual respect? Maybe more than that. Friendship? Perhaps that was it. But there was one big difference – a personality gulf so wide no bridge could span it. Tommy was choosing to embrace the last hours of his life with a fullness and a "fuck it" attitude in a way that Paul, even with his years stretched in front of him like an ocean, could hardly begin to envisage. Tommy was advancing in the face of death. Paul was retreating in the face of life.

Now felt the right time to bring up the question that had been nagging Paul since they'd knocked fruitlessly on the door of the flat in the Edenbridge estate. Tommy seemed relaxed and happy. He'd even told him – in a Tommyesque, roundabout way – that he quite liked him. This was the moment.

"Tommy?"

"Yep?"

"Who's Frances?"

"What...?" Tommy glanced at him, his expression changing from contentment to one of narrow-eyed suspicion.

"I was just wondering who Frances was? Is? When that naked guy answered the door at the flat, you asked if Rose and Frances lived there. Who's he, then? Did Rose marry again or something?"

"It's not a he," muttered Tommy, "it's a she."

"Oh," Paul was still confused. "Is it Rose's sister, then?"

"For Christ's sake!" snapped Tommy with ferocity, "maybe you should ditch a few of those highbrow novels and get yourself a book on biology!"

"Eh?"

Tommy spoke again, much more softly this time. Paul simply didn't understand. He'd none of his own.

"Frances... is my daughter. Frances. That's her real name. With an 'e'. But we call her Frankie."

Paul hadn't bargained for this. Tommy had never mentioned anything about a daughter. He'd talked about Rose, but he'd never

119

said there was a child, too. Paul would have to tread very, very warily.

"Nice name."

"Yes, it is," said Tommy tersely. It had slipped out on the doorstep. He was caught unawares by the muscleman fella and it had dropped out of his mouth like a hot chip. It was so rare for it to be spoken out loud like that. It was a name that was locked away inside his head, the key buried somewhere deep and dark. He didn't think Paul had heard it, but he obviously had. Bloody nosey writer type. The mere mention of the name caused an itchy feeling of guilt to creep up his neck and chest. Plenty leave their wives or husbands behind without a backwards glance, but to do that to kids...

"It... must have been hard, for you and for her."

"I wouldn't know about her. What it was like for her. Though I can imagine."

He knew exactly what it had been like for him. His little girl, his Frankie, with the English tongue and the Irish heart. How he'd loved watching her dance up at the Irish club, the music going like the clappers and she and her little mates all in a line, feet flying like shuttles. But it was Rose who did most of the parenting thing. Not really a man's business. He was too busy oiling the wheels in the pub or greasing palms at the racetrack. But, sure, she was a lovely wee girl. He would get in at night, half-cut, and peep in round the door of her bedroom where she lay asleep. "She's mine," he would think proudly to himself. "I made her."

He left home with a picture of her in his wallet. At first, he would stare at it, night after night, almost retching with a near-lethal mix of guilt and sorrow. Then, in the morning, he would punish himself for being so soft. She was better off without him. They both were. The wallet was lost in some pub fight or other and so his image of her was fixed at the time of the photograph. He hoped she'd fared well, wherever she was.

He sensed Paul was on the verge of another question. He

couldn't, wouldn't, answer it. It was too much. He had to change the subject, get the lad away from it. He couldn't face thinking about her. Too painful.

"So, Paul," he said, straightening up and pushing himself out of the cloud that had enveloped him, "what about you? Daddy dump you too? Or what?"

Paul didn't reply. Instead, he gazed intently out of the windscreen.

"I take that as a 'no comment', then," Tommy said. "You're, er, just practising for your big writer's interview with *The Times*. Is that it?"

This time, Paul didn't take the bait.

"No," he replied, "I'm not being funny with you. I'm just trying to think how to phrase it. I've never had a dad. Well, yes, someone fathered me. I didn't crawl out of a test tube or anything, but I've never met him. Dunno who he is."

"The bastard," muttered Tommy.

"I think that's the technical term for what I am," Paul said, a sardonic laugh accompanying his sentence. "I was the product of a one-night stand. Mum was only young. The guy was some bloke she met in a club. Never saw him again."

Tommy considered what he'd been told. No dad. Every boy needs a dad. Who d'you learn anything off, if not your dad?

"What about your mammy?"

"Well, we were pretty close," said Paul, still staring ahead, "more like brother and sister, I s'pose. Not easy being a teenage mum. Not back then, anyway. Everyone staring at her, whispering about her. She tried not to care, but..."

"But what?" Now it was Tommy's turn to ask the awkward questions.

"She used to cry a lot. At night in the flat. I was only little, but I felt sort of... responsible. Like it was my fault."

"How could it be your fault?" said Tommy, slightly protectively. "You were only wee. Not your fault the fella didn't use a Johnny."

Paul winced at the term. It would have been the one in common

121

currency at the time of his conception. It sounded so old-fashioned now, when you could get them anywhere and it was all above board and responsible. But back then…

"I know," he replied, "but you can't help what you feel. She was only 17. I grew up feeling that I'd ruined her life. Plus, all the stick I got when I went to school. *'Where's Your Daddy Gone…?'* Kids singing stuff like that. Makes you… introverted, I suppose."

"Books are your best mates, eh?"

"Probably, yeah."

"Well, Paul," said Tommy, "that's a bit sad now, isn't it? You could do with a good woman. The caring, sensitive type. Who'll also give you a fecking good ride."

"Is that the answer to everything, then?"

"I dunno, son, but when she's up and on you it certainly feels that way. Even with a Johnny on."

Despite himself, Paul laughed. Tommy had a natural way with words you couldn't take offence at. Even if you did, he'd wrong-foot you with another little gem.

"You know what, Paul, I know a quote from a book. And it's a bloody good one, I'll tell ya."

"Go on then."

Tommy cleared his throat and straightened his tie in mock-solemnity.

"Okay… 'The past is a foreign country. They do things differently there.' – J.R. Hartley, that."

Paul laughed. "It's L.P. Hartley. *The Go Between.* That's the book it's from. Not bloody J.R. Hartley."

"I don't care if it's J.R. Ewing," Tommy retorted, "it's a damn good quote. And very true. Agreed?"

"Agreed."

The M6 through the industrial north-west eventually gave way to a rugged, upland landscape, the snaking threads of old, dry-stone walls clearly visible on the tops of the hills with sheep dotted on distant fells like dandruff on the back of Tommy's jacket. Paul was drinking in the view, soaking up so much of what he'd read by Wordsworth, Coleridge and Southey. In the far distance he could see the tallest of the Lakeland mountains – jagged, brooding giants that dwarfed everything around them and commanded an eerie silence across water-filled valleys and the surrounding villages and hamlets.

Paul looked down at the map. The next junction would take them off the motorway and on to the A590 that would eventually lead to Coniston. From what he could gather, the settlement of houses they were looking for were on the edge of the village. He pointed out to Tommy that they were looking for a sign pointing towards Thirlbeck, but the Irishman seemed to be in a world of his own.

Again, Tommy was feeling anxious. He had no idea what he would say to Rosemary or to Frankie. The story of Paul's absent father was playing on his mind. Supposing he'd messed Frankie up like that? Made her into a nervous wreck, frightened of her own shadow? Too scared to live a normal life and hiding behind something else for protection? Surely her mother wouldn't have let that happen to her... And what about Rosemary? What could she be doing here? Herding sheep?

"Tommy! Stop!"

Instinctively, Tommy hit the brakes, sending him and Paul flying towards the windscreen, held back only by their seatbelts.

"Jesus, you frightened the life out of me," said Tommy. He tugged on his belt. "Nice bit of German engineering, eh? Why the hell have we stopped?"

"You missed it," said Paul, "just back there. The sign for Coniston."

Without comment Tommy reversed and then took a right off the main road in the direction of a terrace of three well-kept, old council houses just in the distance. Paul looked at the address again, tucked into the fold of the atlas's page. They were here.

*

In the middle house, a woman in her late forties, with carefully cut and coloured hair, and wearing a silk striped shirt that clung tightly to her still-shapely body, stood in the window of her kitchen, washing the dishes. Today had been a good day. A couple of nice people around this morning and now, in the late afternoon, the sun getting ready to begin its journey downwards towards the distant shores of the lake. She loved this time of day. When the weather was fine she would sit in her tidy, well-kept and colourful front garden, feeling the warmth on her face and watching the light dapple and shimmer as the afternoon dropped into early evening.

As she briskly scrubbed the dinner plates, placing them carefully into the slots of the crockery tray, something outside caught her eye. A Mercedes, a fine looking one, all gold, was parked outside the house. Mrs Pearson next door hadn't mentioned visitors coming. Still, they could've turned up unexpectedly to give the old girl a surprise. Or maybe they were just tourists, doing the Lakes in a fancy car.

She stared for a moment. There seemed to be someone in the car, maybe a couple of people, but they didn't appear to be getting out. Odd. With a shrug and a wrinkle of her nose she went back to her dishes. She did the final plate, then, wiping the suds from her hands with a brisk movement, took a tea towel from the hook by the sink and picked out the first dish for drying.

A feeling of unease crept over her. She looked again through the window. They were still there, in the car, but they still hadn't got out. She squinted, trying to get a better look at the occupants. Were they lost? She felt duty-bound to ask them. Maybe if she looked out the front door she'd get a better view…

*

Inside the car, Tommy was going through his touching-up routine like a nervous bridegroom minutes from the altar. The hair was licked, the tie straightened and the jacket brushed vigorously for crumbs and other bits and pieces which seemed to stick to him like flies on jam.

He glanced over to the neat, pebbledashed and slate-roofed council house, taking in the manicured lawn and the hanging baskets on either side of the doorway. It looked comfortable, if a little functional compared with some of the more traditional stone-built and whitewashed properties they'd seen on the way.

"Well," he said, "it's not quite the country cottage she dreamed about, but you can't have everything. She'll be happy enough."

He turned back towards Paul for the final inspection and the nod of approval before he emerged from the car, but as he did, the vehicle shuddered with the force of something being hurled violently against the driver's window.

"What the fuck!!!" Tommy and Paul dived for cover instinctively. *Smash!* Again, something shattered against the window. *Smash! Smash! Smash!* The car was taking a hell of a battering.

Together, they gingerly raised their heads and looked just over the level of the dashboard. There, standing at the kitchen window was a well-groomed, forty-something woman in a striped silk shirt, hurling the kind of abuse that would make news in the village magazine. As she screamed and roared, she flung cup after cup through the open window at the vehicle, sometimes missing but more often connecting with the car's vintage paintwork.

Paul glanced at Tommy in fear. "She doesn't seem very pleased to see you," he said, with understatement. "Maybe we should go?"

Tommy, wincing at every crash of crockery across the bodywork, looked back. "Ach, that's just Rosemary," he replied. "Don't worry, she'll run out of cups in a minute."

They paused, still in a semi-crouching position in the footwell of the vehicle. Tommy moved each of his fingers in turn, like a child counting the distance between claps of thunder. When he had counted to ten and there had been no further assault on the Mercedes, he looked at Paul with a grin that said "told-you-so" and, giving his hair one last lick for the luck that had almost run out, tentatively opened the car door and stepped out. As he did, a flying saucer of the crockery kind made painful contact with the top of his curly head.

CHAPTER 13

Tommy, Rosemary and Paul sat in the house in a tense, terse silence, like relatives in a hospital corridor waiting for bad news to come from an emergency operating theatre. The patient, in this case, was a marriage. Considered long since departed, at least by one half of the party, the ghost of it had returned without warning, manifesting its ghastly self in a pinstripe suit and a tie the colour of café ketchup.

They were sitting in Rosemary's front room. It was as neat as a pin, yet comfortable. A bunch of tulips of all shades filled a Waterford crystal vase that sat on top of a bookcase containing neatly filed paperbacks, hardbacks and reference books. A pair of reading glasses lay on a low table next to a single armchair that faced the television. Shades of pale green had been picked out from the pastel wallpaper and used to inform the colour of the curtains, which were patterned into a tasteful tartan. Above the fireplace hung a Victorian print of the Madonna and the child Jesus. On other walls hung watercolours of Lakeland scenes and framed photographs. The whole feeling was one of subtle, unpretentious, if somewhat muted, taste.

With a tight expression, her lips forming a single straight line as though sealed with strong glue, Rosemary cast a sideways glance at her husband, sitting all prim and proper, like some kind of ridiculous vicar, at the end of the sofa. She was perched on the end of her favourite armchair like a canary that has spied a cat under its cage, a tight ball of bristling and quivering nerve endings. Why now? Why, at this moment in time, had he chosen to roll up here, looking like Lord bloody Muck? Who did he think he was? And, more importantly, what the hell did he want?

It was like the last eight years hadn't happened. All she'd gone through – the way she'd pulled her life around, taken her and Frankie away from that damned flat and tried to build a new life here. And now this on the bloody doorstep. Tommy and some goggle-eyed drip of a boy in tow, sitting there looking 40 ways for Sunday. Oh, they didn't have much, her and Frankie, but that was fine. It was certainly an improvement on what they had when he'd done his moonlight flit, which was nothing but a bagful of debts and a whole bunch of questions never to be answered.

With rising venom, she remembered how she'd come home that day to find him gone. She'd set off to pick up the groceries, leaving him sitting there looking like he'd sold his soul to the devil. She knew he was a chancer and charmer, and that there were things going on she'd rather not hear about, but that day was different. He was looking distinctly shifty, fidgeting like a naughty schoolboy, pretending to watch the telly. She'd asked him if he wanted to come with her.

"Ah no," he said, with that stupid, shit-eating smile of his. "I'm grand. I'll just stay here and, er, I'll get the tea on."

Well, she should've known then. That man couldn't make a sandwich without burning it. When she came back, he'd gone. Oh, he'd done it before all right, but he'd always limped home like a wet dog, his tail between his legs. Somehow, this time was different. Something didn't smell right. She rang his phone. Dead. She rang round a few of his boozing buddies. No-one had seen him. Then, for a reason that she still couldn't work out, something drove her towards the bedroom. Their wardrobe door was open. All her clothes were there, on the left side. On the right side, Tommy's side – nothing but a row of empty clothes hangers. She remembered clattering them backwards and forwards, desperately looking, looking. The Lord only knows what she was looking for. Some kind of a clue? But there it was, staring her in the face, the biggest clue of the lot. He'd gone, and he wasn't planning to come back.

Telling Frankie was the hardest part. She cried a bucket of tears, God love her. It affected her terribly. She wasn't the same girl for weeks, months after it. She didn't know what to tell people. Had her Daddy run off with another woman? Was he lying dead somewhere? Did he just hate being her Daddy? She was tormented with it. They had to move away, for the child's sake as much as anyone else's.

All very different from when they first met. He was all over her like a rash. He'd have climbed Liverpool Cathedral naked and painted it green, white and gold if she'd told him to. She was nursing then, over with a few of the girls from the medical college in Cork to fill gaps in the Liverpool hospitals. She might have known never to date a patient. Not that there was much wrong with him that a cold compress over his black eye and a visit to the dentist's couldn't fix. He'd come into casualty on her shift one Friday night, drunk as a skunk and dressed in some terrible, cheap grey suit, all flecked with silver and his sleeves turned up like some low-rent, Paddy version of Miami Vice. He was propped up by a gang of mates, the lot of them three sheets to the wind. But even behind the blood, and the breath that smelled worse than the outflow pipe at the Guinness brewery, he had a certain something. He was back the following week, all spruced up, with flowers in his hand and a great gap in his teeth. She had to laugh. As soon as she did, she was his. Dear God, would you look at him now?

Tommy caught the glance and attempted a half-smile. It was like trying to wink at an iceberg. So, she was still a good aim with the plates. That hadn't changed any.

Trying to avoid another encounter with Rosemary's steely eye, Tommy surreptitiously gazed around the room. A reproduction Victorian wall clock was ticking away the seconds with a leaden beat. He looked up at the Madonna, who appeared to be peering back down at him with an expression of sheer pity. Quickly, he turned away and concentrated on some of the photographs that were dotted around the room. He squinted, seeing if he could spot himself on any of them. But he had appeared to have been exorcised from all of them, carefully cut out and binned like a bad memory.

She was looking fine, though. Very fine. A few more lines around her eyes, maybe, but she was exposed to the elements out here. There wouldn't be much in the way of fancy face creams in the village shop. Still, she was scrubbing up well. That much he could see. Hair all nicely done, figure intact. The house, too, was looking grand. He hadn't thought he stood a cat in hell's chance of seeing inside it, not after a welcome like that, but when she'd calmed down and the last saucer had nearly taken off the top of his head, she'd given a little sideways nod with her head. A gesture to come in. She'd probably given the neighbours enough to talk about for the next decade, and didn't want any more trouble on her front lawn.

He'd have loved to hear her laugh again. When she did, it was like listening to a peal of bells across a mountainside. He'd have her in fits. Well, at the start, anyway. As time went on, there was less and less to laugh about. But when they first got together.... Jesus. He remembered confessing to her one night that he and the boys had tried stealing a car. Somehow, they'd ended up miles out of town, late at night, and all the buses long gone. No-one wanted to walk, so they picked on this old Austin Maxi, an easy ride to break into. Tommy undid the door, and got in the driver's side. But something was wrong; the pedals were almost up at the steering wheel and when he put his feet on them his knees were touching his chin. It was Colm Roche, sat in the back there, who spotted the disabled sticker. The fecking thing belonged to a dwarf! They took the damn car anyway, and the day after Tommy dropped it back round the corner, no harm done. God, Rose was horrified by the theft, but when she heard about the owner she nearly burst her head laughing.

Those were the days, all right. Trouble was, the habits were already there when he first met her, and they were hard to shake off. A man liked his pint after a hard day's work, but for most fellas it was just the one pint. Not Tommy. One turned into three, four, five, six, and before he'd looked at his watch it was kicking out time. She begged him to come home early, and he tried, especially after the wee one was born, but it didn't last. Most times, Rose was away in her bed and the tea in the bin by the time he'd fallen through the door.

If it had just been the booze it might not have been so bad. But the gambling was the icing on the cake. She wanted him to get help to stop, but he was too far gone for that. He had the notion that one last win – and a bloody big one at that – would solve everything. The debts could be paid off, he'd have spare money, and they could start all over again. One last jackpot – the one that never came up trumps. Then there was all the Callaghan business, and the heavy mob asking for their money. And the ring, of course.

Tommy placed his hand in his jacket pocket and felt for the handkerchief. Thank Christ it was still there. There would be a moment he could bring it out, give it to her, apologise, get down on one knee and beg forgiveness. Whatever she wanted. But now wasn't the moment. And he didn't want to do it in front of Paul, sitting there at the other end of the sofa like a gargoyle with running dysentery.

Paul had never experienced a warring couple. At least, not up so close like this. He'd seen couples screaming and shouting on platforms as he'd pulled in to stations on his route, but he'd never been party to such malignant, silent tension such as was going on here. The occasional relationship he'd had – and he could count the number of those on the fingers of a boxing glove – had finished with a whimper, not a bang. Drifted apart, just good friends, that kind of thing. There hadn't been anything like this, a kind of life-force of pent up feeling and mutual history bouncing off every corner of the room. It was like something out of Ibsen – the silences and meaningful glances, the clock ticking away on the wall and the slight breeze coming from under the front door.

Outside, the birds were singing in the trees. Inside was like the aftermath of a nuclear attack. Paul couldn't believe how normal life outside of this room could pass by so oblivious to the malevolent stillness inside. The tension was unbearable. How long would they sit here like this? He longed for Tommy to do something, say something. Give her the ring, tell her he was sorry, and go. Just go. She really didn't want either of them here. What was the point of lingering? Tommy had seen her and she seemed fine in her new life. He and Tommy had had an adventure – that was something he'd remember for the rest of his life. But he was keen to get out of this and go. Monday was just over the horizon.

Paul coughed and slid further forward on his seat. He hoped it might prompt Tommy or Rose to say something, do something. All three glanced at each other briefly, but no-one said a word. The clock ticked and the silence descended once again. At this rate they would be here for hours.

But at that moment, a key turned in the lock of the front door, followed by the sound of someone pushing at it slightly to open it. As one, Paul, Tommy and Rose turned towards the source of the noise. The person opening it sighed over-dramatically with the effort of it, then called out in a cheery tone.

"Mam? Maa-aaamm! I've got the afternoon off. Where are you, mam?"

With a white-faced glance at Tommy, Rosemary answered back in a soft Cork brogue.

"In here, love."

"Have we got visitors?" shouted the female voice, the owner of which was obviously taking off a coat. "Whose is the fancy car?"

A young woman rushed into the living room and stopped dead in her tracks. By anybody's standards, she was beautiful. Punky, but beautiful. Her hair, cut into a sleek bob and dyed red and black, framed her high cheekbones and angular jaw. She was wearing a black T-shirt with a shiny skull-and-crossbones embroidered into it, a bright red tartan mini-skirt over black leggings and high black boots covered with steel fastenings. Paul stared at her, catching her eye, but looked quickly down in embarrassment.

The girl turned to Tommy, the multiple piercings in her ears jangling as she did so. He could hardly believe what he was seeing. She was all big and wild-looking. Was there some mistake?

"Frances," he whispered hoarsely, his speech all but taken away by the presence before him, "is that really you?"

The girl looked away from him with contempt, and glared at Rosemary. Without a word she stormed out of the room and slammed the door so hard that Paul almost flew off the sofa in fear.

"Frankie!"

Tommy jumped to his feet and moved towards the door, shouting her name. But it was no use. Frankie hadn't even bothered to pick up her coat. For good measure, she slammed the front door with equal force.

Tommy turned back to the centre of the living room and picked up a look from his wife that was filled with almost as much contempt as the one his daughter had shot him.

"Now," she said, her voice cold and measured. "Now look what you've done."

CHAPTER 14

The slamming of the front door seemed to stir up every particle of dust in the house. Settled for years, it leapt off every surface and, caught in the shafts of afternoon light which came in through the living room window, tumbled and swirled until gently falling to earth again. Distracted, Paul watched it dance through the light. The echo of the door banging reverberated in his mind. He'd never felt as awkward in the way he did at that moment. He could hear the sound of a jet airliner high in the sky outside. He wished he were on it. He wished he'd stayed in the car. He wished he was anywhere else but here. This – the whole mess of human entanglement and the emotional fallout that seemed to be inevitable when people bumped too close together – was exactly what he wanted to avoid. And yet, he reminded himself, this was real. It was about real things, the kind of experiences writers watched and stole away to make their own. He wanted to watch but he couldn't help feeling that he belonged in the drama. If he hadn't seen Tommy on the bridge, if he hadn't come with him to Liverpool… but it was too late for 'ifs'. He was present in the moment and as the warring parties squared up for the mother of all battles, he felt like he was hanging on to the sidelines only by his fingernails.

Tommy stared at the closed door. He looked like all the air had been sucked out of him by the explosive force of Frankie's reaction. Then Rose's comment – a carefully delivered grenade of blame that would level any remaining doubts that his was an unwanted presence.

"What?" said Tommy incredulously, his palms raised like an Italian restaurateur in the face of a difficult customer. "All I did was say hello."

"You can't just expect to turn up after eight years and expect her

133

to welcome you with open arms," said his wife, with a knowing look.

"What was I supposed to do?"

Rose stared at him. Still the same old Tommy. The poor-me-it-wasn't-my-fault Tommy. The same old mystified surprise that anyone might be in the slightest bit upset, hurt, offended or just generally pissed off with him. He'd never been any different, always getting by on cheek and charm. God, it had worn thin over the years they were together. Rose knew that much.

"You should have thought of that," she said levelly, "before you walked out."

Tommy flushed and his eyes narrowed. "Don't start in, Rosemary," he snapped, using his wife's full name for emphasis, "I've only just walked through the door."

It was the wrong thing to say, and as soon as he'd opened his mouth he knew that his size 10 feet would fit very comfortably in there.

"And you're lucky I let you in over the front step!" she screamed. Her iciness had melted and was now a torrent of anger in full flood. "What d'you mean, 'don't start in'?! Eight years without a bloody word – *eight years!* – and you think you can turn up here in a fancy suit telling me what to do? Start in? I'll bloody start in all right…"

"Ach, come on now Rose," replied Tommy, back-pedalling as fast as he could, "I've driven all the way from London to find you…"

"And you can just get back in your stolen car," she cut in, "and drive back there!"

Tommy protested, trying to explain that he hadn't stolen it. It was pointless. Rose was pouring out her anger and her bitterness and her frustration and Tommy was not going to be able to hold back the tide that threatened to engulf him.

But as soon as she'd begun, she stopped, as though someone had turned off the tap. Biting her lip she looked away from Tommy and towards Paul, who was desperately attempting to appear oblivious to the situation around him, like he was a stick of furniture or some other inanimate object.

Realising the lad's presence had forced Rose to clam up, Tommy mouthed a silent "fuck off" towards him. Paul responded with a quizzical look, forcing Tommy to repeat himself, again silently but this time with emphasis, as though talking to a very old and very deaf man.

Finally he got the message, and picking himself up from the sofa, he shuffled past the couple and, mumbling an excuse about going for a walk, headed towards the door. As he did, he checked his pocket for a book he shoved in there from his bag on the way up the M6. *Naked Lunch*, by William Burroughs. It was still there. He tapped it reassuringly and opened the door, glad to breathe air that didn't crackle with the electricity of conflict. Outside, he looked up and down the lane. There didn't seem to be any signposts or street names or people. He was struck by the power of the silence all around him. Which way should he go? And what would he find when he got there? There were only two choices here, left or right, but he was struck by indecision. To his right, a few more houses and what seemed to be the start of the village proper. To his left, the road they'd come from. He decided to turn right, towards civilisation.

As he walked, he reflected on what had just taken place before his eyes. It was hard to understand why Tommy would risk such a bruising encounter with people he'd obviously hurt so badly. If you did something to someone that upset them, you didn't tend to go back. It was like a dog cocking its leg on a place it had previously pissed on. Why? Surely Tommy knew he wasn't wanted here?

Families, eh? Paul shook his head, puzzled at Tommy's determination to land himself in hot water. It was much better to keep away, he reflected. That had been his way. When his mum got married, had the twins and taken herself off to Spain to run the bar, that was that. He'd known he wasn't wanted, and that hanging around, especially near Steve, the guy she married, was just creating a difficult situation for them all. Steve was so different to the kind of bloke he imagined his mum would meet and fall for – loud, boozy, boorish, full of dreams and schemes and get-rich-quick ideas. The bar in Spain was only one of a long list of business ventures. They'd been there six years now. Paul hadn't visited. Steve wouldn't have wanted him there and besides, pole dancing bars really weren't his thing. Mum had the twins to bring up, Steve had the bar to run. They were busy people. They hadn't time for visitors, especially insular wallflowers like Paul.

Paul turned his pallid face to the afternoon sun, soaking it up like a heat lamp, feeling it seep through his bones and penetrate his natural gloom. Ahead was a low stone wall, alongside which ran a pretty stream. The wall bordered a vast field which swept up the fellside. Somewhere up there, sheep were bleating while rooks cawed overhead. It was idyllic. He would sit on the wall and read a couple of chapters of *The Naked Lunch*. He'd just got to the part where the patrons of the café were about to eat the meat of a giant centipede while Mugwumps dispensed addictive fluid from their heads…

*

Rose handed Tommy his tea, served in a delicate-looking cup and saucer. She sat opposite him and watched, giving no outward hint of any amusement as he struggled to hold the cup and saucer daintily in his workman's mitt.

"Best china, Rose?" He was trying to keep it light.

"You're a guest," she replied curtly. "Guests get china. Anyway, the rest is broken."

Tommy laughed, perhaps a little too loudly. Rose glanced at him, her bottom lip trembling. Not with anger this time, but with pain, sadness and years of suffering. His laughter withered away.

"I thought you were dead, Tommy," she said, her eyes filling with tears, "I thought you were dead. All the other times, you always came back. Maybe a week later. Sometimes longer. But you always came back to me."

She was losing her composure. A tear fell on to her cheek and red patches flushed all around her neck. Putting the cup down gently, Tommy rose and leaned out to put an arm of comfort around his wife but with anger and embarrassment she shoved him away roughly, hurriedly drying her eyes with the sleeve of her blouse.

"I was stupid enough to take you back," she said, casting her damp eyes downwards. The mask was firmly back in place. She paused, then looked up, composed, and with a steely strength Tommy hadn't seen in her before.

"Things are different now," she finally said. "I'm different. What do you want, Tommy?"

He was flustered and confused.

"Nothing. I mean… I thought I could, you know, just look in."

Rose puffed herself up in her seat. If he thought he was going to get away with it so casually, like a neighbour popping round for a spare bin liner, he had another thing coming.

"Oh, 'look in'," she said, her eyes glittering with righteous sarcasm. "Is that what you thought? Right. Well, that's just grand. What a *wonderful* idea. You were always one for the good ideas."

She glared at him, still astonished that he could be so flippant.

"Well now," she said, dropping the sarcasm and sucking in her cheeks, "you've had your look in, so I suggest you finish your tea and get back to whichever boozer you call home these days."

Again, Tommy put up his hands in protest. Rose was having none of it.

"You can't just waltz back in, upset everyone and disappear off again. No way. Which is what you were planning, I would say."

She paused, watching him like a snake watches a rabbit. He stared hard at the carpet.

"It is, isn't it?" she said. "So it's business as usual, hmm? Well I'm not having it, Tommy. I won't have Frankie upset like that again, ever. You've no idea what that little girl was like when you left."

No, he had no idea. None at all. The unique and horrible combination of grief, pain, confused soul-searching and seething, inward anger that comes from being abandoned by a parent. The countless nights that Frankie spent in her mother's bed, crying hard and cuddling up to her like a toddler. Trying to get through days filled with the normal stresses and strains of teenagehood, but overlaid with despair and distraction as she tried to work out why her Daddy had gone without a word. He had no clue about any of that.

"If I could just talk to her…" said Tommy, still not looking up.

"You're too late," said Rose, matter-of-factly. "She won't have anything to do with you." He might as well hear the truth. There was no point telling him anything else.

It was what he expected, but it tore at him all the same. But if she wouldn't – and who could blame her? – maybe her mother might. He stared up, and gave Rose his best little-boy look. It was a high risk strategy. She'd see through it, for sure, but she might allow him a minute's grace.

"And what about you, Rosie?" he said, dropping in the pet name as a softener.

He was hardly worth a fiddler's fart, sitting there putting on those awful cow eyes for her. But perhaps it wasn't worth turfing him out just yet. Her curiosity was beginning to get the better of her. What had he been doing for the past eight years? And did he give a shite about all the upset and the damage he caused? She hardly wanted to know, but still…

She nodded at him, tight-lipped. "I'll hear you out," she said, "and that's as good as it gets. You'll have a sandwich, will you?"

It was more of a statement than a question, but her natural grace and good manners weren't going to desert her, even if her husband had. She stood up and went into the kitchen, but just as her back turned Tommy doubled over in the most excruciating pain. His face scrunched into a tight ball of silent agony as he grabbed his stomach. He didn't want Rose to see him this way.

As she pottered in the kitchen, opening cupboards and clattering around in the drawer for a butter knife, Tommy dosed himself with several of the orange pills from the bottle he had in his jacket pocket. It wasn't good to have had this now, not here, but after some deep breathing he felt the pain subside and he eventually unknotted his body from the pain-wracked foetal position he had suddenly been forced into. He got up, stretched, and walked into the kitchen.

"So," said Rose, placing a plate of ham sandwiches heavily on to the kitchen table at which he now sat, "you might as well come and eat."

He didn't feel like eating after the attack, but to refuse would be fatal. There was more tea, too. The room was warm and comfortable, and Rose looked slightly less fearsome than before. He had to be careful not to provoke her – though it wouldn't be easy.

"How is she then?" he inquired through a mouthful of bread, ham and tomato.

"She's fine. Well, as fine as any young girl can be. I feel like putting up a sign – 'Beware of the Daughter'."

"That's my fault," replied Tommy, keen to acknowledge his guilt.

"Yes. Well. Not all of it, maybe. Ninety five per cent."

Tommy nodded, and paused for reflection for a moment.

"Is she doing well," he asked, "you know, at school and all that?"

"School?" Rosemary was incredulous. What did he think she was? "For the love of God, Tommy, she's 22 years old."

"Right, yes. I knew that," said Tommy, covering up his ignorance. "I meant college, or…"

He tailed off. Christ. Of course she was. She'd only been a wee slip of a thing when he'd last seen her. Missed her 21st and everything.

"She's working now," continued Rose, "up at the Travel Lodge."

"Right you are," said Tommy, still startled at his daughter's maturity. "And, er, boyfriends?"

"Hm," replied his wife tersely, "more than I know, I'm sure.

139

You've seen her."

"Sure, she's a fine looking girl," said Tommy, "just like her mother." He couldn't resist it.

"Just as well."

Tommy grinned at the retort, pleased at the little spark of humour between them. He took another bite of his sandwich and, in lieu of anything else to say for the moment, looked around the room. At the far end was a reclining chair that faced a mirror. Above it, a free-standing hairdryer of the kind usually found in old-fashioned hairdressers.

"What's with all that stuff?" he asked, his mouth bulging with sandwich.

"It's mine."

Well now, this was a surprise. A career woman, was it?

"You? A hairdresser?"

"Yes," replied Rose, "don't sound so shocked. I've found something I love doing and I'm bloody good at it. Just locals, mind, but the money comes in handy."

Tommy smiled and patted his tousled head. "I could do with a bit of a trim meself," he smirked.

"Yes, well I could have done with a husband for the last eight years, but we don't always get what we want, do we Tommy?"

Cowed, Tommy took another bite of his sandwich. He'd overstepped the mark. Better to stick to the facts.

"And your man there," said Rose. "The chatty lad. Who's he?"

Shit. He knew she would ask. He was hardly the type he'd be running round with in normal life, and she knew it.

"Him?" he said breezily. "Oh, he's just a fella I know. Bit of a sad sack, not much going on. Thought I'd take him out for a bit."

The lying arse. But she wasn't going to probe any further. Not her business any more. She picked up Tommy's plate and dunked it into the sink of almost-cold water.

"So what do you think of the suit, Rose?" asked Tommy, keen to move the conversation on. "You always liked me in a pin-stripe, did you not?"

"That I did," she said, raising her eyebrows, "that I did. But, you know, fancy suit aside, you're looking like five pounds of shite in a three pound bag, Tom. I'd say you've not been looking after yourself. Where've you been all this time? What've you been doing?"

Too late, she realised what she'd said. She was curious, but she didn't want to show it. He needed to see that whatever he was up to, she couldn't care less about it. Or him. She turned back to the sink.

"No, forget it," she said sharply, pulling herself up, "I don't want to know."

"Ah well," said Tommy, glad he didn't have to elaborate, "enough about me, anyways. How've you been? I mean, in yourself?"

She hesitated at the sink as the stupid small talk he was trying to make lashed across her shoulders. How the hell did he fecking think she'd been?

"What, you mean after working at four jobs to pay off the debts you left behind?" she spat, not looking round. "Being so tired I thought I was dying? Struggling to put food on our daughter's table and shoes on her feet? Me, I'm *grand*."

Her words hung between them like icicles on a washing line. Tommy, head bowed once more in shame, said nothing. Inside, she was seething. Not so much for the idiot question he'd asked her, but because she'd been forced for a moment to contemplate a past she had worked so hard to escape from. But it was all different now. She took a deep breath and turned to face him.

"Actually, Tommy, I am. Grand, that is. I've made a new life for us up here and for the first time in ages I'm grand. And you know what? I want it to stay that way."

Tommy was quiet. She'd changed so much, and yet, she was still his Rose. The sparkiness and verve he had fallen in love with 25 years ago had not been extinguished. It was time. He put his hand in his jacket pocket and reached for the fresh handkerchief. Carefully he unwrapped it, remembering how her eyes had shone

141

when he took her down to the jewellers, all that cash burning a hole in his pocket and all of it going on this one little thing, the biggest token of affection he'd ever given anyone, before or since.

Again, her eyes widened as she stared at it, this piece of treasure that had been lost for so long, and represented all that had gone sour between them.

"Is that my ring?" she said suspiciously.

He nodded. "It is."

She bit her lip, hardly able to reach out and touch it. So much water had passed under the bridge since she first slipped it on her finger.

"You found it… how?"

There was no way he could explain it. She simply didn't need to know. He had his secrets. This would stay one of them.

"Just… just don't ask."

"I always wanted Frankie to have it," she said.

Tommy stepped closer to her, shadowing her with his whole body. It felt like the first time, all those years ago.

"Put it on," he whispered, "it'll still fit. You haven't put on a pound since…"

He held it out to her. She took it and slipped it on her wedding finger. It fitted perfectly. A radiant smile broke all over her face as she looked at it, turning it this way and that to allow the low afternoon sun to glint off it. She remembered that day at the jewellers, how she had laughed and told him to stop being an idiot when he said he was going to buy it, right there, right then. He'd had it planned, of course, but it still felt like the most wonderfully spontaneous act in the world. And then it disappeared to God knows where – although she had a damned good idea – and along with it went her husband and the father of her child, like a thief in the night.

Tommy smiled, feeling like some old-fashioned hero from a half-forgotten fairy tale. But there was to be no happy ending here. Rose's ray of happiness had gone, eclipsed by the thunder clouds which hung low over her brow. She turned away from him, trembling and hung on to the sink for support.

"You're a bastard, Tommy Cassidy," she breathed, hardly able to get the words out for the sobs racking her entire frame, "you're a bastard."

There was nothing for it. He had dreamt of doing it but, fearful of being on the receiving end of a well-aimed fist, he had resisted. As she pulled the ring from her finger and dropped it into a dish on the window sill, Tommy swept her into his arms, holding her so tightly he thought he'd never let go. Jesus, it was so good to hold her again. It was like bathing in an oasis after years in the wilderness.

Suddenly she screamed, and wrenched herself away from him, staring at the kitchen window in horror and alarm. On the other side, staring back and looking equally startled, was the pallid, skinny face of Paul, his jaw hanging loose in surprise under his striped woolly hat.

CHAPTER 15

Paul had sat on the low stone wall for what had seemed like an eternity. The book was interesting enough, but he'd seen the David Cronenberg film first and somehow he couldn't separate the characters in the novel from those on the screen. It was beginning to distract him. Not only that, but he felt out of place with a novel like *Naked Lunch*. A drug-fuelled road trip across a psychedelic landscape bore little relation to his current resting spot, and the wild, acid-fried antics of Bill Lee and company were in sharp contrast to the groups of mainly elderly, waterproof-jacketed ramblers passing by him at intervals and murmuring their polite "good afternoons". It was nice enough here, but a touch too genteel.

Besides, his bony backside was getting sore and as the sun started to drop behind the fells the air had turned chilly. He looked at his watch. Surely Tommy would have been ejected by now? The mood she was in, he couldn't have lasted more than a few minutes in her frosty company. She looked as hard as nails. Not a woman to be tangled with and definitely not one to walk out on. He was probably sitting in the car right now, nursing his wounds. Paul felt sympathetic to both Rose and Tommy. He'd done a terrible thing to her, leaving her and the girl like that, but he had tried to make it all right in his own cack-handed way. Frankie wasn't going to stand it for a second, and the way things were looking Rosemary wasn't far behind her daughter.

He hopped down from the wall and decided to go back to the house. Tommy might feel like a pint or two on the way home. They could stop at a pub. Let Tommy drown his sorrows. Paul would drive back south. Just go through the night until they hit London, and sleep in on Sunday. Hang around for the rest of the day, and get ready for Monday.

Monday… the thought of that day's events unfolding before his eyes was unsettling, and it pricked at him uncomfortably. He shrugged it off, looking over his shoulder at the vast fellside and the shores of the lake, trying to recall the first lines of Wordsworth's *Prelude* poem that had been so famously inspired by the magisterial power of these very hills.

He trudged back up the lane. 'Oh there is a blessing in this gentle breeze / A visitant that while it fans my cheek…' What came next? Something about green fields and escaping from the vast city. Finding a home in this landscape. He couldn't recall it precisely. No matter. There would be plenty of time and space to study it in the future.

As he reached Rosemary's house he noticed that the Mercedes was still parked outside, and empty. Tommy must still be in there. He didn't want to disturb him, but he didn't want to hang around outside for much longer. It was getting cold, and he needed to know what was going on. He walked up the path to the front door then hesitated. If he knocked, would it be Tommy or Rose who answered? If it was Tommy, that would be okay. But if it was Rosemary… He hadn't yet spoken to her. He hadn't even been introduced to her. He felt embarrassed about standing on her doorstep, trying to explain who he was, why he was there.

He paused on the doorstep. It might be better to be cautious and peep through the window first. If they were still talking, arguing, whatever, he could maybe sit in the car. Unless Tommy was ready to go, of course.

Stealthily he crept to the kitchen window and peered in. There was Tommy, close behind Rosemary. There was some kind of movement. Christ… she was in his arms. It must have gone well, better than he…

"Jesus, who the hell is that??!!"

The screech of fear from Rosemary, clearly audible outside, caused Paul to recoil from the window in shock. *Shit*. He'd clearly intruded on a very private moment. Tommy must have laid on the

145

charm thicker than a triple-decker bus.

He would soon find out exactly what Tommy thought. The front door flew open and out he came, running towards him like a wild bull. He grabbed him by his collar and pushed him out of earshot of Rosemary.

"What the fuck are you doing, gawping through windows?" hissed the Irishman, his face redder than his tie.

"Nothing," coughed Paul, attempting to wrestle himself out of Tommy's grip. "I was just… um…"

"You were just what?" shouted Tommy.

Irritated, Paul pushed Tommy off. "I was bored, alright?" he snapped. "Are you done yet?"

Now it was Tommy's turn to be irritated. Who the hell was he, asking him if he was 'done yet'?

"Bored? You little shite," he snarled. "This is my fucking time and I have 36 hours to do as I please. Got it? Now go and be bored some-place else."

Tommy was about to remind Paul that sheep up here outnumbered people by 20 to 1, and if he played his cards right he might get a date for the evening, but Paul was spared it by the front door swinging open and Rosemary standing in the doorway, hands on hips.

"Everything okay out here?" she called.

"Everything's grand," replied Tommy, turning towards her. "The lad's just asking where he'd find a local hostelry. Weren't you?"

Paul nodded, a little over-enthusiastically. Tommy and Rosemary obviously had unfinished business to attend to and Tommy looked like a man who'd been caught, if not quite with his trousers down, then something approaching it, albeit from a considerable distance.

"Oh," said Rose, "it's just down there by the lake. I'm surprised you didn't see it."

Of course he'd seen it. He just hadn't been in. As a stranger, his presence would have attracted looks from the regulars and he hated drawing attention to himself. So he'd walked by it. Now he was being ordered to go there and if Tommy was playing the long game with Rosemary it would be the only place he could hole up in as night fell.

"Right," he mumbled in the direction of Rosemary, "Okay. Thanks. I'll, um, go and… take another walk then."

Off he went, Tommy's glaring eyes following him down the lane. When he was safely out of sight Tommy indicated to Rose, by pointing to his head and pulling out his tongue, that Paul was quite clearly bananas. Then he strolled up the path to the house, the mild-mannered penitent once again.

*

Paul entered The Crown Pub, his hands shoved deeply into his pockets and without looking left or right, headed for the bar. He ignored a group of young, hearty-looking local lads who were gathered in one corner, idly throwing darts into a dartboard and laughing uproariously at some in-joke. The very act of Paul ignoring them drew attention and a few of the youths nudged one another and nodded in his direction. Compared to them, with their broad shoulders and ruddy, farmers' boys' faces, he looked almost ill, his colourless expression matching the texture of his skin.

In as low a voice as possible, fearful of giving away his southern accent, Paul asked for a pint of bitter and, having already spotted an unoccupied table in the corner of the oak-beamed bar, he mooched over and sat down. He pulled his book from his jacket pocket, opened it at the folded page and started to read, slowly sipping his pint.

But the book still wasn't doing it for him. It was meant to be a classic, but it felt far too chaotic. The jumbled, kaleidoscopic narrative, where everything kind of melted into everything else, reminded him of his existence in London – the noise, unpredictability and edgy people. He couldn't wait to get away from it. The Lake District was exactly the kind of place he hoped he could run away to. So why did he feel almost as intimidated and nervous here as he did at home? Was it the place he was running away from? Or was it himself? And if he found himself out somewhere like this, who was to say that he'd feel any different?

He was looking at the pages, but barely reading the words. He wondered what was going on back at Rosemary's. Had Tommy charmed her into taking him back? He saw himself going back to London alone, fifteen hundred quid lighter and barely a "thank-you" from Tommy for saving his life and helping to patch up his marriage. And, of course, no chance of pulling off the 'Three and Out' rule. Not in the time he had left. Cheers, Tommy. Hope you're happy now.

He took another swig of his pint and looked at his watch. No point going back yet. He didn't want to suffer the embarrassment of having to walk in there for a second time. If he just kept his head down, no-one would notice him anyway.

The heavy door of the pub unlatched itself and swung open. Paul looked towards it. His stomach lurched when he saw Frankie enter with a group of friends. She was greeted warmly by the lads gathered around the bar. Popular girl – which was hardly surprising considering the way she looked. Paul put his head down again, pretending to read. He didn't want to get into a conversation with her and he was sure she wouldn't recognise him anyway. Very few people ever did.

But he was wrong. Frankie had her mother's eye for detail and her father's way of never missing a trick. She had scanned the pub to see if any more of her friends were here and her gaze now rested on Paul. He looked up again, conscious that someone was watching him, and he caught her eye. She squinted slightly as though trying to place him and involuntarily he gave her a feeble little wave.

The penny dropped immediately. Pushing past a small group of resting ramblers, she marched her way over to where he was sat, her face as dark and as hard as the wooden panels on the walls around the bar.

She stood over him, hands on her hips, echoing her mother's determined stance.

"Why did you bring him here?" She wasn't going to mention 'him' by name. She didn't need to.

"He's an arsehole," she continued, "and if you're a mate of his, you're an arsehole too."

Paul began to stammer an excuse – something about not really knowing him. Frankie cut him off mid-flow.

"Look, you can just take him back to whatever hole he crawled out of. He's nothing to me."

She spat out the last sentence with a sneer on her face that wouldn't have disgraced the pages of the *NME*. She looked every inch the punk princess, especially when she was angry.

One of her friends, a beefy, blonde-haired boy wearing a green combat jacket, took a step closer to Paul.

"He bothering you, Frankie?" he said, pushing the question in Paul's direction.

"No," said Paul defensively, "I'm not bothering her."

Frankie didn't speak. She looked Paul up and down. Bit of ratboy. She wondered what he did for a living. Some kind of dealer? Nah, way too nervous-looking for that. Maybe a repair man or a gardener. Something like that.

Then she caught sight of the book on the table and her perception shifted slightly. She'd heard of that book. Wasn't it all about mad people taking drugs somewhere out in the States? She gave him the once-over again. Maybe she hadn't read him quite right.

She turned to the hovering males and, like an ancient Roman empress deciding the outcome of a gladiatorial battle, dismissed them with a wave of her hand and a "leave him".

"I want to hear what he's got to say for himself," she added, curiosity getting the better of her anger.

The boys mooched back to the bar, slightly disappointed that a bit of aggro wasn't going to happen. At least not tonight.

"What's your name?" she asked, still in the commanding hands-on-hips position.

149

"Paul," he mumbled.

"Well, Paul," she said, "seeing as you're here and I want to find out more about what the fuck is going on at home, I reckon you owe me a drink. Then we can have a little chat."

Paul looked towards the bar, and the lads regrouped around it. There was no way out. Reluctantly, he lifted himself off his chair and put his hand in his pocket.

"No," said Frankie, stopping him, "it's okay. I'll go. But you can give me the money."

Gratefully he handed her a fiver and in a few minutes she sat back down, a pair of pints in her ring-bedecked hands.

"So Paul," she said, fixing her gaze on the uncomfortable person sitting opposite her, "if you don't really know him, what are you doing here?"

He could have asked himself the same question and still not got a satisfactory answer. But now he was in the spotlight.

"I'm… erm… it's research. I'm a writer."

Frankie let out a sardonic laugh. "Well I hope you're not writing about that shit-bag. Unless it's a tragedy."

He looked at her sharply. He liked that word. Was it a tragedy, all this?

"No," he said, shaking his head, "it's nothing like that. I'm just here, you know, soaking up the atmosphere, looking for new ideas. I only came along for the ride, really."

It sounded lame, and he knew it. But she didn't seem to care about what he was doing here personally. It was "him" who'd made her angry in the first place.

"Yeah, well," she said, shaking her head, "he's a fucker, so watch yourself."

"Ah, he's alright."

For a moment, Paul had forgotten who he was speaking to. He started to back-pedal. "I mean… no… obviously he's a shit, but…"

Opposite, the heart-shaped face had scrunched into a pained

scowl. Paul's half-justification of Tommy as an alright guy had hurt her. At that moment, he saw through the attitude and glimpsed the damaged young person inside.

"Jeez..." he said finally. "You must really hate him. Did you never get on?"

She wanted to take her time with the answer, but she knew she couldn't. Once upon a time, she'd had the best dad in the world. He was her world. Mam could be bossy, keeping a grip on everything around her, as usual, but Dad... Dad was just a big laugh of a man. He teased her and tickled her, threw her high into the air so she almost bounced off the ceiling of the small flat. He pretended to be a monster and chased her through every room. He peeped in on her at night when he thought she was asleep and gave her big, tender, beery kisses. He picked her up when she was crying and wiped away her fears and her tears. Her heart belonged to him, and in the end he just stamped on it, the fucking shit, and threw it in the nearest rubbish bin.

"I guess so," she said, looking away from Paul. "He was brilliant when I was little. He just filled the place up, like a big bear. And when he left, it was like a big hole where he'd been."

God, that was an understatement. It was like... it was like nothing she could ever explain properly, to anyone. She felt like a tree that had been pulled out by its roots. He didn't even tell her why. He couldn't even be bothered to leave a note or a message on the phone. Nothing. What had they done, her and her mam, that was so terrible to justify such a bloody harsh punishment?

She still couldn't look at Paul. He sensed her pain and saw the slight hint of tears behind her kohl-rimmed eyes. He knew she wouldn't let go in front of him, a complete stranger, and he would not push her any further. Her hurt was plain for all to see.

She turned back to him and forced a half-smile.

"So," she said, "you're a writer, eh? Anything I might have read?"

He looked at her. Christ, it was a serious question.

"No," he replied, smiling shyly, "not yet. One day."

She smiled back and lifted her pint glass. To his surprise, and sneaking admiration for something he couldn't possibly do himself, she drained the rest of it, at least half a pint, in one long go. He laughed as she slammed the glass down on the table, belched and asked him cheekily whether he'd fancy another. Not entirely her mother's daughter, then.

"No," he said, "I'd better get back." The memory of Tommy suddenly loomed large. Surely they'd have finished now?

"Don't be daft," said Frankie, rattling his half-full glass in front of him in a 'drink-up, lightweight' gesture, "it's still early yet. Don't you like being here?"

She cocked her head to one side as she sang out the words. Paul, flustered at her self-confidence, glanced away. The attractive female opposite him compounded his general discomfort.

"No," he began, "I mean… yes. Of course I do. It's just, well, d'you think… they'll be okay? At the house?"

"What?" said Frankie, smiling again, "you think they're gonna kill each other?"

"Well yeah," mumbled Paul, "something like that."

Frankie sighed. "She's never killed him yet. But there's always hope, I suppose."

Chapter 16

"God Almighty," said Rose, sitting down heavily on the chair by the kitchen table. "One minute I'm living a perfectly normal life and the next *you* land up on the doorstep with some Peeping Tom in tow. You don't do things by halves, do you?"

Tommy stood over her, concerned. That fool of a lad he'd landed himself with had shaken her up all right, staring in at them through the bloody window. God knows, he was a liability. Still, he was out of the way now. He wouldn't come back in a hurry. Hopefully…

"You look a bit shaken there, Rose," said Tommy. "Maybe I could make you another cup of tea. Or… something a little stronger, perhaps?"

Rose paused. He was asking her for a drink. The cheek. That damned stuff almost ruined her life. For a long time after he'd gone, she wouldn't have it in the house. Just the smell of it reminded her of him, rolling in at all hours, talking all sorts of crap. After a few years she relented, realising that it wasn't really drink, or gambling for that matter, that had spoiled her marriage. It was the man she married who was to blame.

"And what'll happen if I say yes, Tommy?" she said, her eyes locked firmly on to his. "Will you be joining me for one? Or will you be swimming in it come the end of the night, hmm?"

Tommy shook his head emphatically. "I'm not like that anymore, Rose. Honestly. I've learned me lesson. Besides, I can't…"

He halted in mid-sentence. Sensing something she pressed him.

"You can't what?"

"I… I can't drink a whole lot, anyway," he replied, avoiding her eye. "It gives me a dicky stomach. Christ knows what they're putting in it these days."

"The same as they always did," retorted Rose. "Maybe it's because you put enough of it into yourself over the years. But, you know what, I will have a drink. It's certainly been one of those days."

She stood up and reached into a cupboard, fishing out a bottle of Jameson's whiskey that was three-quarters full and setting it down on the kitchen work surface. She picked a whiskey tumbler from the shelf, then turned to Tommy.

"So… will you have one too? Or will I put the kettle on for you?"

"Ach, you know me Rose," said Tommy, smiling, "one never did me any harm."

"No," she replied, reaching for a second glass, "you're right. One never did you any harm. It was all the ones that followed."

She placed the bottle and the glasses down on the table. She sat down again, Tommy placing himself opposite her. She unscrewed the top of the bottle and carefully poured two decent measures of the amber liquid before screwing the top on again.

"So…" she said, raising her glass, "slainte."

"Slainte."

Tommy raised his glass, returning the traditional Gaelic toast. The whiskey tasted good, with just the right amount of afterburn that momentarily numbs the senses before bringing them back into sharp focus.

They paused, allowing the liquor to seep like lava into their blood. Then, Tommy looked up reflectively from his glass.

"I don't have any answers for you, Rose," he said.

She stared at him. "That's all right, Tommy. I stopped asking the questions years ago."

He wanted to explain, get her to try to understand, say he was sorry. But she'd cut him off at the pass. He had to keep trying to find a way through. That was what he'd come here for. He couldn't rest until he had.

"The closest I can get," he said, pausing while he formulated the words slowly, "is that I'm like a shark, Rose."

Her eyebrows arched. "And what does that mean?"

He sucked his cheeks in while he prepared to explain the nub of his analysis. "I think, like, if I stop swimming, I'll die."

He leaned back slightly, proud of his own profundity. There now. See what she would make of that.

Rosemary sniffed, a dainty one at first, then a couple more, accompanied by a theatrical wrinkling of her nose.

"Can you smell something?" she said, her face turning towards Tommy with a look of slight contempt.

"Ach, come on now Rose…" He knew what she was getting at. She always did have a nose for it.

"Oh, I know what it is," she said. "Bullshit. That's what."

He tried another tack. "So what would you say I am?"

"Well," she replied confidently, knowing she was about to skewer him, "if a shark is a cold-blooded, selfish creature only concerned with its own wants and needs, then you're not far away, Tommy."

The dig hurt him. He was only trying to explain. It was vanity, comparing himself to such an unpredictable, fascinating and dangerous creature, but it was how he saw himself. He'd never seen the shark metaphor from another point of view. Now he knew it wasn't necessarily how others saw him. His bubble was well and truly burst.

"Is that what you think I am, Rose?" he asked, hoping not to hear any further home truths, but knowing that he probably would.

"Me?" she said, in mock-astonishment, "No, Tommy. I think you're a lying, cheating scumbag who gambled away everything we had, and more, pissed the rest up the wall and then disappeared without a word. You're the lowest of the low and I don't know why I have you in the house."

He was submerged in her anger and contempt. And yet, there was a look on her face that suggested a glimmer of something else. He knew his Rose. She would say a thing, and mean it, but she wouldn't totally close down. Not entirely.

"I guess that's not very good, then?" he said, hoping that the deliberate understatement would draw out something softer from her.

"No, Tommy," she said, reaching for the bottle and pouring out two more measures, "it's not."

She was emphatic, sure enough, but the fire that had greeted him when he first arrived had died down now. He might have been mistaking it for pity – she was right, he did look like five pounds of shite, despite the suit – but he was sure he'd seen a flicker in her grey-green eyes. Memories of better times? There were plenty of those, at least in the beginning. Or maybe it was something stronger? The whiskey? Or could it be... well, was it love? He knew what he felt, but did she feel the same?

Outside, the light was fading fast over the hillside and the songbirds were gone. The silence of the remote valleys lay like a blanket of snow across the landscape. As with the fall of night in all mountainous regions, it had suddenly become cold. Rose put on the lights in the living room while Tommy sat in the kitchen in silent contemplation. Automatically, she reached for the small shovel in the coal scuttle and heaped a pile on to the waiting grate. She stopped short and got up from her knees, resting one arm on the mantelpiece. What was she doing?

She was doing what she always did in the evenings – lighting the fire, cooking something for her and Frankie, watching the TV, reading the paper, doing the crossword, going to bed. It was her routine – the way she did things, the way she wanted it to be. It made her feel safe, settled. A response to all the chaos and hell she had been through since...well, since. And here he was again, his feet under the kitchen table, talking about fecking sharks. Why the hell was he bothering? More so, why was she? She didn't love him any more. Did she? No. Not really. Maybe she actually felt sorry for him. Maybe that was it, this odd feeling that had crept over her in the last hour. Pity the poor bugger. He wasn't looking himself that was for sure. But all the same, he had come.

Well, he could have a warm by the fire then take himself off home or find a B&B somewhere. There were plenty of them this time of year. She bent down again and struck a match against the corner of a firelighter which poked out from under the coal. Then she went back into the kitchen.

"Come on out of here," she said to him, "we'll go in the living room. It's a bit more comfortable in there. Oh, and bring the bottle with you. It's not often I have Lazarus round for a drink."

He laughed at the joke and followed her with the whiskey and the glasses like an obedient butler. She motioned him to the sofa and sat in the armchair, perching her stockinged feet on a low coffee table in front of her.

"Well," he said, settling back, "this is nice."

"I've worked hard for it, you know," she said. "It hasn't been easy. But we're getting there. It's a good community up here. They look after each other. You have to."

"I would say you do," he replied. "You know, I went to the flat to find you."

"The Edenbridge? Jesus... if I didn't see that place again in a thousand years I wouldn't be sorry. I imagine I'm not missing much?"

"No," Tommy said. "It looks like an airliner fell on it and no-one bothered to sweep up. Though you know who's got the contract to redevelop it?"

"Go on..."

"Only Mickey Callaghan."

Rose recoiled at the memory of her husband's former friend. "Him? Hitler's evil twin? He's still alive and kicking, is he?"

"Well, he's alive," said Tommy, smirking faintly before remembering the recovery of the ring and changing the subject.

"You still like the music, Rose?"

"I do when I can get to the stereo," she said, raising her eyes to the ceiling and pointing upwards in the vague direction of Frankie's bedroom. "It hasn't bred out, either. I scream at her day and night to turn it down but she can't hear me. So I've given up that particular battle."

"Can't say I blame you," said Tommy. "So... will you put a record on?"

The drink had mellowed her. Some background music would cover the gaps in their conversation. There wasn't going to be any heavy talk now, that was for sure. She walked over to the stereo and after a glance up and down the rack selected a compilation CD of the early 1970s. The first track was Johnny Nash's '*I Can See Clearly Now.*'

Their feet tapped to the gentle reggae beat almost in unison, Rose singing the words softly under her breath. Tommy was sinking further and further into the sofa, the lyrics carrying him back to bright, sun-shining days long gone.

When it had finished, Tommy started chuckling to himself.

"What?" said Rose, coming out of her reverie.

"I was just thinking about Wicklow."

"What about Wicklow? You mean that time you disgraced yourself, running around half naked?"

God, he'd forgotten about that. They had just returned home from a holiday. He and Rose had gone down to Brittas Bay for a few days by the sea. Before he'd left Liverpool a friend working in a garment factory in Bradford had given him a load of knock-off clobber for a good price. He'd put on a brand spanking new shirt and taken Rose out for a meal at some fancy new Italian restaurant. Trouble was, whoever had made the shirt had left a handful of pins sticking out of the collar. The pins wouldn't budge so, in the middle of the restaurant, he simply whipped off the shirt and ate the rest of the meal in his string vest. The drunker he got the louder he became and there were complaints. Finally, he removed the vest and tied it round his head, pretending to be Rambo. To his anger and her deep embarrassment they were asked to leave. He was in the doghouse for many months afterwards, on a diet of bread, water and humble pie.

"No," replied Tommy, shaking his head at the memory. "I meant the singing competition. You were a star that night."

She smiled. Of course. The festival in Wicklow Town – a couple of days before he went streaking through the restaurant. She hadn't even wanted to enter, but he wouldn't let up until she did. There were some mighty fine voices in that part of Ireland back then. She was terribly nervous. The last time she'd sung in front of an audience was at school, and she was so sick with the fear of it all that she almost threw up down her Holy Communion dress. But she got herself on the stage in Wicklow and, shaking with nerves, took a hold of the microphone and, unaccompanied, began to sing.

"My Rosemary," said Tommy, proudly, "first prize. Go on... sing for me, Rose."

He looked at her with an affection she barely remembered.

"Go on," he repeated, "sing for me."

She waved her arm in dismissal. "Ach, get away with you," she said, "who do you think I am? The Rose of fecking Tralee?"

"Ah go on, Rose, please."

"I can't, Tommy," she said, "It's been years..."

"Course you can," he pleaded, "You've a gorgeous voice. Please. For me?"

She hesitated then began to sing softly under her breath. But it wasn't what Tommy wanted to hear. He wanted to listen to every word.

"Do it properly," he urged, "like in Wicklow. Go on."

She pursed her lips. "You're a menace, Tommy Cassidy," she said. Clearing her pipes with a cough she began to sing a melancholic air.

"Oh please ne'r forget me, though the waves now lie o'er me,
I was once young and pretty and my spirit ran free."

She noticed that he had stretched back and closed his eyes. He looked like some mad, mythical Irish warrior in all his finery, regally leaning back to be entertained. The silly bollocks. Still, it made him happy and for that she was glad. An eye for an eye, as some fella once said, makes the whole world blind.

"But destiny tore me from country and loved ones,
And from the new land I was never to see."

Jesus, she could still sing. And what words, too. Ironic, really. Destiny hadn't torn him from loved ones. Nothing so dramatic or noble. Just booze, cards, gee-gees, late nights, lousy fathering and utter selfishness. To think what other people did to keep their families together, emigrating across the world and so forth. He only went from Dublin to Liverpool, but it was still impossible to be a good husband and father. He couldn't make it up to them, not really. At least he'd seen them. Thank God he'd seen them.

"A poor emigrant's daughter, too frightened to know,
I was leaving forever the land of my soul."

But she was not frightened any more. Too much water had passed under the bridge for that. Besides, there was plenty to look forward to in life. The sentimental songs of the past didn't move her much. Though that was a lovely time, there in Wicklow Town, her just pregnant with Frankie and a husband so bloody proud of her he looked fit to burst. They'd seen the two days, all right.

"Amid struggle and fear, my parents did pray,
To place courage to leave o'er the longing to stay."

He opened his eyes and looked around the room, gazing at the photographs of Rose and Frankie. Some were taken before he'd left, some after. The subdued pair in the later photographs a stark contrast to the ones taken in happier times. But the most recent ones showed a mother and daughter reunited in happiness. The shadows of the fire licked across the walls of the song-filled room. What he had lost couldn't ever be counted, even if he spent a hundred years trying. And he didn't have that time left. Not even a fraction of it.

"And that," said Rose emphatically, finishing her song, "is more than you deserve."

He smiled at her with the kind of love and affection that made tears well up in his eyes. He looked away so she couldn't see.

"Beautiful," he said finally. "I'll die a happy man now I've heard that."

She blew out a breath of surprise. "You'll outlive us all. Only the good die young. So... where are you planning on staying? Or haven't you?"

He knew it would eventually come to this. He didn't want to go anywhere, not ever again. Like a siren, her song had called him back to her. He was home. Somehow, he'd get around Frankie, take her back in his arms and call her his little girl. She'd be fine. She just needed a long talk.

"Oh, you know," he said, looking slightly shifty, "I'll find somewhere or sleep in the car. You know me. I can sleep on a rope."

She shook her head and smiled. It was good to see him, she had to admit. He still had it, whatever it was that had sucked her in, God help her, all those years ago. She'd fallen hard for that combination of charm, looks and roguery, to her cost. But Jesus, she'd missed him – missed him so much that she'd almost blocked out the pain of missing him. Which sounded stupid, but it was how it was.

"You're a fecking torment, Tommy Cassidy. Alright then, you can have the spare room."

He grinned, unable to help himself. She saw it and, checking herself, nodded to him.

"But I want you out first thing in the morning."

Chapter 17

The Crown was getting busier. Saturday night brought the lads down from the remote hamlets and isolated farmhouses along the valley for their weekly booze-up. The air was thick with thudding beats from the jukebox and the beered-up shouts of young men on the piss and on the pull. It wasn't how Paul spent his Saturday nights. If he wasn't working, a takeaway, a bit of telly and a good book was his usual recipe for a thrilling weekend evening. In any other circumstances he would have been out of the door of the pub long before the hair gel and Hugo Boss crowd had occupied the bar area.

But tonight was different – very different. For some reason – and he had no idea why – he seemed to be an extremely attractive young woman's object of attention. She was the best-looking girl he'd seen in years. Maybe ever. He searched the limits of his experience but found no-one to compare to the vision that now sat in front of him, with her raucous laugh, wild streaked hair and liquid deep-brown eyes. His only encounter with a glorious specimen of womanhood such as this was between the pages of a Thomas Hardy novel. She was Eustacia Vye incarnate and he was... who was he? He was Paul Callow, an anonymous Tube train driver from London with all the personality of a tunnel-dwelling mouse. Why was she even remotely interested in him? What could he possibly say about his life that would entertain or intrigue her? And yet, it was happening. Here he was talking to her, making her laugh, drawing her in. What the hell was going on? Had someone crept upon him while he wasn't looking and transplanted Daniel Craig's head on to his skinny shoulders?

The truth was that Paul and girls went together like butter and bricks. It wasn't that he didn't have any luck, more that he had no idea how to create it. With no father figure there had been no-one to show him the ropes or teach him the tricks of the trade. He felt he was sensitive to women, but he had no idea how to trade that basic understanding for something more than casual acquaintanceship. When girls addressed him he became tongue-tied, inarticulate and idiotic. This was a cruel world. In all the odd casual encounters he'd had, where he could've made an impression, he'd completely blown it, never to get a second chance.

He simply didn't see himself as boyfriend material, unless she happened to be desperate or strange, or both. There had been a couple in the last few years. Bridget had a bowl haircut like Joan of Arc's and a martyred expression to match. She dressed entirely in black and had been totally unforthcoming with her favours, until she met a female DJ who fed her Ecstasy and married her in a nude ceremony on the island of Lesbos. Then there was Kate, a big, blonde, energetic-looking woman who'd chatted him up at a book club meeting and almost dragged him to her home for a demanding sexual workout, complete with high-pitched screaming and frenzied thrashing. In the morning he awoke to find Kate still asleep and three little pyjama-clad children standing at the end of the bed, smiling at their new "uncle". He gently made his excuses and left. That had been the last time. The *very* last time, he'd told himself.

As they talked, Frankie laughing and sometimes leaning in towards him over the table, he noticed her male friends around the bar occasionally throwing protectively hostile glances in his direction. He tried to ignore them. He could hardly blame them for keeping an eye on her. Despite her self-confidence and beauty, there was a vulnerability about her that brought out the knight in shining armour. He could feel it himself. Although he was shyly pleased to have her all to himself, he also felt oddly protective of her. Maybe it was the way she would raise a serious point then suddenly make light of it, as though she couldn't possibly allow anything more than flippancy or frivolity to enter her head. She was a bright girl, but seemed determined not to show it.

Or maybe it was just the way she drank, knocking back pint after pint with the practised ease of a docker. In his experience, people who drank like that were usually hiding behind it. Or was she simply out for a good, uncomplicated time? He couldn't decide, perhaps because he wasn't really sure himself what a good time was.

She was weaving her way back from the bar with yet another couple of pints on a tray, which also held two shot glasses full of liquid the colour of the Caribbean Sea.

"What the hell is that?" said Paul, eyeing the liquid suspiciously. He'd already had three pints, which was two over his usual limit. Whatever this was it could finish him off completely. He raised the glass and sniffed it.

"Go on," said Frankie, as though talking to an elderly hospital patient shying away from a new medicine, "get it down you. It'll do yer good."

He smiled. She still had a strong Scouse accent. She must have seemed like a visitor from another planet when she first arrived up here – like a flower in the desert.

Simultaneously they raised their glasses and with a "cheers", knocked their drinks back in one. It was some kind of flavoured and coloured vodka. The liquid raced around Paul's chest like a hot coal spat from a fire and he swallowed hard, trying not to cough. Frankie, seemingly unaffected by the drink, slammed down her glass and watched in amusement as her companion manfully struggled with his.

"So," he said, trying to regain his composure along with his breath, "you don't think there's any chance of them getting back together, do you?"

Frankie let out a shriek of alarm. "Mam and Dad? No way!"

No way, not a cat in hell's chance. Mam was well over him. She

164

hardly ever spoke about him and if she did it was in the past tense. Like he was dead, really. Which he might as well be.

It was what Paul wanted to hear, though he was fearful of showing it. He felt terrible for even thinking it, but if they were up at the house now, whispering sweet nothings to one another, that would be it. He'd have to go back alone, the plan in pieces. With so little time left, it was him and Tommy, or nothing. Judging by Frankie's reaction, the long journey south wouldn't be a solitary one.

Spotting a recently vacated space for two people by the open fire in the corner of the pub, Frankie jumped to her feet and indicated Paul to follow. Meekly, he did so and the pair sat opposite one another on old-fashioned but comfortable leather chairs. The drinks, the heat from the fire and the charms of the girl beside him were combining to make Paul feel more relaxed than he had been for weeks, perhaps months, or even years. The shifts spent at work, his teeth almost being rattled out of his head by the movement of the train, and those long, lonely days off, staring into a blank computer screen at a future which might never be his, were melting away. He felt the last hour with Frankie had been like one long sigh of relief, mixed with utter incredulity at his present position and the gorgeous company he was keeping.

She leaned in a little closer, her brown eyes reflecting his sallow features. Catching a glimpse of himself in them, he realised he looked like someone he didn't recognise. He was smiling, nodding, responding. He looked happy. Christ, he *actually looked happy*.

"So, tell me about London," she said with interest.

"Ah, I don't see much of it," he replied, resolving to tell her the truth. It was no less than she deserved. "I'm underground most of the time."

"Underground?"

"Yeah," he said, smiling sheepishly, wondering if this was the moment that her interest would wane and she'd head back to the bar and find her friends. "I'm a Tube driver, too."

She grinned, unable to hide her amusement. So he wasn't some

165

big novelist after all, just a bloody train driver. But she liked the way he'd told her. It was sweet.

"A writer who drives a Tube train, eh?" she teased. "*Very* glamorous. Just research for your novel, I suppose?"

Cheeky girl. He could've ducked out, got on his high horse about having to have a job, moaned about how much he hated it. But she was being playful, not spiteful. He would respond in kind.

"Oh yeah," he replied, trying to sound as deliberately offhand and pseudo-cool as he could, "it's all about a Tube driver… terribly handsome… comes to the Lake District… meets this feisty young girl who gives him a hard time… they get drunk…"

"Oh yeah…"

She was loving the wind-up. He was quite a laugh underneath it all. Not in an obvious way but there was definitely something going on there. A bit of a dork, but quite cute.

"And how does it end?" she said.

Paul took a deep breath, lowered his eyes and shook his head with feigned drama and deep emotion.

"Tragically," he replied, his face a mask of mock-sorrow.

Frankie let out a peal of laughter and, clutching her heart, pretended to swoon like a character out of a Victorian melodrama. Paul laughed too, pleased at her reaction and even more pleased with himself that he'd provoked it. This was like nothing he'd ever really experienced. He'd seen his mum like this when she first met Steve, just messing about, teasing each other, acting stupid. He didn't get it. It was like they were in some play with only themselves for an audience, and a highly appreciative one at that. Now, he was beginning to understand. Maybe Sartre was wrong. Maybe hell wasn't other people. Or maybe it was hell, but it could be heavenly too.

Suddenly his phone on the table in front of them began to vibrate and ring. As he reached to answer it Frankie dived in front of him and grabbed it. Before he could plead with her to give it back she had pressed the green 'answer' button.

"Hello," she chirped, "Paul's phone..."

He held out his hand for it back but it was useless. She was going to have her sport.

"No, I'm sorry, he can't come to the phone right now," she said, in her best posh Scouse receptionist's voice. "Can I take a message?"

As the caller spoke, she screwed up her face in puzzlement. The message had obviously been relayed and she hung up the phone.

"Apparently," she said, looking at him quizzically, "some foreign bloke says he makes tasty crackling and you shouldn't be afraid. What's all that about?"

Paul hesitated before speaking. "Oh, er, yeah, he's just a mate... a chef... wants me to try a new recipe."

For crying out loud. That Maurice freak again. It was nothing less than harassment. When he got back to London he'd have to change his number.

"See," said Frankie, who'd swallowed the excuse without question, "I don't know any fancy foreign chefs. You can't tell me it's not exciting living in London."

No," replied Paul, looking earnestly at her, "it's not exciting living in London."

It was such a myth, the whole London-is-the-capital-of-the-world thing. It was nothing like that. It was a city full of strangers, everyone shoving and pushing, looking like they were going somewhere but actually going nowhere. Some people swimming, others sinking. Most just treading water. It was a soul-destroying grind living in that place. If she wanted the truth about living in London she should ask her dad.

Frankie stared at him in disbelief. She hated it when people said London was rubbish. All the clubs and the bars and the famous people, all the gigs and restaurants and shops and nightlife and glamour. How could anybody say it wasn't exciting? They'd never lived round here, that's for sure.

"Oh come on," she said, "it must be?!"

"It's not," replied Paul, knowing how girls like Frankie were so easily sucked in by London, to be spat out again when their time had passed.

"It's like living in some huge crazy ant hill where nothing seems to work properly. Millions of people just getting in each other's way. No space, no air…"

"Then why don't you leave?" she challenged.

"I'm trying to but it's hard," he said. "If you've got money it's bearable, but if you're skint…you're trapped."

Trapped. He didn't know the meaning of the word.

"Try living here," she said, not prepared to compromise her view. "Everybody knows you and knows everything about you. Nothing changes, nothing ever happens."

She nodded towards the bar, ordering him with her eyes to look. The farm lads were all over a group of village girls. The girls had heard all their clumsy chat-up lines before and witnessed every permutation of their oafish behaviour on thousands of nights previous to this one. And still they were egging them on, flirting and teasing and having a laugh. It was Saturday night, for fuck's sake. They were letting their hair down, and why not?

"Round here," said Frankie, turning back to Paul, her eyes a mixture of contempt and pity, "their idea of a good time is to get shit-faced as quickly as possible and then shag anyone who'll let them. And then do it all again tomorrow. That's being trapped."

Paul smiled. He wanted to tell her that it was the same in London. Or Liverpool. Or Birmingham, Norwich, Leeds, Exeter, Bristol, wherever. That's how it was everywhere, wherever groups of people hung out, got drunk, tried to forget, or tried to remember who they once were. It was all the same the whole world over. He began to feel depressed again. But that wasn't fair. She was young and restless. She was different to these people. She wanted to spread her wings, fly away and find herself. Who was he to tell her that was wrong? After all, it was what he wanted too.

"So why don't *you* leave?" he said, batting back her previous question.

"I don't want to leave Mam on her own," she snapped back

168

instantly, looking regretful. They were so close – sometimes more like sisters than mother and daughter. They looked after one another and held each other close. It was them against the world, or at least it had been. Maybe things were changing now. There was so much more out there, so much she could do. Places she could go where she wouldn't be judged.

She looked up, consciously brightening her face.

"And I'm skint!" she laughed.

He loved how the light and dark sides of her came and went so quickly, like wind-blown clouds across the sun. She had had a rough time, that much was obvious. But she was also a survivor. If she had troubles – and no doubt she did – she carried them lightly. He envied her energy and her positive outlook. Seize the day, eh? Like father like daughter.

He raised his glass in another toast.

"To escaping!"

"To escaping," she replied, clinking her glass against his, "…and a big fat win on the lottery!"

He smiled, but her words threw a long shadow of guilt across his thoughts. He was only here for one thing. To accompany a man who wanted to die on his last journey – a journey that would end on Monday morning beneath the wheels of Paul's train. Paul would benefit handsomely from this man's death – Frankie's father's death. On Monday afternoon, maybe Tuesday, two police officers would arrive at the door of a modest house in Coniston and inform its occupants that the body of a man had been discovered, the cause of death not thought to be suspicious. There would be bereavement, tears, tea, questions, a funeral to organise, regrets, sorrow and heart-searching. A wife briefly reunited with her husband, only to be widowed almost all over again. A daughter who had slammed the door on her father, as he had done to her, now wishing she hadn't. He felt sick and suddenly he wanted to be somewhere else. But Tommy had said it – a deal was a deal. No backing out, no fucking around. They'd shaken on it. The wheels were in motion.

"So," said Frankie, noticing that Paul seemed a little subdued and wanting to keep the flow going, "have you got a girlfriend, then?"

"Nah," he replied, "not for a while. No time really."

"Yeah, I'll bet," Frankie drawled, "You've probably got loads."

With that, she leaned over and ruffled his hair. He was dead cute. Honest, too. She liked that in a man. Not full of shite like most of them. But he looked like he needed to be led astray. Teased a bit, poked in the balls now and again. A bit of colour put back in his cheeks.

"Nice bloke like you," she added, coyly.

He ducked, grabbing his drink and taking an uncharacteristically large swig, his faced flushed with shyness, surprise and embarrassment. Had she really just done that? The little minx. He didn't know what to say. Was she just messing around with him? He couldn't work it out.

From behind the bar the landlord rang a ship's bell to signal last orders. Paul was relieved by the momentary distraction. He shifted in his seat and did his best to drain his glass completely.

"We should go back now," he said. "They might be waiting up for us. Well, for you. Family gathering and all that."

"Christ, I hope not," she replied, suddenly looking worried. "Let's have one more then we'll go back."

Then she smiled, struck with an idea. "I know," she said, "let's walk back past the side of the lake. It is gorgeous down there, especially at night. Though I'd rather be in Soho…"

"You wouldn't, you know," said Paul, smiling. "Okay, just one more then we're out."

Chapter 18

The farm lads and their escorts for the night were way too drunk to notice Frankie and Paul slipping out of the Crown by a side door. Paul was glad. He hated being the object of attention and he couldn't have faced down the inevitable chorus of wolf-whistles, jeers or snide comments if they'd been spotted. But he needn't have worried. Frankie was a city girl at heart and she could bend these country cousins around her little finger. Protectively she steered Paul away from their gaze and out of the side door.

The rich, oxygenated country air that came over them in waves as they left the pub, combined with their alcohol intake, hit them like a ton of Lakeland slate. He was stumbling and giggly, and so was she. They weaved their way unsteadily down the street and towards the sound of water lapping gently against the hulls of moored boats. There was no-one else around, and no other sounds except the eerie cry of a fox barking somewhere out there in the darkness and a motorbike making cautious progress up the pass on the other side of the valley.

Paul was awestruck by the thick, black silence of the night. The soundtrack to his life was one filled with rattling train carriages, automated voices, the ceaseless ocean of cars outside his window, raucous parties above his head, sirens, horns, shrieks, screams and shouts. The total absence of that din was itself a noise in his head, and one he didn't feel entirely comfortable listening to.

He stopped. "Listen," he said, looking round nervously.

"What?" said Frankie, straining to catch whatever it was that he'd heard. "What is it?"

"It's… it's nothing. That's what it is. Nothing. It's so quiet, isn't it?"

"It's the country," she said, shaking her head with the obviousness of it all. "It's always quiet."

Always? He pictured himself in the house on the loch, a single lamp burning in his window as he typed. Not a soul for miles around, only the unseen eyes of foxes, badgers and owls watching him work from the pitch-blackness of their lairs. This little village, with its clutch of pubs and shops, was a metropolis in comparison to where he was planning to go. A small shiver ran up his back and rattled his shoulder blades.

"Bit creepy, really," he said.

"Yeah," she replied, "but look at that sky."

She stared upwards and he followed her gaze. It was a truly amazing sight – like nothing he'd ever seen through the orange-tinted fug over London. The stars shone in the velvet sky like a billion shimmering cats' eyes, appearing and disappearing at random. He felt like a Stone Age man, struck dumb by his own insignificance and inability to comprehend and articulate what unfurled above him like a giant black flag. Either that, or the beer was just stronger up here.

"Look," said Frankie, pointing westwards, "a shooting star!"

"That's a…" He stopped short. He didn't want to sound like a know-all. But she'd already anticipated what he was going to say.

"A satellite, I know," she said, finishing his sentence. "I was just checking."

As they laughed together their eyes met momentarily. He turned away slightly, mentally rewinding the tune that had just popped into his head to get it to the right part.

There it was. Softly, and slightly out of tune, he began to sing. It was an old song, but a good one.

"I saw two shooting stars last night, I wished on them…"

Frankie looked at him in surprise, and took up the tune.

"…but they were only satellites…"

Now it was his turn to look surprised. It must have been around before she was born, but she knew it. His heart leapt, and he beamed at her as he sang the next line.

"Is it wrong to wish on space hardware…"

She smiled. Her turn.

"I wish, I wish, I wish you'd care…"

She took a breath, getting ready for the big moment, and curled her arm around his, pulling him close to her. As she did he tingled with nervous anticipation. He loved the feeling of being connected to someone so intimately. It was rare for him to have any real, meaningful physical contact with another human being. Being shoved up against strangers on his way to work was one thing, to be hooked up to a person he found so utterly amazing in every way – to exist solely in one another's sphere, if only for a moment like this – was quite another.

"I don't want to change the world,
I'm not looking for a new England,
I'm just looking for another girl."

They bellowed the chorus together in joyful disharmony, the words skimming the surface of the lake and echoing off its distant shores. The song broke off into a peal of laughter. Then, looking serious for a second, Frankie leaned forward, grabbed Paul by the hair on the back of his head and pulled his face into hers, kissing him with a ferocity and a passion that contrasted with the gentle clink-clink of rigging tapping against the aluminium spars of the boats on the water, disturbed by a gathering wind.

Deeply she drew him down, her tongue searching out his. Shocked but amazed, he responded in kind. Now he truly understood the American expression, 'sucking face'. Finally, she broke off, taking a breath and smiling at him, her face glowing with the intensity of the moment.

173

He stared at her, stunned. He felt like he'd been pitched head first into a tub of warm honey. What could he say to her that would eloquently describe what had just happened to him?

"Thanks," he burbled.

"Come on," she said, grinning at her own boldness and his face, the flushed colour of a fat tomato, "let's go home."

*

Tommy was so near, yet still so far. The question from Rose about his sleeping arrangements had signalled their night together was at an end, but surely it wouldn't finish like this. He wanted to kneel at her feet and pour out his heart and soul, all his sorrow and his pain and his regret, on to the carpet in front of her. But she had risen out of the armchair and, with an expression like a clucking hen, walked upstairs to gather some bedding for him to take into the spare room.

He followed her upstairs, trying not to let the whiskey affect his footsteps. The last thing he wanted was for her to accuse him of being drunk. Though she'd put enough away, that was for sure. But fair play, she could always hold it better than he could.

He hovered at her bedroom door while she fumbled in a wardrobe for a duvet and a sheet. The room was softly furnished and very feminine. No sign of stale, discarded socks or action novels piled up on the bedside table. A small crucifix hung over the bed. To the left on a dressing table stood a statue of the Virgin Mary next to a box of pastel-pink tissues. It was a woman's realm, alright.

He took another couple of steps into the room and stood at the foot of the bed as she dragged out the bed linen. She turned, her arms full, and gently he took the bedding from her before allowing it to drop almost silently to the floor. She stared at him, but did not speak, her eyes searching his face in anticipation of his next move. He took her hands in his and his gaze met hers. The years of separation and the constant warring leading up to that terrible day he disappeared slid away from them as easily as the discarded bed

174

sheets. Taking her face in his he kissed her, tenderly at first then with more urgency, wrapping his arms around her as he did.

At first she yielded to him, surrendering to the tenderness of the moment and the memories of the good times she had had. What she had seen in him from the beginning – the wit, the charm and the passion – despite everything, would never die.

But even as her heart was opening to him, her head was urging her to think differently. This was the man who'd run out on her and Frankie so cruelly. It was wrong, so, so wrong. Why had she let it go this far in the first place? Gently, but with authority, she pushed him away.

"No, Tommy," she whispered. "No."

If he heard her, he was choosing to ignore it. His hands hung on to her shoulders as he leaned in again.

"You smell gorgeous," he said, nuzzling her neck, instantly recognising the fragrance which he had missed for so long.

She pushed him away again, this time more forcefully. She could more easily put aside any tender feelings for her husband than she could the ones of bitterness for the man who betrayed and abandoned her. The man who now stood in front of her.

"I said 'no'," she repeated, her eyes narrowing.

Tommy was crestfallen. "Ah come on now," he said, trying to inflect his words with sparkle, "you know you love it. A bit of the old Tommy magic…"

"It doesn't work any more, Tommy," she said sadly. It wasn't quite true and she knew it. But she couldn't allow herself the moment. It would be a betrayal of everything that had gone before, all the effort and energy she had put into creating a life after Tommy. It was so sad for him and so sad for her. He looked crushed. Gently, she leaned up and kissed him on the cheek, the way you might say goodnight to a child. Then she bent down, picked up the bedding and handed it to him. He took the bundle reluctantly and looked into her eyes, searching for a sign that the moment had not passed.

"It's down the landing," she said, "first door on the left."

*

When they arrived home the house was in darkness, except for a single light in the living room. With practised, stealthy efficiency Frankie turned her key in the lock and pushed the door open. The living room door was shut. Frankie took a step towards it and, hearing nothing, turned to Paul with her finger on her lips, gesturing him to keep quiet. She crept back to where he was standing and grabbed his hand before standing on the first step of the carpeted staircase. Mutely he followed, with that familiar feeling of trepidation at being in a strange house with potentially threatening occupants. Unlike the crawl upstairs at the Callaghans', this time he was only too willing to accompany the thrill-seeker in front of him. At least she knew where she was going.

They tiptoed down the landing, past two closed bedroom doors and into a room lit by a bedside lamp with a deep red scarf thrown on top. Frankie closed the door firmly behind her and both breathed a deep sigh of relief. She grabbed a CD from a shelf and pushed it into a player while Paul looked around the room. It groaned with the passionate squalor of young adulthood. Clothes were strewn everywhere and every inch of wallpaper was covered by indie band posters, club night flyers, photos of grinning mates, gig tickets, drawings and theatre bills.

Frankie pressed play and Hot Kiss by Juliette and the Licks boomed out. Paul winced, waiting for the door to fly open and an angry Rosemary, in dressing gown and curlers, to march in and demand to know what was going on.

"It's okay," laughed Frankie, seeing his expression, "Mam doesn't mind the music. Anyway, I think she...*they*...are still downstairs. And I'll tell yer what else, it's gonna need to be loud."

With that, she pulled him close to her again and snogged him hard, throwing off her jacket as she did so. His heart was pounding under his clothes, so loudly he was sure she could feel it. His hands shook with fear and his mouth felt dry. With force he pulled away from her. He had to know.

"Just one thing," he gasped, staring at her wildly. "Why me?"

Jesus. She could've laughed in his face. Half the lads in the Lakes would give their back teeth to be where he was, and even as she was starting to pull her clothes off in front of him he was still asking mad questions. But that, of course, was the answer.

"I don't know," she said, pulling the jacket from his back in one go, "because you're… different."

That was all he needed to hear. He had always been different. Outwardly he was the same as anyone else, but inside he was in another place altogether. He had thought it had been to his detriment, the way he moved inarticulately and awkwardly through life, and often it had. He was restless, unfulfilled, lacking in the confidence he needed to get what he wanted. But this was a different context altogether. She liked him…no, she wanted him… because he was different. He hadn't pretended to her or tried to go along with a game. He had just been himself and she had responded. She made him feel like a star. That was incredible.

"Okay then," he shrugged, satisfied with her answer. She smiled and pulled her skull-patterned top over her head, deftly unhooking her black bra to reveal firm breasts with large, brown, inviting nipples. She snogged him again, pressing herself hard against his body. He couldn't wait to feel his skin against hers. She felt his desire too. With her tongue still wrestling against his, she almost tore his T-shirt as she yanked it over his head. Breaking off, and breathing heavily, she pulled him over to her messy single bed, manhandling him on to his back before straddling him and pulling up his hands on to her breasts. With a skill he'd never previously been aware he possessed, he took her nipples between his fingers and rubbed hard, causing her to groan with pleasure and arch her back into a sensuous 'S' shape.

*

177

Rosemary lay in bed, her fingers caressing the rosary beads that had been her comfort for many years. Tomorrow, Tommy would have to go. God love him and look after him, but there was no place for him here. Everything had changed. There was no vacancy, no room at the inn. And yet seeing him, the great stupid head of him trying to be so contrite and humble, had filled her with emotion. Thoughts, memories and long-lost feelings of love – yes, why not admit it, for it was true – came flooding back to her. Once again she was experiencing emotions she thought she'd buried deep enough to suffocate.

Involuntarily she clenched her jaw against the tears she knew were going to fall. Jesus, she didn't want him to hear her crying. He would be through her door like a pack of dogs if he did. She reached over to the dressing table and pulled a tissue from the box and, as stealthily as she could, blew into it and wiped her eyes. Thank God Frankie had that bloody music up loud. She reached into the drawer at the side of her bed and pulled out a photograph. It was of picture of her, Tommy and little Frankie, all eating ice-cream together. On the back she'd written 'Blackpool Beach, June 1990.' Happy days. She smiled at the memories it evoked, particularly the one of Tommy clowning around with a knotted handkerchief on his head. She put the photograph back, shutting the drawer tightly. That was the place for memories and it would stay that way. She turned over and pressed her face into the pillow, craving a dreamless sleep.

*

Frankie jumped off the bed and dragged down her skirt, tights and underwear. Naked, she got back on it from the bottom and slowly crawled up it, slithering along Paul's body, rigid with excitement and anticipation. When her hands were level with his jeans she teased out the opening of his fly buttons, artfully pretending to fumble with each one. He loved the way her bracelets and bangles shook gently as she taunted and tantalised him, her fingers working their way through his boxers to free his bursting erection from its uncomfortable prison. Skilfully she teased his balls and the head of his penis before pausing to haul the rest of his clothing from his legs. When she was done, she straddled him again and took him deep inside her, riding the shaft of his cock whilst leaning over to brush her nipples across his eager lips.

*

In the room next to Frankie's, tired, half-drunk and frustrated, Tommy lay on his back on the single sofa bed. The racket next door from that CD nonsense would waken the bloody dead. It was surprising Rose wasn't down the room to sort it out. He was irritable, annoyed that the long, slow build-up to what he had hardly dared hope for had gone like frost in May. She was still his Rose, but she was her own Rose now – confident, self-assured, doing her own thing. She didn't want him. More to the point, she didn't need him. It was that truth that hurt most of all. True, he had been a lousy provider and fairly hopeless as a father. But he had done what he could, and what he couldn't he'd made up for with his wit, his charm and his playfulness. Now he was redundant, a spare part in the construction of his own family. But he was the one who had unbolted it all, leaving others to put it all back together again to their own design. He could hardly complain now.

He could do something about that sodding noise though. He lifted himself up from the bed and raised his fist in anticipation of slamming it hard against the wall. He stopped and let his arm fall limply to his side. How could he even begin to tell Frankie what to do after all this time? If he tried she would just tell him what to do and where to go, for that matter. And she'd be quite right. She wasn't his little girl any more. She'd made that clear enough. But maybe she'd feel different in the morning. Perhaps Rose would too. He grabbed the pillow from under him and stuffed it over his head. Fuck it. He could sleep on a rope.

*

Next door the tables had turned and now Paul was in command, Frankie yielding gladly under him. Her legs were locked round his back as he thrusted, their mouths finding tongues, ears, necks and hair. Sweat poured off Paul's back as Frankie heaved and groaned, wriggling to find the most satisfying position that she could. Faster and faster they went, the bed shaking in time to their wild rhythm and with the beat from the CD still pumping it out from the player on the shelf.

Then, her breathing changed from one of deep sighs to urgent pants, increasing in rapidity each time. She was coming close to orgasm. Paul could hardly bear to look at her so desperate was he not to come before her. She clenched her teeth together, fighting the animal urge to scream at the top of her voice and right down the valley to the bottom of the lake. Her vaginal muscles clamped round his cock and, as she came, her face buried deep into a pillow to stifle her moans, he could feel the squeeze and release around him. He could wait no longer. His face contorted with ecstatic pleasure. He climaxed into her like a man returned from a long, dry season.

Exhausted, they fell into one another's arms, hardly daring to speak of their now-sated lust. The sex and the drink had done for them. Within minutes of Frankie turning off the CD player and curling back into Paul's arms, she was asleep. He lay on his back, wide-eyed, unable to believe the events of the evening. Him and her, and *this*. Last night he'd been at the wrong end of a sawn-off shotgun. Tonight he'd met the most stunning girl he'd ever seen, and not only had she flirted with him like mad, she'd dragged him to her house, practically thrown him on the bed and shagged him like there was no tomorrow.

Which, of course, there wouldn't be if her father found out. That was a thought he hardly dared to address. Not at this moment, when somehow all the planets in the cosmos had somehow lined up to grant him the most incredible good fortune. But there it was in his mind's eye, Tommy's face glaring down at him, like a

Minotaur in a red tie ready to wreak revenge for the defilement of his daughter. He'd just have to take his chances and hope he could somehow slip out of the room before Tommy sensed trouble. There was Rosemary, too. Christ, he hadn't even spoken to her yet and here he was in bed with her daughter. If anything, she might be even more fearsome than her estranged husband.

Frankie snuggled up closer to him, wrapping her arms round his puny chest. To hell with it. Whatever tomorrow brought he would live in the present, the midnight hour mixing with the heady fragrances of sex and sleep. He pulled her in closer and she responded, curling her body round his. Even if he was the best writer in the world, he couldn't make this up.

CHAPTER 19

Tommy slept only fitfully that night, the events of the previous day playing and re-playing through his mind. He'd tried so hard to show restraint and do everything by Rosemary's rules. He hadn't attempted to justify himself or given her a set of lame answers. Anyway, she hadn't asked the questions in the first place. Nevertheless, he knew there was still something between them. Although it was buried deeply, covered over with thick layers of anger, betrayal and bitterness, it was just still alive. Sure, she hadn't invited him into her bed, but he could hardly expect that she would've. God knows, it had taken him long enough the first time round, she being a good Catholic girl and all.

Now it was morning, the dawn breaking rosily over the eastern fells and casting subtle shades of pink and yellow on the tops of the trees in the distant Grizedale Forest. He raised himself up from the single sofa bed and rubbed the back of his stiff neck. Hostel beds were only marginally more uncomfortable than this, but at least he hadn't had to sleep in the Merc. Somewhere in the distance, a solitary sheep bleated. For some reason, Tommy thought of Paul. Where the hell had he got to last night? Maybe Paul had slept in the car. He'd never hear the end of it today, if so. Still, at least he'd cleared off and not come back, giving Tommy and Rosemary some space.

But what had it achieved? They'd talked, he'd given her the ring, witnessed her distress, taken pleasure in the good manners of her hospitality, delighted in her song and been disappointed by the closing bedroom door. She hadn't slit his throat or called the police. She couldn't have thought he was that bad. "You're a fecking torment, Tommy Cassidy," she'd said. That wasn't the same as,

"Feck off and die! I never want to see you again." Surely, then, there was a chance, even the slimmest one, of a new understanding between them? After all, Elizabeth Taylor married Richard Burton twice.

He picked the sleep out of the corner of his eyes and automatically wiped it on his boxers. Jesus, he felt tired. Yesterday had been like a month spent on the same ride at Disneyland. Up, down, up, down, up, down. He'd have slept soundly in Rose's arms, if only she'd let him. Ah well. Softly, softly and all that. There was time. Rose said she wanted him out in the morning but he might be able to somehow extend that into lunchtime, the afternoon, or may be even into the evening.

In truth, Tommy didn't know what would happen next. There was still Frankie to contend with. He was surprised at how much she'd grown up. She was a woman in full cry, just like her mammy, and all the soft-soaping in the world might not bring her round. Jesus, it was some racket she was kicking up when she came in last night.

Tommy looked around the box room he'd been banished to. It was packed floor to ceiling with memories. Books he'd read to Frankie, toys he'd bought her, board games they'd played. He recognised some of Rose's clothes spilling out of a wardrobe. It was all there – the remnants of his former life tided up and set aside. He pulled a dusty teddy-bear from a drawer and turned it over in his hands. Frankie was so delighted with it that he'd forgotten to tell Rose he'd purchased it with petrol station coupons. Just as well. She would've tutted at him, reminded him of his responsibilities as a father and a bread-winner and held it up as an example of his priorities where cash was concerned.

There was no point crying over a moth-eaten teddy bear. Not now, when there was still time to repair the damage. His suit lay in a crumpled heap on the floor where he'd discarded it, in disappointment and frustration, the previous night. He didn't want to put it on. Not yet. He didn't want to give the impression

183

he was making a move homewards. If he could eke out his time in the cottage for a while longer he might – just might – be able to sweet-talk Rose into a Sunday lunch at the pub or a nice walk by the lake. He'd prove to her that he'd changed.

Hung on a peg behind the door was a dressing gown. In truth, it was more of a kimono, all silky red with a Japanese white blossom motif. It would have to do. Otherwise it was a stroll downstairs in his vest and underpants. Not the best way to rekindle a great romance. He took the kimono from the peg and put it on. He looked a sight for sore eyes, but it was his wife he was dealing it. She knew him. And it might just make her laugh. Now wouldn't hearing that be a grand way to start the day?

He opened the bedroom door softly and tip-toed across the landing to the top of the stairs. She'd still be asleep and he didn't want to wake her before her morning cuppa. It was the one thing that gave her unfailing pleasure, a cup of tea in bed. Even if he'd crawled in with the milkman, she usually forgave him once she had a cup in her hand.

In her room, Rose heard the creak of heavy footsteps at the foot of the stairs. Like Tommy, she had had a rotten night's sleep. The vision of him standing there at the doorway last night, looking like a man who'd lost a grand and found a shilling, had kept her awake. She could've made room for him in the bed. Whoever the hell he was now, he was still her husband.

She was already dressed. She knew Tommy would go downstairs and start brewing a pot of tea. Jesus, he might have been eight years gone but some things hadn't changed, and that included his predictability where guilt was concerned. And boy, he had plenty to be guilty about. But they needed to talk and soon. She had things to say. She had to be up and about, not lounging in bed.

She opened the curtains and fussed around her dressing table, tidying up the bits and pieces that lay scattered across its surface. She wondered how Frankie was today. Maybe she wouldn't even come out of her room. She was in late, and what with all that went on the previous day, plus all the booze she'd probably drowned her sorrows with, she wasn't likely to surface before the end of the afternoon. By then, he and that scarecrow he called his mate might be long gone.

Downstairs, Tommy carefully washed and dried the best china he and Rose had drunk from and set two cups on a tray. After opening several drawers and cupboards he eventually found a box of tea bags. He then placed two bags in a pot, poured hot water into it and left it to brew. Did she have sugar? He could hardly remember and she might have changed her tastes. If she did he would go back down for it once he'd seen her. Tommy picked up the tray and started for the foot of the stairs, but as she did he spied a vase of flowers on the kitchen table. There, in the middle of the display, was a single rose. He placed the tray on the table and carefully lifted the rose from the centre of the vase. It was beautiful – deep red in colour and perfectly sculpted into a tight knot of intertwining petals. He smelled it and instantly it reminded him of his brief, intoxicating encounter with Rosemary's neck. Gently he laid the flower on the tray and picked it up again. It was a little touch like this that could make all the difference, he was sure.

Rosemary heard him ascend the stairs and smoothed down the corner of the pink duvet into a neat fold. A cloud of butterflies suddenly fluttered in her stomach and instinctively she lifted her chin up, steeling herself for his re-appearance at the doorway of the bedroom.

With the cheek of his arse, and trying not to get the kimono caught, he pushed down the door handle to Rosemary's bedroom and shouldered it open. She could've laughed at loud when she saw him, dressed like some eejit escaped from a magic show in that old silk robe, but she kept her composure.

"You're up," he said, unable to hide the disappointment in his face. "I thought I'd bring you a cup of tea."

She smiled nervously, but did not thank him. Instead, she sat down primly on the end of the bed and with her hand, patted the space next to her.

"Come and sit down, Tommy," she said, her eyes searching out his. "There's something I've got to tell you."

Something in her expression, the way she pursed her lips and furrowed her brow, set off alarm bells of concern in him. Why was she up and looking all business-like? What was this about?

She swallowed hard. She had to make her intentions very clear to Tommy, a man who wouldn't take 'no' for an answer if there were a thousand more complicated questions he could knock back. She had to tell him in no uncertain terms.

"I'm going to divorce you, Tommy," she said softly, but with resolution in her voice. "I want to get married again. He's a good man. He lives in the next village. He's a plumber."

There. He'd heard it – the truth. There was nothing he could say or do that would change her mind. Bill Davis *was* a good man. A widower. Not an old one, but old enough to find the hunt for a new mate something of an uphill task. A neighbour had recommended him when she started up with the hairdressing and had to get a sink fitted downstairs. They'd talked over cups of tea. He was a lonely man, no doubt about that, but not a desperate one. He'd worked out a way of living on his own that had suited him and although he missed his wife terribly he was resolved to carry on and do what he could to get through the weeks, months and years ahead.

They had so much in common in that way. She hadn't told him much about Tommy, only that there had been a husband once who'd abandoned her and their wee girl, disappearing without trace. She'd never bad-mouthed him, but neither had she praised him. She'd simply acknowledged his existence in her past life and got on with living happily without him. Occasionally, she had wondered out loud what had become of him and whether he would ever be in touch again. Dependable, practical Bill advised her to cross that bridge when she came to it and she listened to him. Eventually, she came to trust him – something she swore she would never do again after Tommy left – and finally she fell for him, or rather they fell for each other in a quiet, understated sort of way. It was not the mad spark of heart-leaping excitement like it was in the beginning with Tommy, but she examined her feelings closely and with honesty, finding them to be real.

And Frankie liked him too. He didn't try to talk down to her, or tell her what to do or who to be. He accepted her for who she was. She, still bristling with hurt, even after all this time, had found it in her heart to accept, begrudgingly, that there was a new rival for her mother's affections. In a way, she was quite glad. For while her Mam and Bill were out roaming the fells or visiting the shops in Carlisle she could get on with the business of being an attractive, available and sought-after young woman, with all that entailed.

Tommy stared at the wall, stunned into silence. *Divorce?* It was the last thing he expected. Even when Rosemary was in full battlecry, the term divorce would never have fallen from her lips. She'd have sooner boiled her own head than suggest divorce. What the feck would the Pope say? Obviously, the Holy See didn't stretch as far as the Lakes. There must be something in the mountain air. And a plumber... Dear God alive. He might have a brass washer to slip over her finger come the wedding day, but he wouldn't have a sapphire like the one he'd risked his bloody life to get back. No way.

"Come on, Tommy," she whispered gently, anxious not to twist the knife. "You didn't think I'd want to grow old on my own, did you?"

Of course he didn't. But he just couldn't imagine her with anyone else. She was his. She'd always been his. Even when she wasn't his and he'd left her to fend for herself and sort out the mess he'd left behind, she was still his. Tommy and Rose. That's who they were. That's who they'd always be. My Rose. My beautiful Rosie.

She bit her lip. In all the years they'd been together she had rarely seen him lost for words. It made her anxious to see him this way. What was he thinking? Did he approve? Did she care whether he did or not? Of course she cared. She could not so easily put aside her concern for him.

"Well, speak to me then," she prompted.

He looked at the tray with the flower lying limply across it. What she wanted was for him to say he was happy for her. But he couldn't quite form the words. Not just yet. He needed a moment to gather his thoughts and get over the shock of the announcement. If she was happy then he had to be happy for her. She deserved that. But Christ, he wished it could be different.

"I'll take this into Frances," he said, still staring at the tray and the pot of cooling tea. "She'll be glad for a cup."

He stood up and clutching the tray, wandered out of the room, the kimono hanging dejectedly above his black socks. "God, look after him," thought Rose, "because I know that I can't."

CHAPTER 20

Tommy tapped softly on his daughter's door. He knew from personal experience that waking party animals prematurely was never a good move. But she might as well have this tea now he'd made it. It might perk her up or at least put her in a half-decent mood.

The truth was he just wanted to talk to her and get her to listen to what he had to say. There might be an onslaught of objects hurled at him, but he'd have to brave it out. There was no point shying away from her, whatever she thought of him. It might well be the last time she ever saw him.

"Frankie," he said in a low voice, "it's me. Can I come in?"

Inside the bedroom, Frankie bolted upright. *Shit.* No him. Not now. He'd want some great long heart-to-heart, trying to make himself comfortable on the end of the bed. The tension rose in her throat then quickly subsided. This was her room, her space. She could let in whoever she wanted and bar anyone she didn't. Her father definitely belonged in the latter category. God, he picked his moments to turf up, looking for a friendly chinwag. Well he wasn't coming in. No way.

"No!" she shouted, determined not to give in. "No, go away…"

She was always a stubborn one. Got that from her mother. Actually, they both shared equal responsibility for that trait. But dammit, she was his daughter. He couldn't tell her what to do, but he could tell her how he felt.

"Ah, come on now, Frances," he wheedled, "please. Just hear me out. I've brought you some tea."

God, he wasn't going to go away. She could hardly jump out of bed without a stitch on and try to block the door. Anything could happen then. She'd just have to brave it out.

Tommy took the silence from inside the room to be a sign of tacit approval for him to enter. He pushed open the door using the bum-on-handle method and went in. As he did, his eyes took a moment or two to adjust to the gloom. The dark curtains were tightly shut against the morning sun and the poster-covered walls reflected little natural light, turning the whole room into a kind of dark and slightly squalid pit.

At the far end of the room Frankie was sitting up in bed, a patchwork-patterned duvet cover tucked tightly under her arms. He noticed a large tattoo on her right shoulder. God, was that real? He wouldn't have given the okay for that if he'd been around.

"Don't you listen?" she said, visibly bristling, "I said 'no'."

Their eyes met and she looked away towards the curtains. She seemed nervous. So was he. This was going to be so bloody difficult. The thoughts in his head were only half-formed. What did you say to a child – a woman now, yes, but still his child – you'd ratted on by running away almost a decade ago? She looked tense. No surprise, really. She must have thought that he was... God knows what she must have thought. There was nothing much her mother could've done to comfort her, either.

Despite her persistence and obvious hostility he wasn't going to leave the room without something being said. He placed the tray down on a small table. A wicker chair draped with discarded clothes was the only obvious place to park himself in the cluttered room. He pulled the chair closer to the bed for the big talk.

"Frankie, please," he said, in the most reasonable tone of voice he could muster, "I just want to talk. Though, I don't know where to start. I..."

He paused and reflected. This wasn't going to work, him blathering on like an idiot.

"Perhaps I should let you talk. Tell me what you feel, how I've let you down..."

He looked at her, waiting for a whirlwind of words to come

190

flying straight into his face. All the years of pent-up anger, plus the normal teenage stuff, were about to be unleashed and it wouldn't be pretty. But it had to come out.

She paused, as though forming a sentence in her head. Then she cast her eyes downwards. "Please," she whispered, "not now."

Poor girl. It was all too much for her, him turning up like this without a word of warning. She was just the same. She didn't know what to say or how to say it. She was only young and while he didn't want to voice her feelings, he was supposed to be the grown-up here. It was up to him – his fatherly duty even – to do the talking.

"No, you're right," he said, nodding and gravely assuming the mantle of responsibility. "It's my call."

Like an MP making his maiden speech in the House of Commons, Tommy cleared his throat and clasped his hands together.

"The thing is, Frankie," he said, taking a deep breath, "I *hate* myself for what I've done, more than you ever could. I know that's no excuse."

She looked at him from under her eyelids. The gesture involuntarily caused him to sit lower in the chair, his elbows on his knees in a position of humility.

"I know I'm not very good at this," he continued, articulating his contrition with earnest hand gestures, "but what I want to say is that I've…"

He paused, slightly distracted. Had he heard something? It sounded like a cough or something like that, coming from under the covers. What was it?

"What I want to say," he said, his eyes now turned away from Frankie and his attention focused on the bed, "… is that I've been a bad father, but it doesn't mean that…"

His voice tailed off. There was a shape, a shape under the bloody covers. Somebody was in there with her. Jesus Christ.

He looked at his daughter, who stared wordlessly back. Slowly, but with curiosity and a bad feeling rising up in him, Tommy lifted the corner of the patchwork-patterned duvet. There was a foot, then two feet with hair on them. He pulled back the bed linen another few inches, revealing a pair of very white, very skinny legs. Upwards again and a pair of hands were exposed, clutching a bunny in a hopeless attempt to cover limp genitals.

Tommy whipped the duvet back completely and stared, open-mouthed, into the face of Paul, whose naked body was rigid with guilt and fear.

Suddenly, it was like a tornado had hit the room. With an almighty roar Tommy leapt up, sending the tea tray flying off the table and scattering the cups across the floor. He lunged at the bed, but Paul was quick and dived off it on to the floor. Frankie screamed like a banshee, desperately trying to stop the bellowing Tommy from belting Paul within an inch of his life. Frankie howled at her father to get out, punching and pushing him in the direction of the door while scrambling to keep the duvet around her top half.

The scream alerted Rose, who tore across the landing and into the room, immediately entering the fray. With a pugnacious look on her face she jumped in between the warring parties, elbows flying as she tried to separate father and daughter.

Paul was now swiftly throwing on his clothes like a man three hours late for his own wedding. Everything seemed to be tangling and tumbling as though it was in a washing machine, but he got his boxer shorts on and the T-shirt over his head. Wildly, he looked round. The whole room was a mass of flailing arms, screams, shouts, bellows and threats. The door was blocked by Tommy's sizeable frame, writhing and struggling like a guard dog at the end of its leash, straining to attack.

But there was the window. He threw the curtains aside and hauled up the old-fashioned window frame. It was a drop to the ground, but it wasn't the certain death that faced him if he stayed a second longer. Grabbing his jeans he scrambled out of the window and quickly lowered himself down, hanging by his fingers for an agonising second before dropping to the grass.

Christ, it hurt! But he was down and he had a precious few seconds to pull on his jeans. He almost tripped into them, stumbling as he hopped desperately on the spot, wriggling them up over his knees.

"Paul!"

A scream from the window he'd just leapt from. It was Frankie, her mouth open in an expression of panic and his trainers in her hand. She hurled them down and he pulled them on.

As he did, the front door was flung open and Tommy flew out, still in his kimono, vest and boxers. Now, there wasn't a second to lose. Paul started running, his ankle still aching from the fall, with Tommy in hot pursuit.

But not for long. The broken crockery hurled at him by Rose the previous day was still strewn along the path and Tommy's stockinged feet ran right into it. Cursing and roaring with the pain of the broken shards in his soles, he hopped back into the house, found his black slip-on shoes, slammed his feet into them and ran out again, keen to get the skinny bag of shite who was now down the path and tearing along the lane.

"Tommy, wait!" shouted Paul, terrified at the sight of the bellowing figure bearing down on him like a red-sailed galleon.

"I'll take a fucking bar to you!" howled the Irishman, determined not to lose his quarry.

On the road ahead was a priest, making his way to church for morning mass. He stopped dead at the sight of Tommy, the kimono flapping behind him and his face as red as its flimsy material.

"Morning, Father," nodded Tommy, remembering his manners as he raced by.

The pursuit continued up the hill. The Irishman was almost 30 years older than Paul, but he was giving a good account of himself. The younger man hadn't expected him to get this far. He spotted a stile leading to a field and took it at speed before hitting the ground and panting up the coarse, marshy grass.

"I'll rip yer fucking head from your shoulders, you little bollicks!"

193

roared Tommy, as he scrambled over the same stile, catching his knackers on the wood before jumping down and charging up the hill.

Paul was now at the other side, but sitting in the cab of an Underground train all day had made him unfit. A stitch was tearing at his side and he was so out of breath he felt his lungs might leap from his throat at any moment. He stood with his back to another stile, his hands on his knees as he fought for air. Meanwhile, Tommy was approaching from over the brow of the hill.

"Come on Tommy," panted Paul, holding his palms upwards in a gesture of peace and reconciliation, "let's talk about this. Be reasonable…"

"Oh, I'll be reasonable," said Tommy, advancing, "I'll be bloody reasonable all right!"

But it was like trying to reason with a ravenous crocodile. Paul scrambled over the wall and along a rough uphill track. Tommy took the stile and although he was beginning to flag he was far from giving up.

The track led down to the banks of a stream. Paul ran through the icy water, hoping that Tommy wouldn't want to get his legs wet. He was wrong. Tommy stumbled through it and on to the far bank, his shoes squelching and spitting with excess water.

Ahead was a gate. Maybe it would lead to a better road surface and the chance of a faster run. Paul dashed through it and on to a stone bridge over the river, but as he turned to see how closely Tommy was on his heels he slipped forwards and landed face first into a thick, semi-liquid heap of steaming cow shit.

He heard Tommy give a low, harsh laugh of triumph behind him and looked up. There, facing him on the other side of a five-barred gate was a herd of cows, their huge heads pressed against the metalwork, their tongues lolling and steam coming out of their open mouths and nostrils.

He could do it. He could get over that gate and past those cows. No… no he couldn't. They were just too big and scary. At least

Tommy had a tongue that enabled him to speak. He could reason with him. He could just explain that...

"So," said Tommy, advancing slowly on the mud-spattered and panting Paul, "is that what you like to do to young girls is it?"

"It wasn't my fault," pleaded Paul, his eyes staring wildly through the mask of manure. Christ, he hadn't asked to go to bed with Miss bloody Cumbria. It just kind of happened.

"No, it never fecking is," snarled Tommy.

Paul was desperately thinking of a way out, something to throw back at Tommy.

"You're the one who said 'seize the day', he shouted accusingly.

"Seize the day!" roared Tommy, "Not me fecking daughter!"

"You weren't that bothered about her two days ago," Paul blustered. "She won't even talk to you."

The cheeky shite! Tommy's eyes flashed with rage and he grabbed Paul by the front of his T-shirt, dragging him to the metal railings along the top of the bridge. He was going over, and no mistake. Paul's stomach lurched with a mixture of fear and horror as the strong hands forced him over the side of the bridge and held him only by the waistband of his jeans. Fifteen feet below was the stream with vicious, jagged rocks thrusting from its bed.

"No, please, Tommy," hollered Paul, the blood rushing to his head. "Please God, no! Don't drop me! Oh fuck! Shit! Fuck!"

"My own fecking daughter," shouted Tommy, inching his victim even further over the bridge side.

As Paul panicked and struggled, the water and the rocks loomed in and out of his focus. And then, as though it had been breathed into him by some spirit of devilment lurking high up on the fells, he started to laugh. Once he started, he couldn't stop. Just feet from death he was literally shaking with hysterical laughter.

Tommy stopped, shocked. He grabbed Paul's T-shirt, hauling him back over the railings and on to terra firma. Paul was still laughing.

"What the fuck's so funny?" snapped Tommy, almost as puzzled as he was angry.

"You…" said Paul, hanging on to the railings, "… us… this… life."

"Life," snorted Tommy, "is that what you'd call it? You ought to start leading one instead of just following one around."

The words jabbed Paul like a bee-sting.

"Yeah, well," he snapped back, pointing straight at Tommy, "you're the one who's topping yourself, mate."

"Like you give a fuck," said Tommy. "You never even asked me why."

So he wanted philosophy with his fifteen hundred quid, did he? Well, he was going to hear a few home truths, and no mistake.

"You're right," Paul said with a swagger, taking the moral high ground, "and I don't care, that's why. You think you're the only one who ever screwed up? Well boo-hoo, Tommy. Life sucks sometimes and that's all there is to it, but not all of us are so full of self-pity we feel the need to kill ourselves."

The little bollicks. Full of his own fecking self-importance. Lecturing a man of the world like he was some bloody politician.

"How the fuck would you know?" sneered Tommy. "You just sit with your head up your arse all day."

A young boy had appeared at the gate. He clutched a stick, occasionally employing it to keep the straining cows in check. A farmer's lad, he was moving his dad's cattle from one field to another and thoroughly enjoying this unexpected and colourful spectacle that was playing out in front of him.

"How the fuck would I know?" shouted Paul, hurt by the accusation that had got right into the heart and soul of all his worst fears about himself. "Because I'm standing on a bridge in the middle of FUCK KNOWS WHERE covered in cow shit, fighting a fat old Irishman dressed in a kimono and all because his daughter hates him and seems to quite like me!"

The young boy exploded into laughter and as he did Tommy lunged at Paul. Down they went, scrabbling and wrestling on the filthy ground, their blows racked with gasps from their exhausted frames.

196

The boy looked at his watch. No matter how much fun this was, these cows needed to get moving. He pulled the spring-loaded bar which fastened the gate and with the aid of his stick, shooed the lowing, bellowing animals through the gate. Seeing the beasts heading towards them, Tommy and Paul jumped up and backed themselves against the metal rail over the bridge as the cows squeezed past.

After the cows had passed, with their young keeper whistling at the back of the herd, the shit-splattered pair sat down by the railing. Fishing roughly in the pocket of the kimono, Tommy pulled out a packet of cigarettes. He offered one to Paul, which he accepted. They were beyond words now.

Paul looked around. What was he doing here? This was insane, the whole thing. He had to be somewhere else. He'd have to get the rest of his stuff then… then fuck knows what? Was there still a plan? He was almost past caring. Wearily, he staggered to his feet and headed towards the gate without a backwards glance.

"Where are you going?" shouted Tommy. "Hey! Where are you off to?"

Paul didn't answer, but he was aware of Tommy getting to his feet and following.

"Paul, wait!" shouted the Irishman, staggering in the wake of the younger man. "Wait, you fucker… wait for me!"

Paul didn't acknowledge him. He really, really had had enough. Enough of him, enough of this place, enough of all the madness.

"Well, you can forget about tomorrow!" yelled Tommy, frustrated.

"Good!" shouted Paul in reply, but still not turning around.

"You'll have to find some other poor fucker," threatened Tommy, "because I won't be there."

"So?" said Paul. He couldn't give a damn. It wasn't worth it.

"Fuck you!" shouted Tommy, frustrated that he was just pissing in the wind here.

"No," shouted Paul, "fuck you!"

He trudged on. Tommy could make all the threats he wanted. They were just sliding off Paul like the cow crap from the end of his nose.

"Aaaarrrggggghhhhh!!!"

Suddenly, Paul heard a terrible, shredding scream from behind. He whipped around to see Tommy stumble and then fall to the hard earth, clutching his chest and letting out unearthly groans.

He watched as the Irishman lay on the ground. Pathetic. Was this as good as he could give? Trying to pull the old soldier, out here in the middle of nowhere? Well, it wouldn't work.

"Tommy, you're an arsehole," Paul sneered, laughing.

Tommy was huddled in the foetal position, the wind gently tugging at the flaps of the kimono. He wasn't moving.

"That's so childish, Tommy," said Paul, with less certainty than before.

"Tommy?" There was still no response.

"Tommy? Oh shit... Tommy!"

Paul ran over to where he was crouched. Now he could see the agony creasing his face, the whites of his knuckles digging into the side where the pain was.

"Tommy, don't you dare..." The panic was rising in Paul's voice. He looked round. Out here there was nothing, just the cawing of rooks overhead, the burbling stream below and the bleat of sheep. But he had his phone. Thank God.

He pulled it out. There was just enough reception to make a call. He hit the nine button three times, urging it to connect.

"Tommy," he pleaded, almost weeping and hugging the prone body, "please. Please don't do this to me. Please, Tommy, please!!"

198

CHAPTER 21

"Is he gonna die?"

Paul hovered anxiously at the edge of the circle of paramedics gently coaxing Tommy on to his back, whispering the question to the ambulance driver who'd guided the converted Land Rover up the rough, rugged path to where the sick man lay on the ground, barely moving and emitting only the occasional agonised groan. Paul didn't want Tommy to hear the question, but he had to get some kind of answer.

"Difficult to say," said the ambulance driver, hedging his bets. "We pick a lot of people off these fells and most times they're all right. But he doesn't look very well at all, to be honest."

The red-jacket paramedics now had Tommy lying flat on his back and were easing him on to a stretcher. An oxygen mask to aid his breathing had been placed over his face and already the routine checks to try to establish the cause of his collapse were being made.

The ambulance driver sucked his teeth and nodded towards Paul as he watched his colleagues lift the stretcher to waist level.

"It isn't what I'd choose to go hill-walking in, a woman's dressing gown and old man's underpants," he said laconically. "He looks like something from a charity shop window. What the 'ell was going on up here?"

"It's a long story," said Paul wearily.

"Yeah well, it's gonna have to stay that way for the moment," replied the driver. "We need to get him some treatment ASAP."

Paul watched helplessly as the ambulance driver opened the back door of the vehicle and the paramedics prepared to lift the stretchered Tommy inside. But as they did, and with superhuman effort on his part, Tommy turned to Paul and removed his oxygen mask.

"Don't let them see me like this," he pleaded, fighting for breath, "... Rose and Frankie."

Paul muttered a non-committal 'all right', still shocked at the scene unfolding in front of him, but it wasn't good enough for Tommy.

"I'm serious!" he shouted, as he was loaded in. The paramedics climbed in behind, the last occupant slamming the rear doors of the rescue vehicle.

"Don't worry, lad," said the ambulance driver to Paul, as he opened the door to the driver's cab and stepped up to his seat, "we'll do our best for him."

He gestured to the back of the vehicle. "I'd take you with us," he said sympathetically, "but it's a bit cramped back in there. Sorry."

"It's okay," said Paul, "I'll walk. I've got some people to see, anyway."

The driver's door was pulled shut and the vehicle trundled carefully away down the path and towards the main road, its emergency lights flashing.

Paul was alone. Not just physically alone, but separated from Tommy, the man he'd come to regard as... a friend? Was that strong enough? Anyone would have been forgiven for thinking they were sworn enemies, especially in the last hour or so. Barely a word of kindness had passed between them. On the contrary, some bitter accusations had been thrown that couldn't be taken lightly.

But even those words, the "head up your arse" slur from Tommy and Paul's "self-pity" taunt back, showed a level of mutual understanding, if it was the right phrase, that Paul had barely experienced until now. Tommy had held up a mirror to Paul and forced him to look at himself. Tommy had grabbed him by the throat, not always metaphorically either, and pushed him into situations he could never have imagined himself in. And despite everything, he'd coped. He'd coped with a gun in his face. He'd taken care of the ring, dealt with Callaghan on his own doorstep and sprung Tommy from custody. And made passionate love to a woman who wasn't even in his dreams, so far out of his league was she. He'd done all this. *Him*. Paul Callow. Day-dreaming, friendless, lonely Paul Callow, the aspiring-writer-who-never-would-be had done this. And all because of the bond he'd formed with Tommy.

He started to walk back towards the village, dazed with emotion. *Bond*. That was the word. They had bonded. They weren't buddies or drinking pals or life-long soul mates, but they had bonded. Seeing Tommy lying there like a wounded stag had wrenched feelings from him he never knew he had. He was so cut off and out-of-touch with himself that he had no idea what it was like to feel this deeply for someone. He would've changed places with him if he could have done. He would have taken on his pain, carried his burden gladly. He had glimpsed into Tommy's world, and while he had seen selfishness at its worst, he had also seen what it was like to live. To truly live a life, with all its twists and turns, its pains and its joys. To have a story to tell at the end of it. Not, as Paul had done up to now, to have lived life by proxy, always judging your own worth by the achievements of others, especially those from the pages of a book. It wasn't healthy and he saw now how he was almost paralysed by his own introspection. But Tommy – mad, bad and random Tommy – had torn a hole in the fabric of Paul's humdrum existence and, forcing his head through the gap, made him breathe the cool, clean refreshing air of real life.

But as he walked he was struck with another thought. Supposing, in his own way, he was just as selfish as Tommy? Were his reasons for not wanting him to die on that fellside – or in a Lakeland hospital, for that matter – truly as honourable as he was making out? Because if Tommy died now, the whole point of their relationship was dead, too. A dead man could not walk under a train the day after he had passed away. If he did die, it was the end of the Big Game. There would be no Three and

201

Out, no six-figure pay-off, no chance of living the life he wanted to live.

Paul sighed deeply and looked around as he walked. This was a beautiful landscape, all deep browns and luscious greens tinged with blue and red and gold. Birds sang joyfully as though revelling in the beauty of their surroundings. The brooks and streams that fed the great lakes of Coniston, Windermere, Grasmere and Thirlmere tumbled like liquid crystal down the fellsides. Even the bloody sheep looked content. The peace and quiet of a place like this was what he craved with every bone in his body. It was a hundred million miles away from Horn Lane and the ever-present drone of too many people squeezed into too small a place. Yes, it was what he wanted. But did he really want the silence, the insularity and the isolation. What was it Frankie had said? *"Everybody knows you, knows everything about you. Nothing changes, nothing ever happens."* Tommy made things happen. Tommy was the spark, the catalyst. Tommy was a life-force and even as he lay in the back of an ambulance that bounced its way down a rutted and pot-holed road, he was more alive than many so-called healthy people. If he isolated himself, cut his ties with the rest of humanity, he would never meet people like Tommy again, or Frankie for that matter. A life without either of them, and all they stood for. Was that what he *really* wanted? And how hypocritical was it of him to want Tommy to live today, in order that he died more conveniently tomorrow?

Over the brow of the hill, Rosemary's cottage came into view. What was he going to say to them? How was he going to describe the scene he had just witnessed? He suddenly felt sick with nervous anticipation. He still hadn't spoken to Rosemary, and as well as being the accomplice in a very unwelcome visit, he'd also bedded her daughter and been caught with his pants down. This could even be worse than fronting up Mickey Callaghan, but he'd managed that. And if Frankie had somehow persuaded her mother that he was an all-right bloke, and not some voracious sex fiend from the dirty streets of the capital, he could manage this too.

As he walked up the cottage path, dirty, dishevelled and knotted with various scenarios running through his head, the door opened and Rosemary stepped out. She had obviously been waiting by the window, concerned about the combatants who'd fled the cottage and who had so far failed to return.

The sight of Paul alone made her heart lurch. Tommy was absent, and the lad looked very sheepish. He was covered in muck, too.

"Well," she said, her arms folded, "what happened? You look like you've been wrestling in a pig-sty. Though it's no better than you deserve. Animals, the pair of youse."

Frankie joined her mother on the step. She was wearing a green vest and a pair of shorts. Paul smiled wanly at her, but she looked away.

"So what have you done with him, then?" asked Rose, her face hardening. Paul couldn't tell if she was angry or concerned or both.

"I'm really sorry..." he said, trying to form the words. "There's been... I dunno what you'd call it. An accident, I suppose."

"What kind of an accident?" she snapped. "Where's Tommy?"

"We were running. We were both knacke... we were both tired. Then we stopped by a bridge. We didn't fight. Well, not really. I started to walk off and he followed. Then he... just collapsed."

"Collapsed?"

"Yeah. Look I'm really sorry. But I think he's had a heart attack."

"Oh dear God!" exclaimed Rose, clasping her hands to her face. Silently, Frankie turned on her heel and pounded upstairs. Then the sound of her bedroom door slamming was heard.

Rose's eyes now filled with tears. "Where is he now?" she asked. "Is he all right? Oh God. I should be surprised, but I'm not. He looked like a plateful of bad fat when he walked in here yesterday. The man's not well. But a heart attack?"

"I rung an ambulance as soon as it happened," said Paul, trying to reassure her. "They've been and taken him to hospital."

203

"And what did they say," she said, "the ambulance people, I mean?"

Paul hesitated. He couldn't lie. Bad news was heading in her direction one way or another.

"They said he didn't look well at all. I think… it probably doesn't look too good for him. I'm really sorry."

She could hardly take it in. After all this time, he turns up here, just to die on the doorstep. That was so bloody typical of Tommy. Selfish to the bitter end.

She looked at Paul, a forlorn figure covered in cow dung, the unlikely bearer of bad tidings. Whoever he was – and she would be giving him a mighty earful about her daughter when all this mess was sorted out – he deserved a bit of humanity.

"Come in," she said, looking him up and down, "and get that muck cleaned off you. You can't go over to the hospital looking like that."

*

Paul showered and went back outside to the car to retrieve a clean T-shirt he had stuffed into his sports bag. When he came back in, Rosemary was waiting for him again, her arms folded.

"You'll be wanting to talk to Frankie, no doubt?" she said, eyeing him suspiciously.

"If I could?" he replied uncertainly.

"You can," she said, indicating the stairs "she's still in her room. But don't be long. She's upset. All this has been a shock for her. So no heavy stuff. Understand?"

Paul nodded in tacit agreement and ascended the stairs.

*

Frankie sat on the end of her bed, her back to the door. In her hand was a faded photograph, twenty years old, maybe. In it, a father crouched beside a toddler on a beach. Happier times for Frankie and her father. The days when he delighted in her presence, and she in his. Sunny days on the beach,

204

before dark clouds scudded over and poured sadness on the memories of her childhood. She stared at the picture and bit her lip, her eyes brimming with unshed tears. *My Daddy...* Even as she struggled to hold back her emotions, she swore she would never cry over him. Not that bastard. And yet, her whole body shook as she thought of him on a drip in a hospital bed, his heart on its last few beats.

There was a soft knock at the door which temporarily shook her out of her misery. As the handle turned and the door opened, she stuffed the photograph under her pillow.

She knew who it would be and, catching a half-glimpse of him in the doorway, she knew she was right. She didn't want him to see her like this. Couldn't he leave her alone?

Paul paused for a moment, unsure of what to say. He wanted to walk over, sit down, put his arms around her and tell her it would be alright. But he didn't know whether it would be all right. Not today, not tomorrow.

"I'm off to see him now," he muttered, still standing uneasily in the doorway.

Again she bit her lip and did not turn round.

"Well, I'm not going," she said, defiantly. "If he thinks having a heart attack is going to make up for... well, he can think again."

She had to see him. She just had to. He felt a thick lump of guilt rise in his throat.

"Maybe you should go and see him," he said, making a half-hearted attempt at a persuasive tone.

"Why?" she replied.

"I don't know," he replied, desperately thinking of a way of getting her to him. "You never know when you'll see him again."

"Like I care," she sniffed.

Oh God. But you would... You would care, if only...

"But what if something happens?" he said, taking a step closer to her. "What if it is the last time?"

She didn't reply or turn round. It was hopeless.

"I'll see you later then," he said resignedly.

"No you won't."

"I will, I promise…"

"No," she said, her voice more emphatic now, "I mean, I don't want to."

"Oh. Okay." Paul hung his head. She didn't want to see him, ever again. The pain swept over him like the tentacles of a stinging jellyfish. Last night, when she'd said he was different. Did she mean it, or was she just saying it? Or, in the harsh light of the day after, was he just *too* different? He felt crushed, confused, hurt and disappointed all at once. He wanted to ask her why, plead with her, ask for another chance. She was… she was wonderful. Truly wonderful. This might never happen to him again.

"Just go, Paul," she whispered softly, sensing his hesitation

He had no choice but to swallow his pain. He nodded, accepted the verdict and turned slowly away from her room, closing the door behind him. As he did, she was unable to contain herself any longer, her shoulders shaking as sobs of anguish tumbled from her.

At the bottom of the stairs Paul picked up his jacket. Rosemary came out of the kitchen with Tommy's suit and shirt, tidily placed on a coat hanger and neatly folded. Paul thanked her, and fished in the jacket pocket for the keys to the Mercedes.

He smiled at her awkwardly. She seemed a lovely woman. She'd done a good job raising Frankie. It couldn't have been easy.

"Well," he said, "I'd better get off."

He stepped out of the doorway and into the fresh air. Rosemary followed him out.

"You'll call me," she said, pressing a phone number into his hand, "and let me know how he is?"

He nodded, then caught her gaze. Like Tommy at the ambulance doors, she wanted something more from him than simple reassurance.

"Will you see that he's alright?" she said anxiously. "Look out for him?"

"I… I hardly know him, really," he said.

But she wasn't budging.

"Promise me," she whispered fiercely.

Again, he nodded, not wishing to commit. Again, it wasn't enough.

"*So say it,*" she hissed, looking deeply into his eyes, her jaw set firm.

"Alright," he replied, deeply uncomfortable at her insistence, "I promise."

She nodded, satisfied, and turned away. He trudged over to the Mercedes, the piece of paper with the phone number and address of the hospital in his hand. *'Promise me you'll look out for him'*. He gulped, not wishing to think about the implications of her words. If only she knew…

CHAPTER 22

Paul took the road that bordered the shores of Lake Coniston. Sunlight glinted on the water and a gentle breeze blew along the many sailboats that were out. Behind the wheel of the Mercedes, and alone again, he felt relaxed and contemplative. Even so, Rosemary's demand that he make a promise to her about Tommy still weighed on his mind. He wanted to fulfil the promise and look out for her husband, as she had asked, but there was still Monday to consider and Tommy's equally forceful demand that a "deal was a deal".

Oh well. What would be would be. If Tommy needed emergency surgery, or was being transferred to a larger hospital – Carlisle, maybe, or even somewhere in Scotland – the decision would be made for them both. The deal was off. The Big Game would end without result. Tommy would live – or, at best, he wouldn't die under a train – and Paul would… Well, what would Paul do?

He would go back to London, carry on with the job and try to start the novel again. Or would he? Somehow, he wasn't so sure that he would. Everything was different now. He couldn't see himself slipping back into his old life with the same kind of resigned attitude he'd had in the past. Up there on the fellside, Tommy accused him of having his head up his arse. It was true. He lived life in black holes, the black holes of the tunnels he drove his train through and the black hole of his mind, stumbling and tripping over itself to find a way out. Well, he had found a way out and Tommy had shown him the path. The least he could do would be to take it, wherever it led. If it wasn't to the front door of Loch Tyne house, so be it. There would be something else. Tommy had shown him that there was always another way.

*

208

He arrived at the hospital and parked up. It looked to be more of a cottage hospital than anything else. Paul hoped they were looking after Tommy properly. It couldn't have many modern facilities, surely? Still, the ambulance guy had said they took many people off the fells, so this would be the place they came to. It must be okay, he decided.

He went in through the wooden doors and followed a sign for reception.

"Can I help you?" said the uniformed receptionist, a blue cardigan slung over her shoulders.

"Yes," said Paul, looking beyond her to see if he could catch a glimpse of Tommy, "I'm looking for someone. His name's Cassidy. Tommy Cassidy. He was brought in this morning."

"Oh yes," smiled the receptionist, "Mr Cassidy – the kimono man. Yes, he's here."

"How is he?" asked Paul anxiously.

"The doctor's just been to see him, actually," she said, gesturing to a white-coated, bespectacled man in an office behind her, making notes in a file. "Would you like to have a word with him?"

Paul nodded so the receptionist knocked at the window of the office. The silver-haired doctor stopped what he was doing and came out.

"I hope you don't mind, doctor" she said, "but this gentleman has come to visit Mr Cassidy. I've told him that you've just seen him. Could you give him a progress report?"

"Sure," he said, stretching out his hand to Paul, "I'm Dr Calderbank."

"Hi, I'm Paul. Paul Callow. I'm Mr Cassidy's… friend."

"Ah, good," said the doctor, smiling. "Now, I've just been to see him and he's fine. Well, actually he's not fine because we suspect he's had a heart attack, but he's as well as can be expected given the circumstances."

Relief swept over Paul at the news of his friend's survival. But it was followed by a wave of guilt. Tommy wasn't dead. A deal could still be a deal.

"Thank God," Paul said. "So what happens next?"

"Well," replied the doctor, "he's comfortable enough. He's asked for a pen and paper and he's been scribbling away, so that's a good sign. But he is under observation and I would like to keep him in overnight, maybe even for a few days, just to see how he's getting along. We'd like to run some tests on him too, just to make sure everything else is all right."

So that was it. Game over. Tommy was going nowhere. The deadline would pass without incident. There would be no pay-off or island retreat. But there would be Tommy, and maybe Frankie too. Despite himself, he felt relieved. The decision had been made for him. Now it was his priority to see that Tommy got better. He would take him back to London. He would look after him. They could do stuff together. Whatever he wanted. Suddenly he realised he'd never felt so close to someone before. He needed him.

"Okay," said Paul, distractedly. "That's… great. Can I go and see him now?"

"Of course," said the doctor, "he's still awake. Or he was when I left him. Go out of here, turn left, down the corridor and it's the ward at the end."

Paul followed Dr Calderbank's instructions and walked down the corridor to the ward, Tommy's clothes tucked under his arm. He looked down the row of beds until he spotted him in the third one along, dressed in a hospital gown and lying on his back, staring at the ceiling. Attached to his body were wires which fed into a heart-monitor by the side of his bed.

Spying him, Tommy greeted Paul with all his usual charm and enthusiastic warmth.

"Where the hell have you been?" he snarled.

Paul ignored him. Poor sod. He must still be feeling pretty out of sorts.

"How's it going?" he asked as brightly as he could.

"Did you bring my kit?" said Tommy, swinging his legs out of the side of the bed and removing a wire from his arm, casting it aside seemingly without a care.

"Hey," said Paul, putting his arm on Tommy's shoulder and attempting to pull him back into bed, "don't get too excited. The doctor wants you to stay in overnight for observation."

Tommy stared at Paul, hardly able to believe what he was hearing.

"I'm not staying in here all night," he huffed. "I've got things to be doing."

"Tommy, you've just had a heart attack," said Paul, desperately trying to restrain him. "For Christ's sake, just lie down!"

"Heart attack me arse!" said Tommy scornfully. "It was angina. Just a bit more lively than usual."

"Forget it," said Paul, his face set in determination, "you're staying here."

"What's it to you, anyway?" Tommy snarled, before turning away pulling monitor pads off his chest. Suddenly he stopped and leaned forward slightly, clutching his stomach. The pain was back. He clenched his teeth, forcing down a moan of agony. He needed to get out of this place, right now.

Tommy turned back to Paul, his face wracked with suffering. But there was something else, an expression Paul had never seen on him before. It told a story of fear, of real, gut-wrenching, terror. He didn't know Tommy could be frightened, but here he was, his eyes telling him a very different story.

"Don't leave me in here, Paul," he pleaded, almost begging, "please don't leave me here."

Paul stepped back, shocked. Tommy was in the best place. They would look after him, feed him and make him better. Why did he want to leave now, against the doctor's advice? It was mad. But the way Tommy had implored him and the hunted look in his eyes persuaded Paul that he could do nothing other than agree to his request. He nodded and pulled the curtains around the bed, passing Tommy his suit.

Paul stood watching the Irishman for a few moments as he

threw off his hospital gown and pulled his shirt on.

"What d'you want me to do, Tommy? I mean, where do you want to go now?"

"Back to Rosemary's," Tommy muttered, sliding his legs into his trousers and fastening them up. "I've one more thing to do."

*

Dr Calderbank argued, warning Tommy that he couldn't be responsible for his health if he left, but he was adamant. He was discharging himself, thanks very much. He felt fine and now he wanted to be on his way. The doctor stood at the doorway, shaking his head, as Tommy, supported by Paul, made his way back to the Mercedes.

Within half an hour they were back at the cottage in Coniston. Paul pulled up in the same spot they parked the day before and switched off the engine. But as he took the keys out of the ignition and went to unfasten his seatbelt, Tommy stayed his hand.

"You stay here," he said.

Something wasn't right, but Paul wasn't going to challenge him.

"Okay," he muttered, as the Irishman opened the door and gingerly hauled himself from the seat.

Paul watched as Tommy walked slowly to the door, taking an envelope from his jacket as he did so. At the door he paused, but he did not knock. He raised the envelope to his lips and kissed it tenderly. Then he lifted the flap of the letter box and posted it through, before turning and slowly walking back to the car.

Without a word he climbed back in, staring straight ahead as he settled into his seat. Paul had seen sorrow written all over him as he plodded back to the car. Why hadn't he knocked? What was going on?

"But what about…I mean, don't you want to…?"

Tommy said nothing. He wasn't about to offer an explanation.

"But… everything you wanted to say to her?" continued Paul,

212

trying to understand.

Tommy turned to him, an expression of weary resignation on his face.

"Just take me home," he said sadly.

As Paul reversed out of the drive, he noticed Tommy gazing at the disappearing view of the cottage, particularly the front door which remained firmly closed. Paul straightened up the car at the end of the drive and headed off up the lane to the turn-off for the motorway. Nothing was said. They were going back to London. Paul switched on the radio, hoping to drown out the awful, ominous silence that had grown between them.

*

Still lying on her bed, Frankie's thoughts were spinning out of control, tormenting her to the point of tears. She heard the click of the letter box. Her mother was in the back garden, weeding, so Frankie slowly pulled herself up and padded slowly downstairs to see what had come through the door.

She picked up the thick white envelope and looked at it. On the front, in neat, sloping letters was one word: 'Frances'. Her stomach turned over. Cautiously she opened the door and looked out. But no one was there, only the cries of birds high above the fells and the rushing sound of the wind in the trees.

She walked upstairs and into her room, shutting the door behind her. With trembling hands she pulled open the envelope. It was stuffed full of money – what looked to be hundreds of pounds. The bastard. He was trying to buy her affection. He'd come all the way up here, caused all this trouble, churned everything up, and now he was trying to buy his way in. Well he could just *get lost!*

With a force born of anger, she flung the wad of notes against the bedroom mirror. And as she watched them, fluttering down harmlessly like falling leaves, she slumped heavily into a chair and burst into unstoppable tears.

*

Tommy and Paul had been on the road for three-quarters of an hour, and not a word had passed between them. The skies were darkening over the fells and the weather seemed to be closing in on them. Angry black and grey clouds lay heavily across the landscape in anticipation of a storm. The roads were silent.

A dreary play on Radio 4 was coming to an end. The story was some kind of petty, middle-class affair involving an opera singer losing her voice. Neither had listened to it with interest, but like an old married couple with little left to say to one another, it had filled a void.

Paul, however, had plenty to say to Tommy. There were so many unanswered questions running through his head that he hardly knew where to begin. But he had to voice them. Alarm bells were ringing. There were things he suspected of being left unsaid. And whatever it was, Paul wanted to hear it. Tommy had to come clean. He owed him that much.

He turned to Tommy, who was still staring fixedly ahead, and paused before he spoke.

"It's because you're ill, isn't it?" he said gently.

"What?" The Irishman was suddenly shaken out of his stupor by Paul's question.

"That you agreed to… you know."

Tommy tutted and turned away from Paul in contempt.

"I've never heard of someone killing themselves because they had angina," he sneered.

"It's not though, is it?" replied Paul, matter-of-factly. "It's not just angina. What is it then, what…?"

"Alright," snapped Tommy, interrupting, "it's not just angina."

Paul persisted. "So what is it then?"

Tommy paused and sighed. Jesus. Why now? Hadn't he enough on his mind? But then, Paul had done as he'd been asked. He'd helped Tommy out of the hospital. And fair enough, they'd made it this far together. They were a team, of sorts.

"It's terminal," said Tommy, "that's all you need to know."

The words turned Paul's blood to ice. *Terminal*. Now it all made sense. "Seize the day". That's exactly what you would do, should do, if you didn't have many days left to seize. Grab any opportunity you could and take as many risks as you wanted. It didn't matter. Christ almighty. No wonder he wanted to get out of the hospital so fast.

"Come on, Tommy," said Paul, "don't keep it to yourself. You know you can tell me. We've been through a lot together, haven't we? How terminal is terminal? Please tell me."

"No." Tommy was adamant.

Paul stared ahead, stunned into silence. Then Tommy spoke again, this time with a nervy energy.

"I don't want to die alone," he said suddenly, "in some piss-stinking nursing home surrounded by people dribbling and making farm noises."

He paused, wrestling with the appalling image in his head.

"And however long I've got left," he continued, "whether it's six months or six years, it's not gonna be some fucking golden age, oh no. It's gonna be shite and every day will be worse than the last. I refuse to live life looking over my shoulder the whole time. I won't have it!"

Paul could feel the anger coming off him, hotter than a roaring fire.

"I'm going to pull out when *I* say," he declared indignantly, "not when they decide to pull the fucking plug. I'm a stubborn, selfish bastard and I want to *choose* when I die."

With that, he leaned backwards slightly and turned his face towards the car's side window, shutting his eyes. There. He could stick that in his pipe and smoke it. No more needed to be said on the subject.

Paul fell into silence again. He could sense Tommy didn't want to talk any more. And who could blame him? The bravado of Tommy's words only partially papered over all the fear, pain, anxiety and dread he must be feeling. If he was in Tommy's shoes, he'd feel exactly the same. He'd want to be dead already and not have to walk around with the shadow of the Grim Reaper a foot behind him. No wonder he was prepared to jump from a bridge. No wonder he was willing to fall under a Tube train.

"*Six months or six years…*" It was quite a gap between the two. Surely something could be done? He could care for Tommy. Maybe he could somehow get a bigger flat with a couple of bedrooms and have him to stay. You could get an allowance for looking after very ill people. God, he wouldn't be the easiest patient, but at least he'd have everything he wanted – his own room, a telly, books. Plenty of those. He could come and go as he pleased. Frankie and Rosemary could visit.

Paul began to see the possibilities. It might not be easy, but they'd work it out. He felt a duty of care towards him now. No, it was more than that. Christ… he loved the guy. In spite of everything, he genuinely loved him. He'd seen him, warts and all, and he still loved him. He'd been the best friend he'd ever had, in a desert of friendlessness. He wanted no harm to come to him and he wanted to make whatever time he had left as warm, comfortable and as pleasant as he possibly could.

But then it was Tommy he was dealing with. Stubborn bastard Tommy. He was a hard man, who was ready to stare Death squarely in the face like some Western gunslinger and tell him to bring it on. A man who'd brokered a deal with Death and who'd be very unwilling to walk away from it. That was his style. If he was going to die, he would do it his way. That's what he wanted. If Paul killed him tomorrow, as planned, he would be… doing him a favour. Of course. Tommy not only wanted to die, he had a bloody good reason for wanting it, and soon. It was not for macabre or miserable reasons, this planned suicide. It was the only practical solution to an intractable problem. If Tommy died beneath the wheels of the train, it would be nothing less than a mercy killing, plain and simple. If he loved him, he had to let him go.

Paul pulled up to the roundabout before the slip-road on to

216

the M6. He looked at Tommy, his eyes full of sympathy for him. He seemed to be asleep now. Gently, he turned down the radio. It was the shipping forecast being broadcast "… Tyne, Dogger, Fisher, German Bight. West or Southwest 6 or 7, Gale 8 later. Rain at times…"

The miles and the hours stretched out in front of him as he joined the motorway. Tomorrow was Monday. Three and Out Day. If he wanted it, it was there for the taking.

CHAPTER 23

They came out of the darkness and into the light again. As he drove, Paul couldn't help noticing how everything seemed to be brighter once the brooding fells and valleys of the rural north of England were left behind. Factories, football stadiums, blocks of flats, housing estates and leisure parks suddenly came into view once more, all bathed in the neon glow of a million sodium lamps. On the way up, Paul felt he never wanted to see such sights again. Now, re-entering the atmosphere of the big city he felt curiously pleased to be reunited with it. It was still too crowded, dirty, noisy and dangerous, but it was home. His attitude had changed. He no longer wanted to be friendless, isolated and alone. The break away had made him think very deeply about his life. From now on, he would explore possibilities, take opportunities, talk to people, socialise. He would immerse himself in it, start living. That way, he was sure he would find the path he wanted to follow.

By his side, Tommy shifted awkwardly in the seat, trying to find a comfortable spot to rest his head. Eventually he gave in and sat up straight, twisting his neck from side to side to shake off the aches of the long sleep he'd had.

"Where are we?" he murmured to Paul, rubbing his eyes.

"About a mile or so from the North Circular," replied Paul. "You had a good sleep?"

"It was a sleep," said Tommy, grumpily. "Whether it was a good one is very fecking debatable."

"How are you feeling?" asked Paul.

The Irishman paused before answering. Of course. He'd told him about the illness thing. He hoped Paul wasn't going to start

218

going all mushy on him. The last thing he wanted was sympathy. Not now. It was too bloody late for all that. Still, the lad had pulled him from that god-awful hospital and its doctors, prodding and poking and wanting to test this, that and the other. The least he could do was be civil.

"I'm okay, thanks," he said, a note of weariness in his voice. "Better now I'm away from the quacks. Who needs 'em, eh?"

"I would say you do, Tommy," replied Paul quietly. "You're a sick man."

Tommy dismissed the suggestion with a wave of his hand. "I've got me tablets," he announced, "and that's enough. If I want to take them I will, and if I don't, I won't. My choice."

"Anyway," he went on, "the whole subject is so boring, just sitting here talking over it brings me out in piles. It's an auld woman's habit, is blathering about illness and death. The minute you're born you're on a countdown. We all are. So we should all stop yakking and get on with living."

"Fair enough," said Paul, "let's change the subject."

"Agreed."

They sat in silence for a moment, unable to think of anything else to say. Then, Tommy laughed.

"It's been a mad weekend, eh?" he said.

"I can't say I've ever had one like it," replied Paul.

"I'll bet you've not," smiled Tommy. "Your fecking face when Callaghan pointed that shotgun at you. 'Oh shit, oh no, oh please, oh God!' If it hadn't been so bloody terrifying I might a' wet me trousers on the spot. And yours too, for that matter."

Paul laughed. "I thought I was a goner," he said.

"So did I, to be honest," Tommy retorted. "If that thing had been loaded we'd have been dog meat. He's a vicious bastard, you know. Still, Maureen was always worse. I just hope he's booked an appointment with the jewellers."

"It was good to meet Rosemary," said Paul, "…and Frankie."

"You've still got some beggin' to do before I forgive you that

219

little episode," said Tommy, turning to face Paul and shaking his head. "Me own daughter. Me own fecking daughter."

"So you keep saying," said Paul meekly. "Look, Tommy, I'm sorry. I didn't mean for it to happen. I was in the pub and she came in, then she sat down and…"

"Look, I don't wanna know," said Tommy, interrupting. "I don't want to hear the ins and outs of it. In fact, I *really, really* don't want to know the ins and outs. So shut your hole."

"She's a lovely girl," muttered Paul, aglow with the memory of her asleep next to him in the single bed.

"She is," said Tommy. "Pity I couldn't talk to… ah well. At least I had the chance to see Rose. She was looking grand. Me out of her life has taken 20 years off her."

The car turned into the top of Horn Lane, Acton. Almost home. He pulled up the Mercedes almost parallel with the front window of his flat and right behind his wreck of a Fiesta. The noise coming from an open window in the flat above him indicated that Yvonne was having yet another of her parties. As Paul reached over for his sports bag and opened the car door, the racket coming from the upstairs flat mingled with sounds from the street – the constant thrum of traffic, car horns, stereos booming, distant sirens, low flying aircraft overhead. So nothing had changed along Horn Lane, but for Paul, everything had changed. He looked at his street with new eyes.

Paul rooted for his keys in his jacket pocket then climbed the steps to the front door of the flat, Tommy a couple of steps behind him. They went through the main door and stood outside the entrance to Paul's flat as he selected the correct key.

The noise from upstairs was almost unbearable. Tommy looked up at the direction it was coming from, realising with weary resignation that a good night's sleep was probably out of the question. Paul put the key in the lock then hesitated. It wasn't that late and it sounded like they were having fun up there. He looked at Tommy and laid a hand gently on the Irishman's arm.

220

"Come on," he said, indicating the stairs. "Change of plan."

Tommy groaned hesitantly. The last thing he wanted was to be whooping it up with a bunch of kids at this time of night. He shook his head, but Paul seemed adamant.

"Come on," he repeated, "let's just go and have the one drink. It's been a long drive."

Paul led the way with Tommy following reluctantly behind. At the top of the stairs they went through the open door into the flat, buzzing with party-goers, music, noise, laughter, smoke and good times.

Paul turned to Tommy as they squeezed past the revellers, many of them Yvonne's attractive female friends. He did look tired, but a drink might do him good. Paul headed for the kitchen where a table stood packed to the edges with beer, wine and spirits. He grabbed a can of lager for himself and a half-full bottle of whiskey for Tommy.

"Will this do for you?" he shouted to Tommy over the relentless disco beat, passing him the bottle.

"You know what they say, Paul," he roared back, suddenly perked up, "it's either kill or cure! So I'll take me chances!"

They grinned at one another then clinked can and bottle together in a toast.

"Slainte!" shouted Tommy.

"What?"

"Slainte!" shouted the Irishman again.

"What?!!"

"Ah, fuck it," said Tommy, laughing at Paul's puzzled face. "Cheers!!"

"Oh yeah… cheers!"

They toasted then leaned back against the living room wall to take in the scene. It was a small flat, the same size as Paul's, but it bubbled and brimmed with life. Paul looked around at the happy faces of the party-goers, wall-to-wall in this flat. It was so different to the lifelessness of his own living accommodation.

221

"I'll tell you something," said Tommy with surprise, leaning over to speak in Paul's ear, "this place is a nest o'birds, is it not? Look at the women here… Jeez, it's like being backstage at a Tom Jones gig!"

Paul laughed. "I suppose so," he said. "I've never been up here before."

"What?" Tommy was incredulous. "You live in the flat downstairs and you never come up here on the hunt for a bit of the old leg-over? Jesus, son, you really are a one-off aren't you?"

"I've lived a quiet life," Paul said, suddenly thoughtful. Too damn quiet. Too quiet and too still. But it would change. It had to change.

"Right," said Tommy, taking a big swig from the whiskey bottle and suddenly looking mischievous, "I'm not standing next to a bloody wallflower all night. I'm off to try a bit of the old Tommy magic. Watch and learn, Paul, watch and learn."

Bottle in hand, Tommy edged his way towards a small group of twentysomething females in glamorous party dresses. They looked surprised at first, but as Tommy politely introduced himself, then started to crack a few jokes and tell a few tall tales, they began to smile and laugh uproariously.

He was holding court, and they loved it. The circle of women was enthralled by him, his accent, his humour and his manner. Paul could now see what Rosemary saw all those years ago. So this was the old Tommy magic being worked, was it?

"… I've done many things in me time," he heard him saying, as the girls hung on his every word, "some I'm more proud of than others. I'm like a shark, you know… if I stop swimming, I die…" He raised his arm in imitation of a shark's fin, slicing through the surface of the ocean. The girls laughed and he winked at them cheekily.

Paul smiled to himself. He was pleased to see Tommy looking so happy. Then, someone touched his arm. It was Yvonne, the party queen herself. She looked delighted to see Paul.

"Hey," she said, beaming at him, "how are you? Not too loud is it?"

"No," replied Paul, "not at all. I just figured... if you can't beat them..."

"Cool," said Yvonne, "good for you." She turned to a blonde haired girl who was squeezing by, a beer in her hand.

"Have you met Katie?" she said to Paul, holding each of them by the hand. "She's an archivist in the British Library. I reckon you guys'll get on really well."

Paul smiled, slightly awkwardly, but instead of wanting to run away as he usually did, he began to chat instead. She responded to his questions, asked him about himself, seemed interested. But in truth, he was somewhat detached and distracted. He was too busy looking over at Tommy, making sure he was okay, hoping he was bearing up. His thoughts were even further away, back in the Lake District and with a girl he'd met and just couldn't forget. There were plenty of lovely women in this room, but not a single one of them compared to Frankie. He wondered if he would see her again. Maybe, if he was to look after Tommy through his illness, she would come to visit her father. Then they could talk and say all the things they didn't say.

Yvonne came past again, holding a CD case.

"I've got a brilliant record I'm gonna put on for your mate," she said. "Irish, isn't he? God, he's a laugh. This'll get him going."

She showed Paul the CD cover. He recognised it and smiled, waiting for the moment when Tommy would hear it.

She took off the disco music and slipped the CD into the player. In a split second the room was filled with a wild, raucous reel, driven by accordion, banjo and drums, and featuring the vocals of a singer who sounded like he'd woken up in the world's biggest ashtray after a night in a distillery. It was Shane MacGowan and the Pogues.

Yvonne grabbed Tommy's hands and dragged him into the middle of the room, flinging him round with a manic scream of laughter. He just had time to put down his drink as she twirled him around, clapping her hands to the Irish triple-time beat. People jumped off chairs and sofas to join in. The room became hot with dancers, rocking and reeling to the song. Tommy was beaming, and as he moved his feet to the music and sang the words, he spotted Paul in the corner, looking at him with his head slightly to one side.

Tommy raised his finger and beckoned him to join in. Shyly, Paul shook his head, but Tommy was having none of it. He danced over and grabbed him in a headlock, pulling him on to the makeshift dance floor. Paul felt Tommy's broad arm around his shoulders and the pair danced together like a pair of drunken sailors.

Tommy swung Paul around, whooping and singing at the top of his voice. Paul stared admiringly at him from the corner of his eye. In his black jacket and white open-necked shirt, he reminded him of Brendan Behan, the great Irish playwright. It was the sort of gathering Behan loved, one where he could take centre-stage and show the world how the Irish could party. With his stories and his sharks and his magic, Tommy could play that character too.

The song flew along. Tommy and Paul linked arms, Riverdanced like idiots and jumped up and down on the spot, drawing in the rest of the party with their antics. As the last two beats of the song drew it to a close, Paul flung his arms round Tommy's neck and hugged him tightly, the Irishman responding in the same way. The bond between them was sealed. Paul shut his eyes, revelling in the moment of deep affection he held for Tommy Cassidy, his friend for life.

CHAPTER 24

The party was winding slowly down. After their exertions on the dance floor, Tommy had resumed his role as king for the night, sitting among his handmaidens who congratulated him on his dancing skills and kept a regular stream of whiskey flowing down his throat.

Paul retired, exhausted but flushed with happiness, to the kitchen, where a small hardcore of guests seemed determined to see out the dawn. He felt like he had never felt before when surrounded by people of his own age. He felt like one of them. As he made conversation with strangers and swapped small-talk, he no longer considered himself an outsider, an unsociable freak of nature whom Destiny had forced into a small, book-strewn cell for the rest of eternity. He could do this. He had a lot to learn, but he could do it. He could still read, for sure, but he could also live a little. Or a lot, if that was his choice.

More importantly, he felt that other people didn't see him as an outsider. It had always seemed that way in the past, but here everyone appeared to be friendly enough and willing to take him for who he was at that moment. He no longer felt he had a sign over his head saying 'Weirdo – Please Don't Touch'. He could be whoever he wanted to be and at this moment he was a young guy – a bit shy, maybe, but willing to let his hair down – with a mad mate who was the life and soul of the party. New people, he had discovered, were no longer a threat. Indeed, they were an opportunity.

Paul was sitting by the kitchen window talking to Yvonne. He realised that in all the time he'd spent in the flat, he'd never spoken more than a few sentences to her. He'd had her down as an air-headed party girl with reading skills that could just about extend to a weekly celeb trash-mag and an interest in current affairs that was only sparked when a bottle of chardonnay went up by 10p in the Budget. So he was surprised – and somewhat humbled – to discover that she was a PhD graduate with an important job in the Ministry of Agriculture. She read, too – Jane Austen, George Eliot – and so they chatted about favourite books and authors, book groups, signings and shops. She wasn't Frankie, but she was better and more interesting company than he'd ever assumed. He began to wonder whether a lot of what he assumed about life and people wasn't quite how it really was.

He was just telling her about a signing he'd been to where the author flounced out after a couple of awkward questions from an obsessive fan, when Tommy came over.

He leaned over Yvonne and, smiling at her, interrupted the conversation.

"You got the keys, Paul?" he asked.

Paul was momentarily shocked. A minute ago, he'd observed Tommy through the kitchen door, laughing and winking away at his female admirers. He looked like he was going nowhere fast.

"What?" said Paul, unable to conceal his surprise, fishing in his pockets to find the keys and passing them to Tommy. "You don't want to go yet, do you?"

Tommy leaned in further, the red neon sign from the hotel across the road illuminating his face and giving him a serious look.

"Better get some sleep," he said. "We've both got a big day tomorrow."

Paul's face fell. He could not speak. Surely Tommy couldn't mean…? But the Irishman was staring at him with an expression of intense determination.

"Now don't tell me you've forgotten our little arrangement," he said, his eyes hard.

Paul stared back at him. He couldn't be serious. Not now. Not after tonight? They'd danced, laughed, embraced, got drunk. Who cared about tomorrow? They were mates.

Tommy saw the hesitation in Paul's face and, ignoring Yvonne's bewildered look, slowly raised a finger and pointed it at the younger man.

"I'll see you tomorrow," he said, "at six minutes past ten. Like we agreed."

As he turned, Tommy turned to Yvonne and thanked her for the party.

"Sweet dreams!" she shouted after him as he walked through the remaining party-goers and out of the door to the flat. She turned back to resume the conversation with Paul, but he'd already gathered up his jacket and with a hurried 'thanks' followed Tommy out of the flat.

"Tommy, wait!" he shouted, belting down the stairs towards the figure who was about to put the key into the lock of Paul's flat.

Tommy turned in the darkened hallway, his face lit only by a street lamp which glowed through the window about the front door.

"I can't do it, Tommy," said Paul, his eyes bulging with fear.

"Oh yes you can," he whispered calmly, "a deal's a deal."

"No," said Paul, this time with more urgency in his voice, "I can't. Anyway, I promised Rosemary."

"What the feck did you tell her?" replied the Irishman savagely.

"Nothing," said Paul. "I said nothing. She just asked me to look out for you."

"Oh, right, that's great," said Tommy sarcastically, "and that's all I'm asking. Look out for me. And when you see, don't fecking stop. Then you won't break any promises to anyone."

He nodded emphatically at Paul and put the key in the lock. He opened the door and went inside, leaving Paul where he was, one hand over his eyes in disbelief. This was some kind of a nightmare, he was sure. But Tommy looked deadly serious. In a few hours he was going to die and he seemed determined about it. But there was still time to try to persuade him otherwise. Their story couldn't end like this, could it?

Paul entered the living room and found Tommy reflectively staring out of the window at the street.

Tommy heard the door open and sensed Paul entering, but he didn't turn round.

"Tell me, Paul," he said in a low voice, "why do you want me under your train?"

Paul paused. He'd never asked the question, and because he hadn't asked, he hadn't told him. He assumed that the Irishman didn't want to know or didn't care. He walked across the room and perched on a small sofa by the window, his head in his hands.

"It's just that… well, I've had two people under my train this month…" he said, wincing with embarrassment and hardly daring to voice the rest of what now appeared to be a ridiculously self-indulgent plan.

"Jesus," Tommy said, turning to face him, "you're a serial killer!"

Paul didn't know if he was joking or not. On the face of it, it might look as though it was part of some twisted fantasy. He had to explain.

"No," he said, staring at the threadbare carpet, "they weren't my fault. But they've got a rule at work… if you have three in a month then they pay you off. Ten years' pay. A lump sum."

Tommy whistled in surprised admiration as he digested the information. He made a quick calculation in his head. A very good six-figure sum was what Paul would get.

"And what are you going to do with your pay-off?" Tommy said, looking round the flat. "Buy more books?"

Paul didn't want to say. It sounded so stupid now.

"No," he said finally. "I want to get out of London and live in Scotland on an island. Get away from everything."

Tommy looked at him with incredulity. A young fella like him, living in a city like this, and he just wanted to sit on his own in the middle of feck all.

"Really?" he said, "a hermit at your age? Life in the fast lane got too much for you, did it?"

Tommy sat down in the green leather chair by the unlit electric fire and shook his head in amusement.

"Feck," he said, stretching back, "youth is wasted on the young. Somebody famous said that."

He looked over at Paul, who was sitting awkwardly on the sofa.

"And what do you plan to do on this island?" Tommy asked him.

"Write, I guess," mumbled Paul.

This was going from bad to worse. Sitting there on his own, the rain belting down outside and not a soul for miles, just writing.

"About what?" Tommy sneered, "You've had no life."

The dig was as nasty as it had been on the fell side, just before Tommy's collapse, but this time it simply went over Paul's head. There was too much at stake now for him to start taking comments like that personally.

"Anyway, it doesn't matter," said Paul, suddenly getting up from his seat and taking a step closer to Tommy. "I don't want it any more...I didn't know you before... You were just some guy... but now... we're friends, I think. And I don't want to do it. The money's not important."

Tommy sat up in his chair and looked at the anxious figure above him.

"It might not be to you," he interrupted, "but it is to me. I want some of it to go to Frances. Ten grand."

Paul felt like he had been punched in the face. He heard what Tommy was saying. An opportunity had opened up for him that only Paul could deliver. The man was terminally ill. His daughter could use the money. It all appeared so simple. But it wasn't. He was being asked to kill his friend, the only friend he'd ever had. It would be like killing a part of himself.

Tommy paused. He could see Paul was upset. He felt for him.

The lad was an honest sort. A bit spineless here and there, but a decent skin all the same.

"Paul... son," he said, softening his tone, "if this weekend has shown me anything, it's that I want some good to come from my passing. If I'd have jumped from that bridge, the only thing I'd have left behind would be a traffic jam all the way up to Highgate."

He paused, reflecting on that night. The noise of the traffic below. The final cigarette. The sickening view from the rail. Then the hand grabbing him...

"This way, I get to give my little girl more than I ever managed when I was alive," he continued. "Everyone's a winner! That's the way I want it. You'll have your money."

"For fuck's sake, don't you see!" shouted Paul, his stomach lurching with the realisation that Tommy had it all worked out, "I don't want the money!"

Paul kicked over a small pile of newspapers in frustration. This wasn't happening.

"I'm an idiot!" he shouted, "I... I didn't think things through. It seemed like a good idea at the time, but it's not. It's crazy. I can't do it. *I won't do it.*"

Tommy stood up from the green chair. The lad wasn't listening.

"Do you know how many times I've stood on that bridge?!" he shouted. "You know how many times I've climbed over and stood on that parapet, wanting to jump, wanting to put an end to it all? You want the truth? The truth is... I'm a coward. I'm fecking scared."

He paused, biting his lip, his face red with temper and embarrassment. He turned once more to the window, staring out.

"I need your help," he said softly. "I need you to be there for me."

Tommy turned towards Paul, his face imploring him to listen, to take him seriously.

"The only way I can do this is if you help me," he said. "You said we're friends. Then do this for me. Please, Paul. As a friend."

As he spoke, he laid his arm on Paul's shoulder. The younger man was speechless. He knew he would burst into tears if he heard any more. He wanted to embrace him, tell him he didn't want to let him go, not ever. Without speaking, he turned away from Tommy and walked towards the door of the living room.

"10.06, Paul," said Tommy to the departing figure. "Don't be late for me."

*

Paul sat on the side of his bed, trying to smoke a cigarette. He'd found it in an old packet at the back of a drawer, kept as an antidote to stressful situations. This was most definitely one of those. He wanted so desperately for Tommy to care about their friendship that he would see sense and call the whole thing off. But Tommy seemed to be beyond caring about anything other than his daughter's welfare. Paul understood that. But why did it have to be this way? Couldn't they work out some other means of helping Frankie out? Paul tried desperately to think of something.

He realised that that wasn't the point. Tommy had already made up his mind to die. Or, more correctly, he'd had his mind made up for him. All he wanted to do was choose how and when, and he had chosen. He cast his mind back to the previous two incidents. They were too horrible to contemplate. The sheer pace of the weekend had forced the memories away but here they were again, in all their sickening detail. He hadn't known the youth or the businessman. Hadn't known a thing about them. Not even their names. But he knew Tommy, almost better than he did anyone. Even his own mother he hardly knew any more, since Steve and the twins. Tommy was different. Even if he hadn't really wanted to, he'd let Paul into his world. Like it or not, they had formed an attachment. Now, he felt like a farmer who'd given one of his animals a pet name, only to slaughter it when it was fattened up. It was a betrayal of Tommy, and of Rosemary and Frankie too, and yet it was Tommy who wanted to go through with this.

Paul stubbed out the half-smoked cigarette and climbed into

231

bed, almost weeping in frustration. For what seemed like an age he writhed and turned, trying to get comfortable. He wondered what Tommy would be thinking next door. He was probably already asleep, happy in the knowledge that everything was going to work out all right. Well it wasn't all right. It was all very fucking wrong. He was tempted to go back in there and throw Tommy out. But he was in too deep. He punched the pillow in anger, trying not to cry. He'd started this chain of events and here were the consequences, tormenting him and playing with his head. He could stand it no longer. He placed the pillow over his head, blocking out the light from the moon which fell across his bed as well as the turmoil of his own thoughts, and finally drifted off to a nightmare-filled sleep.

*

Contrary to what Paul believed, Tommy wasn't asleep. Far from it. His own thoughts were turning darker by the second. He imagined himself standing on a line, the train thundering nearer and nearer. The thought twisted at his guts like a knife. He took a couple of pills from the bottle in his jacket pocket and dry-swallowed them. He wanted as settled a night as he could get.

Tommy turned on the TV and flicked through a selection of channels, pausing idly on the 24-hour rolling news show.

"And finally," said the presenter, half-smiling, "a man in North London is in intensive care tonight following a bizarre attempt to cook and eat his own body parts. The native Frenchman was rushed to St. Thomas' Hospital after the incident that is alleged to have…"

Tommy sighed heavily and turned the TV off. The silly bollicks. He'd met many madmen during his time out there and nothing surprised him any more. There wasn't a scrap of news worth listening to.

He settled back in the chair and shut his eyes. He thought of Rosemary. The whiskey, the song, the ring. And the handing over of the duvet by the bedroom door. Ach, it would never have worked, anyway. Too much water – or maybe whiskey – under the bridge now. Still, she'd asked the lad to "look out for him". That was kind of her. It showed she still cared. "Look out for him". He thought of Paul next door. Probably in a terrible state. *"Look out for him..."* The words tumbled around his mind as he nodded off.

Chapter 25

Paul didn't know what woke him so suddenly that morning. Maybe it was a thud from upstairs, as a hung-over Yvonne rushed out of her flat to work. Or maybe it was his body telling him he had an important appointment to keep, the way the body sometimes does when a person needs to be in a certain place and at a certain time.

He blinked hard as he surfaced from under the duvet. It was Monday. Shit. The implications of the day ahead hit him like a bullet and he fell back on to his pillow, his hands over his face.

He could just lie there all day. He could call in sick or simply not turn up. There would be no inquiry. Everyone knew he'd had a rough time of it. Someone else would cover his shift. Someone else would...

No. There was no way he could let one of his workmates carry the can for that. To do that to someone would be unforgivable. If it was going to happen, he had to be the one at the scene. He had sought out an accomplice. Now he had to face the consequences and, if necessary, do it himself.

He sat up again in bed, a faint ray of hope entering his heart like a shaft of sunlight from the gap in the untidily-drawn curtains. Tommy might still be asleep next door. They'd been up late at the party and Tommy wasn't a well man. He'd had a fair bit of whiskey, too. There was every possibility he was still crashed out in the chair.

Daring not to be over-optimistic, Paul gently pushed open the door of the living room. There was the usual clutter – books, papers, clothes, magazines and tatty furniture. But the chair where Tommy had lain was empty. Paul stared at it for what felt like minutes, almost willing the Irishman to somehow reappear in it. It was hopeless. He had gone.

Shoulders slumped, he walked across the room to his desk by the window. There was nothing, no note, no scribbled 'goodbye'. No trace of the man who had taken over his room, and his life. Paul looked out of the window to the street below. The Mercedes had gone too, leaving an empty parking space. He had lost him, and nothing but a gap remained.

*

Far away, in a cottage on the outskirts of Coniston, Frankie walked back from the shower into her room. Her mother was downstairs with Bill the plumber, who had dropped in for a cup of tea. Frankie checked herself in her mirror and reached down for her make-up box. As she did, she noticed the bundle of notes lying on her dressing table. She had no idea what to do with the money. Yesterday, she could've happily flushed it down the loo and never thought about it again. Today? Today felt a little different. He must have wanted her to have it. She ought to spend it then. Or save it. She'd get a bloody good holiday out of it.

Frankie gathered up a handful of the notes and picked up the envelope they had arrived in, intending to put them back in. As she did, she noticed something in the envelope. It wasn't a banknote, but a folded piece of A4 file paper, covered in writing on one side. A letter. Her stomach turned over as she pulled it out, unfolded it, and read the first words:

"My Dearest Frances…"

"I know you are angry and hurt and you don't want to hear anything I have to say…"

*

"Five pounds of shite in a three pound bag, eh? Well not this morning," Tommy thought, as he carefully smoothed an inch-long path through the snow of shaving cream across his cheeks. He'd crept back into the hostel quietly, not wanting to wake the drunks and the down-and-outs who occupied its flea-ridden, dingy beds. He showered and lathered up the old-fashioned way, with brush and shaving cream, in the small, dirty sink next to his bunk bed.

*

"I don't want you to feel bad for not speaking to me. I don't blame you at all."

*

Paul, too, was about to shave. London Underground liked its employees to look the part. After all, it was a customer service they were performing. He wiped steam from the bathroom mirror and sprayed a meringue of foam from a can on to his hand. He went to put it towards his face and then stopped, dropping it into the water in the sink. What the hell was he doing, trying to look his best? It was insane. He threw the razor down and walked out of the bathroom.

*

"I accept I have no place in your life any more. You realised a long time ago that you're better off without me..."

*

Paul stood at the side of the road, looking murderous. Today, of all bloody days... He turned the Fiesta's engine over again, but it simply sputtered out. There was no-one around to give him a push start, and even if there was he'd be lucky if anyone offered to help. Bloody car! Bloody place! He got out and in an uncharacteristic fit of temper he slammed the door hard, kicking the metal again and again and again. It would have to be the bus.

*

"And of course you're right. I can't expect you to understand why I've done the things I've done. I don't even understand, though my pals Arthur Guinness and Jack Daniels might have an idea. Anyway, I need you to know it was never my intention to hurt you..."

*

Tommy had borrowed the communal iron and given his shirt,

236

trousers and even his jacket a good press with it. He put on his clothes, still warm from the heat of the appliance, and made his way back to the small mirror in his shared room. He looked the part. There might not be time for a hearty breakfast as well, but at least he looked tip-top. He spotted an almost-empty bottle of cologne on the window sill and, snaffling it, poured a hefty glug on to his upturned palm before applying it to his cheeks and his neck. He gave himself a final once-over and wiped a small stain from the lapel of his jacket with his finger. The old Tommy magic. He still had it, right enough. He turned and left the room without a backwards glance.

*

"I've been stupid and selfish and pig-headed, and I don't have much to show for my time. Except you. And I couldn't ask for more."

*

It had to be the bus, and there was one coming down Horn Lane. Paul got on, fishing in his pockets for some loose change. He found a spare seat and sat down. Stop-start, stop-start. Would he ever get to the bloody depot… on time?

*

"Look after your mother. You don't need me to tell you she's one of life's good ones, far too good for someone like me. Tell her I'm pleased about her and the plumber. It's always handy to have a man with a trade about the house. She deserves a bit of happiness."

*

Rosemary turned from the work surface and put the mug of tea in front of the man in overalls who was sitting at the kitchen table. She looked at him, saw his sheer ordinariness and his kindly, down-to-earth expression, and she smiled. She loved Bill with all her heart. Well, perhaps not all of it, but the best part of it. He smiled back at her, the woman who would soon be his wife.

*

"I know I was never the father you needed or deserved, but you will

237

always be my beautiful girl and I will always love you. Always, always, always."

Frankie could hardly breathe. The tenderness of the words, and all the love and loss and guilt they conveyed, stung her eyes and her throat. She felt like she was being smothered. As she read the final three words, her hands clutching at her lips, trying in vain to stop them trembling, she could stand it no longer. She dissolved into a heap of uncontrollable sobs as the years of grief and loss and bewilderment flowed out of her. She fell back on to her bed, clutching the crumpled piece of paper torn so pathetically carefully from a large pad, and wept like she had never wept before.

*

The bigger man's face peered into the mouse cage, an expression of mock-outrage playing across his flabby features. He'd just come in off his shift to find the door of the cage empty and its occupant gone.

"He still had six weeks in solitary," said Vic vexedly. "If people don't respect the law, then what've you got? Anarchy. Mob Rule. And mice in your Garibaldis."

At Vic's side stood Ash, also just in on his break. The pair always seemed to time their breaks together so they could get back to the depot and indulge themselves in their puerile humour.

"What are you going on about?" said Ash, bending down to have a closer look. "Maybe some of his rodent brothers came and busted him out?"

He stared more closely at the cage and pointed his finger. "Look," he said dramatically, "I think I can see a tunnel."

As the pair dissolved into sniggers, the door of the locker room opened and Paul walked in. As he spotted Ash and Vic, his heart sank. They were the last two people he wanted to see this morning. He walked to his locker, hoping that they might not notice him. But it was a futile hope. Vic looked over to see who was coming in and on seeing Paul a broad beam cracked his features.

"Oohh," he said, "back already?"

Paul ignored him, and, taking off his coat, opened his locker. His uniform polo shirt and overcoat were in there. Paul reached up to bring them down from the peg.

"There's your culprit, Vic," said Ash, delighted that an object for some sport had just walked in. "A bleedin'-heart liberal like Paul."

Paul was in no mood to be the butt of their jokes. Why was it always him? He felt like he'd never been away from this place.

"Nailed on," continued Ash, hitting his stride. "He's got the hump about that 'Three and Out' wind-up. He's come down here and let Mickey have it away on his toes. He's your man, Vic. Look at him... he even looks guilty."

Paul stared at them uncomfortably. He had no idea what they were going on about. But something they'd mentioned had pricked up his ears.

Ever placatory, Vic stepped forward. "Paul," he said, donning his sympathetic expression, "it was only a joke, mate. We were only having a laugh."

"A laugh about what?" said Paul, confused. "What are you talking about?"

"You know," said Ash, "The 'Rule'. The Big Game. *Three and Out*."

Paul swallowed hard. They were trying to tell him something. Something he really, really didn't want to hear.

"What about it?" he said, his voice almost at a whisper.

Ash leaned into him, inspecting the haggard, haunted face.

"You know what, Vic?" he exclaimed, his voice rising to a higher pitch, "I think he believed us."

"You knew it was a joke, a wind-up, didn't you?" Vic watched as Paul sat heavily at a trestle table covered in coffee mugs, what little colour there was rapidly draining from his face.

"What?" said Vic, unable to believe it. "You fell for it? Jesus, if it was true everybody would be looking for someone to run down.

Come on, you didn't believe us, did you?"

Paul stammered a denial, but he wasn't listening any more. It was all bullshit. The whole fucking thing. It didn't exist. There was no rule. No pay-off. No nothing. It was a lie. A wind-up. A joke. He could have almost laughed. All the time and effort and searching. And then Tommy. Finding Tommy. Taking a weekend off from his life and thinking he'd changed it completely. And now, this... He began to shake uncontrollably.

"You know what, Vic?" said Ash, nodding to his mate in the direction of the forlorn figure at the table. "Maybe it wasn't him who let that mouse out."

The schoolboy pair sniggered and walked out of the room, still chuckling. Paul slumped forward, his head in his hands. His shift began in less than five minutes. Outside the door was a train he was required to drive. If he didn't do it, someone else would. He stood up and as though in a dream, wandered to his locker. He pulled off his T-shirt, threw it in, put on his uniform blue polo shirt and jacket then robotically walked out of the rest room towards the platform. He felt compelled to go. If he tried to back out from his shift now, the bosses would want to know why. What could he tell them? That he'd arranged for a man to die on the line? They'd think he'd gone mad and send him home. Then, someone else would have to do his shift. Someone else would kill Tommy.

He thought of Tommy, standing there, waiting. If he was going to be there. Maybe he'd changed his mind. Gone back to wherever he was staying, thought about it and thought better of it. Maybe that's what had happened. But maybe not.

His head spun and his stomach churned like a washing machine. As he reached the door of the cab, he leaned forward and vomited forcefully in front of the train. He didn't want to go forward, but he couldn't turn back. Paul pushed the door open and, wiping his mouth, stepped inside. He sat at the seat, and went through the routine checks. He felt like he was on auto-pilot.

Within a minute the signal changed from red to green. His

prompt to move off. He pressed the lever and the train lurched forward into the darkness of the tunnel.

Normally the journey up the Northern Line was laboriously slow, but not today. The stations below ground went by as though he was driving a Japanese bullet train. He felt like he was being moved along by an invisible and malignant force, driving him on to the destination he hoped he would never reach.

Finally, the train emerged from the darkness and headed into the above-ground East Finchley station. Paul pressed the 'open' button and a clutch of passengers got on, taking their seats, settling down with their books and their papers. Paul stared ahead at the red light, almost frozen with anxiety.

It changed to green. He wouldn't be allowed to hesitate. It could cause catastrophe. As the bile in his throat rose for the second time that morning, he turned the train's starting handle and pushed it forward. As he did, he looked at his watch. 10.04. Just two minutes to go.

The train lumbered out of the station, every rattle and jolt of its forward motion remorselessly reminding Paul of what he had done and what he might be about to do.

He drove on, hardly daring to look up yet almost morbidly fascinated with the landscape that passed by. Colourless, lifeless and grey and yet somehow steeped in the significance of the seconds that ticked by on his watch.

10.05. He rounded the bend which he knew would take him into the long, straight stretch that was to be the deadly rendezvous point with Tommy. There appeared to be nothing ahead. A shaft of sunlight glinted off the rails which seemed to stretch into infinity. He wasn't there. Christ, he wasn't there…

Then, a sudden movement from the side of the track. A figure was striding with determination across the southbound line. Paul reacted instinctively, slamming on the brake and bringing the train to a shuddering halt.

There was no mistaking him. White shirt, tieless and open at the collar, pinstriped jacket and trousers. Tommy stood, proud and defiant, right in the middle of the northbound rail, as the wind tugged gently at his jacket and ruffled his hair. It was 10.06. He had made the appointment with perfect timing.

"Jesus, Tommy, no," hissed Paul, his teeth clenched and his eyes bulging as he stared fixedly ahead. "Please… no."

Everything seemed to have fallen silent. The wind buffeted the side of his cab and shook the trees along the edges of the track. Then, a voice crackled through the speakers in the cab.

"Train 208," it said, "is there a problem? You are signalled go."

It was the controller. The progress of each train was electronically monitored and any unscheduled stops were noticed and acted upon immediately. The result of not doing so could be disaster.

Paul knew the controller was demanding an answer. Sweat was dripping from his palms and his mouth was sandpaper-dry. He could not go backwards. There was only one way and the figure blocking his path looked to be as solid as a rock.

"Fuck, fuck, fuck, fuck!" He rubbed his face, panicking.

A hundred yards away, Tommy watched as the train remained motionless. He knew how terrible the young driver – his mate – would be feeling. But it was the best way – everyone a winner and no regrets.

He sensed Paul's hesitation and shouted at the very top of his voice up the track.

"A deal's a deal!"

Even if Paul didn't hear, Tommy felt the need to remind him. And maybe himself, too. His teeth chattered slightly and he clenched his jaw tight.

"Please Paul," he said anxiously, not wanting to lose his grip on the situation, "for the love of God, hurry up!"

In the cab, Paul was wracked with horror and fear. Tears were beginning to tumble down his cheeks as he desperately fought back a choking feeling in his throat. He felt paralysed within the grip of a monster he had created which was about to destroy him

242

and the only friend he'd ever had.

"Driver, are you in control?" The bored monotone of the controller emitted from the speakers again, but this time with more urgency. "Come in train 208, are you in control?!"

He had to tell them something. There would be panic in the control room by now. He picked up the intercom handset and just about fought the rapid gasps of breath from his chest.

"Driver 208," Paul replied, his voice trembling. "Animal on the track."

Tommy was not moving. He had made up his mind. Paul now had to make up his. He gulped hard, fighting the almost overwhelming urge to open the cab and just start running. Then he spoke into the handset again.

"Line clear. Proceeding now."

He put down the handset and slowly, agonisingly, he released the brake. The train moved forward and started to pick up speed.

"You stubborn old bastard!" sobbed Paul, his face twisted with anguish. "A deal's a deal. God help you!"

Down the line, Tommy saw the train start forward and sucked in a breath. Thank Christ he'd seen sense. He took a deep breath and braced himself as though he was standing at the very edge of the world, looking over into the abyss. Then, he started to recite a poem by Yeats he had learned many years ago in school, back in the times when every day had a golden beginning and end, and there was no sadness, regret or guilt. He had rehearsed it many times in his head. Now, he was ready for its final performance.

"I will arise and go now, and go to Innisfree,
And a small cabin build there, of clay and wattles made;
Nine bean-rows will I have there, a hive for the honey bee,
And live alone in the bee-loud glade."

He roared out the words, defying the noise of the wind pushing through the trees and the hideous, unstoppable racket of wheels rattling over tracks.

"And I shall have some peace there, for peace comes dropping slow,
Dropping from the veils of the morning to where the cricket sings;
There midnight's all a glimmer, and noon a purple glow,
And evening full of the linnet's wings..."

"NOOOOOOOOOOOOOOOOOOOO!!!!"

Paul screwed up his eyes and howled like a banshee as the train bore down on his friend. Second by second he sped nearer, the inevitable, thudding horror of flesh against metal, the animal squeal of brakes and the cries of passengers flashing before him as he sat, just screaming and screaming and screaming...

CHAPTER 26

Even now, almost a year later, the memories of that day and its immediate aftermath, are still vague. I've been told by people who are meant to know about these things that I'm blocking out those memories, but it isn't quite true. In my mind's eye I can still see it unfolding in front of me – the fear building, movement on the line, the train stopping, the controller's voice – all those elements are as clear as they would've been if it had happened yesterday. It's what took place next that appears to be difficult.

I remember telling the controller there was an animal on the line. I suppose it's how you define 'animal', really. We're all animals under the surface, after all. I was hoping that it would buy me time, give me a moment to think rationally. But I was beyond rational thinking. I felt the whole train was being pulled towards its destination by some invisible force, a force so strong that it could not be resisted. The figure ahead of me was stubbornly willing me on. We had shaken on it and a deal was a deal. If I was ever to retain any bond with the man I called my best friend, I had to carry out his final wish – whether I liked it or not.

Of course, from my point of view, the deal was off. It was invalid, for there was no deal to begin with. I had been duped and made a complete fool of. There was no 'Three and Out'. There was no money for me, no ten grand for Frankie and no house on an island. Our dreams – Tommy's and mine – had disappeared. By then, I knew that, but he didn't and I couldn't tell him. Would it have made any difference if he had? Knowing Tommy as we do, I think we know the answer to that. Tommy's wish to choose how and when he would die would not have altered. A cruel twist of fate brought us together and it parted us too.

I told the controller the line was clear and set the train into motion. I think I said some kind of prayer and then I shut my eyes. Remember, I'd already seen two people die on the line in front of me. I wasn't about to be a willing spectator at the death of my best friend. I felt the grotesque thud of impact as the train hit Tommy and I knew at that instant that he was dead. And even if by some miracle he wasn't, the wheels going over his body would've... well, I'm sure it's easy to guess the rest.

I hit the brake almost immediately after the collision, as any good driver would've done. The controller was on the blower just seconds afterwards, demanding to know why I'd stopped again. This time, I couldn't hold it in. "I think I've hit someone," I sobbed. "I dunno, but I think I've hit someone... I saw something on the line before... I thought it was an animal... but I don't think it was. Please help me..."

I was babbling, crying, tripping over my words in shock and horror. Credit to her, the controller was good. She just talked me down, very calmly and rationally, and told me not to open my cab door until I was truly ready to do so. I was even worrying about the passengers. I knew they'd be getting restless and angry back there, but the controller said to calm down. I was the priority, not them.

And after that? Then it all starts to blur. I felt like I'd sat in the cab for what seemed like hours, just staring ahead. At some stage I remember seeing a couple of Transport Police in yellow reflective vests climb up the banking and head towards the front of the train. Their expressions were very grim. One kept looking at the front of the train then got on his radio and talked rapidly into it. The other guy knocked at the door of the cab. At first, I couldn't remember how to open the door. Just had no idea how it worked. Somehow, it came to me eventually and I let him in.

He asked me my name and how I was feeling. The shock had really kicked in by then. How the fuck did he think I was feeling? I felt like every part of my body had been anaesthetised, except for my eyes which were just staring, staring. Then he asked me what happened. I told him I thought I'd run a guy over. I tried to be helpful, I tried to picture the scene, but it was like watching a film that kept stopping at a certain point. I just couldn't get past that bit so I said no more.

Somehow, and I can't remember how, the cop persuaded me to leave the cab and walk back down the line. He told me to shut my eyes, and I did, happy to obey the law. I imagined all the irate faces of the passengers staring angrily at me, furious that I, and the selfish sod under my train, had spoiled their commute.

A car took me back to the depot. I'm guessing now it was a police car, as the driver seemed to be acknowledging police vehicles travelling in the opposite direction, their lights flashing, as we drove. I suppose they were going to the scene. I heard later that the area around the train was sealed off and all the passengers were escorted out before the police and the railway engineers started their investigation. It took them a good few hours before it was complete, stuffing up the Northern Line for the rest of the day, far worse than a traffic jam all the way up to Highgate. Good old Tommy Cassidy, eh? As inconsiderate as ever.

God knows how much tea was poured into me at the depot. It felt like it was going to emerge from every orifice. The guys were good. One of them even gave me a book voucher he didn't want, which was sweet of him. I didn't like to say that my eyes were too sore from crying to read. A bit later on – must have been lunchtime – the door opened and in came Ash and Vic. They'd obviously heard and I'd never seen them so subdued, especially Ash. He was like a character from a fairy-tale, struck dumb by a witch's curse. I heard that a couple of weeks later he left the job and went to work in a bar abroad. Vic's still around, I believe, though he confines his practical jokes to his caged mice now.

I saw the trauma team that day, too. They wanted me to

talk through my feelings, share my thoughts and explore any possibilities of achieving "closure". Closure… Christ! As though I could simply slam the door shut on everything that had happened, all my feelings, thoughts and emotions, and lock it all away in a dusty room while I sat there and waited for it to die of starvation.

Funnily enough, that's almost exactly what I did do, except I was in that room too. I was given a month's compassionate leave by a manager who seemed to be edging away from me even as he signed the letter. I was a dark talisman, a bad omen. A walking number 13, an unlucky third light glowing in the darkness, encouraging an invisible sniper to strike. I knew then that a month away from my job would not be enough. Maybe a couple of lifetimes might have seen me back, but I doubted it. I couldn't have driven out of East Finchley again, across the spot that marked Tommy's demise and over the grave of the person I once was.

So I just went home, back to my flat and books and my non-existent novel, back to the dried-up remains of the life I thought I'd left behind on the road to Liverpool. Everything had changed and yet, when I put my key in the door lock and stared at the rows and rows of books, many of them unread and just up there for show, in the highly unlikely event of anyone interesting coming to visit, I realised that absolutely nothing had changed at all. My life was as still and as flat as a week-old glass of water left under a dusty bed. I closed the door behind me, and when I did I seemed to shut out all the possibilities in life that had been so wonderfully, but so briefly, revealed to me that weekend.

For weeks, I did nothing. I sat in the chair that Tommy slept in and I watched day turn to night and night turn to day. The cars hissed by my window and people went on with their lives, not knowing, not caring. I was unable to drag myself into my bedroom to sleep – because there was no sleep to be had. So itchy was I with tiredness that I could feel a million ants crawling across my face, digging into my eyes with their jaws, but still sleep would

248

not come. I did not wash or change my clothes. I couldn't eat, at least not for a few days. Then I started to feel very ill and I knew I was beginning to starve myself. I could quite happily have done that, but somehow I didn't. Call it the survival instinct. Call it being plain bloody hungry, perhaps. So one night I waited until 2am, 3am – when I knew Yvonne wouldn't be hanging around, trying to see if I was okay – and went out, like a prowling wolf, in search of something to eat.

I took home the cheapest frozen pizza, bought from a guy in a 24-hour corner shop who saw just one more insane crack addict in front of his till. I cooked it and cut it into seven slices. Every day I ate one slice and after I'd eaten them all I crawled from my hole once more to get another one. It was my way of marking time in the hermitage I had created for myself here on Horn Lane. It was a long, long way, physically and mentally, from the imagined kingdom of Loch Tyne.

The weeks turned into months. A short appointment with my doctor resulted in me being signed off as long-term sick. No doubt my employers were pleased. The last thing they wanted was a jinx around the place and who could blame them? I had no word from them, other than a letter confirming my sickness and an offer of further counselling. Kind, but unnecessary. A confessional box would've been more use, except I'm a Protestant, as Tommy sarcastically reminded me that day in the church. After three months I wrote to my bosses, telling them that I would never be coming back to work. It didn't seem right to carry on taking their money. Besides, I had a little bit accumulated from the sick pay I had already received, and it was enough to keep me at the subsistence level I was now used to.

It would be trite to say there was a Tommy-shaped hole in my life. Trite, but true. I missed the uncouth bastard terribly. He couldn't have altered my life so dramatically if he'd punched me out and left me in a coma. Tommy turned on its head everything I thought I stood for. He breathed energy into me, forced me to see things from a new perspective. He came along with a large knife and ripped an irreparable hole in the fabric of my existence, but instead of just shrivelling away deflated, I was replenished with all the fiery air he could breathe at me. He said I had no life – almost his last words to me – but it wasn't true. I did have life, the new one that he'd gifted me.

And as I thought about his life, so I dwelled on his death. I hadn't looked, hadn't seen, but I knew what had happened. After all, I was experienced in these things. Had I killed him? Yes. Did I want to kill him? No – and, to be truthful, yes. I didn't want to let him down. He was my best friend. I didn't want him to suffer from whatever it was that was killing him anyway. Despite everything, he had a strong moral streak running through the middle of him. He believed in doing the right thing, even if he often didn't manage it himself. Maybe more accurately, he believed in redemption and I had offered him the chance to redeem himself one last time. Death, then, was the final, inevitable, paragraph of his moral code.

Not that it was any great comfort to me. Wherever Tommy had ascended (or possibly descended), there was no denying he was at peace and free from stress, worry or pain. But of course it isn't the dead who experience death, it's the living. I thought of him day and night. He was there in the books I tried to read and cast aside, in the faces of the drivers whose cars I watched going by my window. Whatever I did, wherever I went, whoever I saw, he appeared in my thoughts. I became convinced he was haunting me, but I couldn't work out why. It couldn't be for reasons of revenge, because I had done what he'd asked. Was he trying to tell me something? I wracked my brain trying to think of what that might be, and finally I wondered if it was in some way connected to Frankie and Rosemary.

I was their only true link to Tommy and yet, I couldn't stand the thought of having to tell them he was dead. Why? Because, like him, I was a coward. I just couldn't make that leap into the unknown. I was too scared to answer the questions they would ask, too jumbled in my thoughts to work out a way of telling them that I had killed a father and a husband, but with his full consent and for a sum of money, which had enabled him to visit them for the final time, throwing their emotions in the air like confetti. Besides – and this was my biggest concern – I had been trusted with the responsibility of having to "look out for him". On the face of it, I had failed in the worst way possible. Not only had I not looked out for him, I had actually killed him. In terms of duty of care, there is no greater failure than that. So I did not contact them and to this day they don't know if he is alive or dead.

After five months hardly seeing daylight from one week to the next, a new mood entered me. I wouldn't go as far as to describe it as 'optimism' – that was still a long way off – but the tiniest shoot of a new start was beginning to appear. The dreams I had when I did manage more than an hour or two's sleep were slightly less tormented and I only thought of Tommy every other minute. I still ignored the occasional knock on the door, knowing whose concerned 'come-to-my-party-it'll-do-you-good' face was behind it, but I did manage to take short walks around the area without feeling I had crawled from under a tombstone in Highgate Cemetery.

Then, one evening when I knew no-one would be around, I sneaked to the front door and picked up that morning's post. I sorted through the letters quickly and pulled out a brown envelope with my name on it. It was postmarked with the words 'HM Courts Service'.

'Dear Mr Callow,' the letter read. 'This is to inform you that your presence is required as a witness at the inquest into the death of Mr Thomas Francis Cassidy, which occurred at East Finchley…

You will be required, under oath, to provide the Coroner with full information about what you witnessed in relation to

Mr Cassidy's death. Please be at the Magistrates' Court, at the address given above, at 10am on Friday…'

I could feel the pores on my palms beginning to clog up with sweat as I read. Another grim invitation to do something I did not want to do. I could refuse, but if I refused I would be ordered to appear. Besides, a non-appearance would be almost like sticking my hands up and shouting, "I'm guilty! Put me away now!"

I sat for hours in what I now thought of as Tommy's chair, trying to make sense of it all. In the past month I had been asked to write two inquest statements into the deaths of the youth with the Rottweiler and the heart-attack man. These I had done, simply and straightforwardly. I posted them back and I had heard nothing more. But this was different. I decided that somehow, they knew what had happened. They'd found out that I'd cooked this up and recruited Tommy as a willing accomplice. And even though the 'Three and Out' rule was fiction, what Tommy and I had done was made of hard, cold fact. I had helped him to die and now they knew it.

There was only one person who could save me now and he was dead. I wondered what he would do in these circumstances. Would he pack up his troubles and run? Yes, that would have been an option for Tommy. When the going got tough in Liverpool he abandoned his wife and child and did not see them again for eight years, and only then because an opportunity fell into his lap.

Opportunity. Of course. Seize the day. The hope that had begun to grow in me suddenly took on a new shoot, that of courage. I would go to the inquest and I would tell the coroner, the police and the press all about Tommy Cassidy and I. How and why we met. What we talked about. Where we went. Why we came back. Why our paths crossed so bloodily that day on the Northern Line. I would tell them who he was, how we became friends and who his family were. The truth, the whole truth and nothing but the truth. Then, there would be no doubt, and just as Tommy drove

252

up that country road to Coniston not knowing what he might encounter at the end of it, so I would walk up the steps to that Magistrates' Court and take whatever was coming to me – good, bad or downright damnable in the eyes of the law.

There was one more thing I had to do. The day before my appearance at the court I took a bus to Oxford Street. I hadn't been more than half a mile from my flat in almost six months and I felt extremely agoraphobic. Jostling, sweating bodies seemed to surround me, pressing against me everywhere I went. I had to fight the urge to turn back and crawl once again into the protective squalor of my flat, but I would not do it. I had to battle through my fears, bottle them up for later. I walked nervously into a men's clothing shop and looked around. I had lost a lot of weight and I couldn't afford to lose much more, but I knew that this chain did clothes for the skinniest of frames. I spotted it almost immediately – a black, pin-striped, two-piece suit. I wouldn't fill it quite as well as Tommy did, but it would do. I selected a white shirt, a pair of black shoes and, to top off the look, a tie the colour of café ketchup. I paid for them and, clutching my bundle, headed for the bus stop.

The following day I woke up early, having set my alarm. It was a gorgeous, early autumn morning, the kind that poets write about and the rest of us just take for granted. My stomach turned over as I wondered what the day would bring for me, but once I'd showered, shaved, donned the new suit and tie and slapped half a bottle of cheap aftershave across my chops, I knew I was ready for anything.

Again, I used the bus to take me to my destination. Tommy, of course, would have driven there in style, but the Fiesta was hardly what you would call a high-rolling ride. Besides, it had been towed away months ago, banged up in some compound for the crime of possessing an out-of-date tax disc. I smiled as I wondered whether the court would take this offence into account.

I arrived at the courthouse just before ten. I went through the metal detector and was met at reception by an older man in a black gown.

"Good morning, sir," he said. "Which case are you looking for?"

The place was buzzing with solicitors, defendants, police officers, witnesses and administrative staff. An air of brisk efficiency hung about the place as people marched by with huge bundles of bound files or black boxes, while others just watched nonchalantly from slumped positions behind their tabloids.

"Erm, it's an inquest," I said. "Cassidy."

"Ah yes," said the usher almost immediately, "the coroner has now arrived for that one. Are you family?"

"No, I'm a witness," I said. "My name is Paul Callow."

"Okay, Mr Callow, you've been expected and now you're here I can mark you off. Up the stairs, turn left, through the double doors. Court Five is just on your right."

I followed his instructions, and tentatively pushed open the door marked 'Inquest In Progress'. It hadn't started and I was met by a friendly usher, female this time, who asked my name and invited me to sit at the back of the court room.

"But I'm a witness," I said, surprised. "Aren't I supposed to stay outside until I'm called?"

"Oh no," she said, "it isn't a trial you're at. You can listen to all the proceedings. So please do make yourself comfortable."

Two British Transport police officers were sitting up the back. They nodded to me in greeting and I wondered if they'd brought their handcuffs. They'd need them by the end of the morning. Next to them was an older, bespectacled man with a black briefcase between his feet and to his right a younger man in a blue shirt, orange tie and some kind of pass hanging around his neck.

The Coroner entered and we stood up. He motioned us down with a wave of his hand, clearly keen to get on with business.

254

He was a balding man with an old-fashioned watch and chain dangling across his prominent, waistcoated belly.

"This is an inquest into the death of Mr Thomas Francis Cassidy," he said, "who died on the Underground railway line near East Finchley. The purpose of this inquest is not to apportion blame, but to establish the cause of death."

No blame, eh? Wait until he hears my statement, I thought.

Then, after taking the oath, some sort of an official began to read from a statement. He announced himself as the Coroner's Officer and said it was his job to outline the facts as they had been established so far.

"The body of Thomas Francis Cassidy was found on the Underground line just north of East Finchley at 10.30am," he said. "The body was badly mutilated, having been passed over by an Underground train. At the side of the track, British Transport police officers discovered a large quantity of empty bottled-water bottles, a pair of men's shoes and a note."

What? I could hardly believe what I was hearing. What was he doing drinking water? Surely Tommy's last beverage would have been an alcoholic one? And why the hell had he taken his shoes off?

"In normal circumstances I would not read such a note in open court," the officer went on, "but as we were unable to trace any relatives who might have attended and the press aren't present, I will make an exception in this case."

From a file he produced a tatty piece of file paper and, after unfolding it gently from the corner, began to read it.

"My name is Thomas Cassidy," he read. "I'm writing this letter to tell whoever finds it that I have committed suicide by electrocution on this track today. I did it in front of an oncoming train, just to make double sure I would die. Please say sorry to the driver for me. It's not his fault."

I clenched my jaw tightly as the words echoed around the court room walls. Electrocution? Surely they'd made a mistake.

But those were Tommy's words in his own handwriting.

The Coroner's Officer stood down and the British Transport policeman was called. He turned out to be a sergeant, with 30 years' experience on the force. He told the court about the significance of the shoes and how taking them off before standing on a live line would improve the conductivity of the current.

"What about the water?" asked the Coroner?

"Well," said the sergeant, "if the gentleman had doused himself in water before he placed his foot on the live rail, that act would also improve conductivity."

At first, I failed to understand, but as the evidence unfolded, it started to become clear. Somewhere, somehow, Tommy had changed his mind. He had decided not to die under the train, if at all possible, but to take his own life *before* the wheels of my train rolled over him. He knew I didn't want to do it, but he also knew that a deal was a deal and I would be there. Jesus…

Then, a call went up for the pathologist and the man with the glasses and briefcase on my bench stood up. He confirmed his name and his qualifications and started to talk about the post-mortem he had carried out on Tommy's body.

It made for grim listening, but the pathologist was methodical and matter-of-fact. He went through everything, describing internal burns to various parts of Tommy's body.

"As you might imagine," he concluded, "due to the severity of Mr Cassidy's external injuries it has not been easy to establish the cause of death. But I can say, with a strong degree of certainty, that he died almost instantly as a result of an electric shock sustained when his body came into contact with the live rail."

I felt as though the same shock had momentarily entered me. Tommy had worked this out perfectly. But why? Why had he gone to all this bother? Surely he didn't care that much about me?

Next up was the young guy in the blue shirt, who turned out to be a hospital consultant. He told the inquest he had seen Tommy at irregular intervals over a period of months before his death. Mr Cassidy, he said, was suffering from a number of conditions including liver failure, angina and stomach ulcers.

"Mr Cassidy was not a well man," he said, "and I have to tell the court this…about a month before he died, he was brought into hospital for a complaint quite unrelated to his various conditions. In short, he had been in a fight and sustained a blow to the head. It was routinely X-rayed and while we discovered no internal injury as a result of the blow, the radiologist spotted something else. A shadow on the negative."

He paused, taking a sip from a glass of water before continuing.

"A sample was taken which, when analysed, turned out to be malignant. Unfortunately, Mr Cassidy had the beginnings of a brain tumour. If it had gone untreated it would've killed him eventually. I had the unfortunate task of breaking this news to Mr Cassidy. He did not react well and that was the last I ever saw of him."

"It's terminal. That's all you need to know…" Tommy's words in the car floated back to me. He was a brave man, who knew, finally, what his limits were.

"Now," said the Coroner, clearing his throat, "may we have the final witness? Mr Paul Callow, please."

I felt I could barely stand up. Bracing myself on the bench in front, I stood up slowly and walked towards the witness box, feeling every pair of eyes following my progress.

I swore the oath and confirmed my name and occupation.

"I'm sure this is not an easy experience for you, Mr Callow," said the Coroner, looking at me with sympathy, "but I would be very grateful if you could describe to the Court, as clearly as possible, what happened on that morning."

I stammered something about getting out of bed late and the car breaking down. I talked about getting into the train cab, reaching East Finchley and then leaving it. I was rabbitting on

257

and I knew it. As I came to the part about the bend, I faltered, but as I did, I felt what I can only describe as an invisible hand on my shoulder and a faint smell of whiskey in the air. It seems ridiculous, even as I write it, but the sensation was accompanied in my mind's eye by a large, flat face – a bit weather-beaten but still handsome – staring at me and winking cheekily.

"Go on," said the Coroner, in measured tones.

"I stopped," I said, "because I thought I'd seen something on the line."

"Oh yes?" said the coroner, leaning forward, "and what was that?"

"It looked like an animal, sir. A large animal."

"Indeed," said the coroner, "and you reported this to your controller. Do carry on."

"The line seemed to be clear, sir," I stammered, "and I reported that back to control. I carried on, increasing in speed. Then…then I don't know what happened, sir."

"Please try, Mr Callow," said the coroner. "We do appreciate this is a painful experience."

"I… I… I think whatever I'd seen – whoever, I suppose I should say – had come back or had never gone away. I just don't know. All I knew was that I hit someone, sir. Killed them. And I feel very bad about that."

As I said it, I dissolved into tears and sat heavily on the chair in the witness box. The usher offered me a tissue which I took, wiping my eyes before I started to twist it around my finger with nervousness.

The Coroner looked at me and, when I had calmed down slightly, began to speak.

"Thank you for coming here today, Mr Callow," he said, "and sharing what must be an awful experience for any Tube driver. I am told you've been off with long-term sickness since this incident and I think we've subjected you to enough this morning. You are free to go, but if you wish to stay I shall be summing up now."

I resumed my seat at the back, my head in my hands. I wanted to say it all, tell the whole truth and nothing but. Somehow, though, it seemed rather irrelevant. Tommy Cassidy had played his final hand and at last he had scooped the pot.

The Coroner began his summation. He went through the evidence from all the witnesses, including me, before he reached his verdict.

"It seems very clear indeed that Mr Cassidy intended to take his own life," he said. "He clearly had his reasons for this and his final act was a carefully planned, well-executed operation. He also left a note, stating his intentions clearly, and leaving no-one in any doubt how he intended to die. The only verdict I can reach in this sad case is one of suicide."

Then, he looked over at me. "Mr Callow… just before you go. Please don't feel guilty about anything. Mr Cassidy was a determined man. There is nothing to feel guilty about. You didn't kill anyone."

I left the court room in a daze. I was free. I'd looked out for Tommy, and in turn, he'd looked out for me. He'd asked for my help during those final moments we had together, and although I was reluctant, I had given it. Then, he had helped me and he was still helping me.

I walked home, savouring the fragrance of liberty. I was getting a noseful of pollution from every angle, of course, as I trudged back through those congested roads, but Christ, it smelled good. Again, the world seemed alive with possibilities and as I walked I felt new strength grow within me. I would not accept what I thought I could not change. Tommy never did and neither would I. Wherever possible, I would try to do things differently, attempt to create new ways of looking at my world and beyond it, too.

I tramped up to my front door and let myself in to my flat. Almost immediately, I did something I hadn't done for months.

I took my laptop from its case and plugged it in. I switched it on and opened the Word document entitled 'BOOK'. Up came the familiar sentence across the top of the screen:

'Love Song for a Lost Generation – A Novel by Paul Callow'

I stared at it, but the words wouldn't come. What the fuck was a 'love song for a lost generation' anyway? It was bollocks. I snapped the lid shut and turned away from the desk, sighing. If I wasn't going to be a writer I would have to be something else. But what?

I ran through the driving options – cabbie, long-distance lorry, delivery, courier. They didn't appeal. Burglar, maybe, or fell runner? I had a bit of experience in both of those now. I wanted to be a writer so, so desperately. But what would I write about? Let's face it, I'd had no life. That's what Tommy said.

Then, for the second time that day, that winking face appeared in my mind's eye. True, I'd not had much of a life, but I'd had an experience, the kind of experience that you'd tell people about and add the line 'honestly, you couldn't make it up' on to the end. No, you couldn't make it up. So why bother trying?

Cautiously, I opened the lid of my laptop and clicked on 'BOOK' again. That title had been with me for ages and it hadn't provided one squeak of inspiration. I aimed my mouse pointer at it and swiped over it. Then, pausing for a second and holding my breath, I pressed the button marked 'DELETE'.

There. It was gone, lost forever. It had disappeared up its own arse with the lost generation, whatever that was. I didn't know – never had known – and now I simply didn't care. In its place I typed another title – shorter, punchier and more enigmatic.

'Three&Out – A Novel by Paul Callow'

I thought about Dylan Thomas and I began at the beginning.

And I didn't stop. Somewhere along the line I drafted out a plan, but it was all in my head anyway. I just told the story. Tommy's story. Rosemary and Frankie's story. The Callaghans. Mad Maurice. Dirty Mary Loughlin. Vic and Ash. Oh, and mine too. They were all there, queuing up for a part, standing in line like X-Factor contestants just waiting to be noticed. I gave them all a star turn and within a week I had the elusive three chapters, the lucky three that you send off to publishers in the vain hope of them landing on the right desk at the right time.

I didn't care about publication that much. Of course I wanted to see it in print, but the bottom line was that I just wanted to tell this story, even if I might be the only person ever to read it. Tommy stopped me having my moment in court, but he was urging me on to do this, that much I knew. I wrote and wrote and while I did, I waited and waited.

For a while, nothing. Then two rejection letters. 'We think your chapters have potential, however...' Blah, blah, blah. I didn't care. Somehow, I had a feeling that it would all turn out well in the end. A phone call one afternoon confirmed my new-found trust in my instincts. 'Three and in', you might say. "I've read this," said the well-bred female voice on the end of the line, "and I think it's fascinating. What a premise!"

"Thanks," I said, not knowing what else to say. "I've done some more. Would you like to see it?"

"Yes I would," said the voice, "but more importantly, perhaps, I'd like to see you."

Well, that was what clinched it. That and a certain suit I wore for our appointment. I handed over a few more taster chapters and within 24 hours I had another phone call. Would I be interested in a publishing deal with them and how about a £20,000 advance for *Three&Out*, ten thousand now and ten thousand on completion, with the option of signing for a second novel with them? Would I be interested? Damn bloody right I would.

As I finish this, the last chapter, I'd like to make a prediction.

It's not really in my nature, being the cautious type, but I'm going to do it anyway, because I'm pretty certain it's going to come true. When I receive the first advance copy of *Three&Out*, I'm going to go to the Post Office at the end of the road and buy a large envelope. Then, I'm going to take the copy of the book and surreptitiously slide a cheque in between the front cover and the first page. This is for the grand total of £10,000, made out to Frances Sheridan, according to the wishes of her late father. I will also include a slip of paper with my own address on it and an invitation to visit London sometime very soon.

Then, I will take out a scrappy piece of paper that I've hung on to, but never had occasion to use, since I was in Liverpool with Tommy, and I'll copy the Lake District address on to the envelope. I will then pay for the postage and packaging and hand the book over, watching it tumble into the parcels sack hung up behind the counter.

What happens then is this. The book arrives by postal van one sunny morning at a pleasant, homely house on the outskirts of Coniston. A beautiful young woman picks it up and sees it is addressed to her. She opens it and stares at the front cover. It makes no sense to her at first. She turns the first page and sees the cheque made out to her. In shock, she picks it up, but underneath it there is another surprise – a dedication printed on the flyleaf.

'In memory of Tommy Cassidy.'

She puts her hand up to her mouth as the tears well up at the sight of her father's name, and at the implication of the words 'In Memory Of…' Then, she remembers. Paul… in the pub… laughter, drinks, a conversation… *"it's all about a Tube driver… terribly handsome… comes to the Lake District… meets this feisty young girl who gives him a hard time… they get drunk… how does it end?… tragically…"*

So it was true, Frankie. I was a writer. Technically, at least. I just spent rather a long time in search of a plot. And, like all the best things in life, it was under my nose the whole time.

And, Frankie, you know what? I was wrong. It doesn't end tragically after all. Not if it doesn't have to. Now you have read this book, pack a bag, get on a train to London and come to see me. I need to see you. I want you more than anything I've ever wanted in my entire life. Even more than seeing this book in print. And when you arrive, you'll fall into my arms and weep like a tragic heroine. And so will I, for that matter. Then you'll say to me, "pack your bags, there's something we've got to do."

And as we stand, hand-in-hand in our scuba-diving gear on the back of the specially-adapted fishing boat anchored in the greeny-blue waters off Gansbaai, South Africa, we will know exactly what it is that we have to do. We've been waiting for this moment and now it's finally here. We will be fulfilling a dream, the dream of a man who always wanted to swim with the sharks. And look, there he is, a dreamy, half-glimpsed figure hanging out by the cabin of the boat in that pinstripe suit and a fag leaning from the corner of his mouth, making his shark's-fin gesture, willing us on to do it, seize the day, and feck the consequences. We will take the plunge into the shark-infested seas with abandon, just as we will with everything we do from now on. Come on Frankie, tomorrow is another day – let's jump together.